T0328565

Snake

Snake

Tracey Farren

modjaji books

Publication © Modjaji Books 2011
Text © Tracey Farren 2011
First published in 2011 by Modjaji Books PTY Ltd
PO Box 385, Athlone, 7760, South Africa
modjaji.books@gmail.com
http://modjaji.bookslive.co.za
www.modjajibooks.co.za
ISBN 978-1-920397-38-8
Cover artwork and lettering by Kirsten Beets
Book and cover design by Natascha Mostert
Author photograped by Karin Schermbrucker
Printed and bound by Mega Digital, Cape Town
Set in Garamond

All rights reserved. No part of this manuscript may be
reproduced, stored in a retrieval system or transmitted
in any form or by any means, electronic, mechanical,
photocopying, recording or otherwise, without the
prior written permission of the copyright holder,
Tracey Farren.

For Janey,
who would have taken Stella under her
wing if she was real,
and for Maire,
who cared for her words

It slides wild past the grader, it speeds towards my tree!

I shut my eyes for the shock.

The engine stops.

Its name is Renault, it's the colour of old blood. A lady springs out with a big black bag and a black pen in her hand. Her shirt is see through, I can see her black bra. 'Hello, hello, hello everyone!' she says in a rush. 'I'm Melinda. From the Truth.'

'Sorry?' Ma says.

'Truth magazine. Do you know it?'

Ma's lips go shivery.

'Can you give me some of your time?' But it's *her* who's rushing in her own red dust.

She's got a long nose and a round bald dot. I can see from my tree. Her hair is black, but the sun shines dyed red stripes. It looks like strings from the top. It needs a wash. She must have a shower in her house, with hot water in her pipes?

Her black shoes have got shiny black bows on top. They crunch through our coals. Black dust flies up. Her lipstick is dark purple, like grapes that no one's picked, the ones that stink, and shrink in the sun. When she smiles, purple stains leak on her teeth. And it looks like she stole all her teeth from someone bigger.

'Let's not beat the bush. I'll pay you two thousand for your story. Cash. Right now.'

Kunng, Ma drops the kettle on the grid.

'We'll run the story early,' she says, like it needs some exercise.

Ma says, 'But how can you write it if there's a court case coming?'

'Oh, we just say, maybe and what if? That way they can't say that we're writing lies.'

Ma watches the kettle like she's trying to boil it with her eyes.

'It's too ugly,' Ma says. 'I don't want them to see.'

The Truth Lady says, 'If you want, I'll change your names.'

Ma folds her arms.

'I won't even say the name of the place. I'll just say, Somewhere on the way to Worcester.'

'I can't.'

The Truth Lady's purple lipstick shrinks. 'Look. I only really need to talk to the kid.' She looks to the hut.

Quietly, quietly, I pull my legs up.

'She doesn't even sing,' Ma says.

'Hey?'

'Stella's not even singing anymore.'

The Truth Lady smiles her big stolen teeth. '*I'll* get her to sing, don't you worry.' She calls to the hut, 'Stella?'

A hadeda cries, up high.

The Truth Lady gets a voice like tight wire. 'Look, I'm writing it anyway. I want to end it like this …' The Truth Lady hangs imaginary words with her hands, 'The little girl is their only hope. God only knows if the judge will believe her.'

I talk above her bald dot, 'Will the judge read it?'

Her book slaps on the sand. She grabs it and shakes it, its white wings try to fly. She clamps it in her armpit. 'Of course! I'll put my head on a block.' I look far away from our chopping block. I don't want to see a head with red shreds.

The Truth Lady walks right under my feet. She says very soft, 'I know the judge, Stella. He *always* reads my stories.'

Her hair looks like a old cat with stripes.

She says, 'You're very, very lucky that I came today.'

I slide slowly down my tree.

Ma says, 'Stella, you don't have to.'

I turn our metal tub over. I drag it far to our thorn tree, just like he did. I drop it down, *dumm.*

The Truth Lady sits, her thin legs twist like old vines. She ruks a black plastic thing from her pocket. She smiles her grape teeth, 'Don't worry, it won't bite.'

Ma shouts from the hut, 'Stella, are you sure?'

'Ja, Ma!'

I say to the Truth Lady, 'I've been practising.'

'Hey?'

'For the judge.'

Ma still watches, with thin worried lips.

The Truth Lady spins. 'Let's face the other way, so you can concentrate.'

The Truth Lady's face shines blue in the shade. She flicks a red switch. It hums like Ma's tapes, but softer.

She says, 'Where do you want to start?'

'The first day.'

'Hey?'

'The day that he came.'

Her big teeth jump alive. 'Can you tell it like it's happening right now?'

She traps her book in her lap, she grips her black pen like it also might run. It says Independent Inc along the side. It's only weak plastic, it's easy to crack. But I don't want to watch her grape nails writing. I don't want to see her violent smile.

I hold my head in my hands, just like he did. I stare at my feet, but I don't see my toes.

I only see the terrible trouble that I'm telling.

The nun's got red strings in her eyes and deep roads in her forehead. She taps them with her finger. She's got brown spots on her hands, like someone's burnt her with a magnifying glass. She cuts her fingernails so short, sometimes they bleed. Sometimes me and Nita can see the dried blood.

Nita's up there with the Musicians. She's on the top step where Mary's skirt ends. Mary's got no feet, just a cement dress. The wagtails and weavers usually sit on her head, but David's scaring the birds today. Last year, Pa said he played like someone sat on a cat. This year, David's better. He plays Silent Night like a lady being killed. I'll tell Pa the joke when I get home.

'Stop!' The nun's little finger is bent like a bird's foot. The skin on her palm is thin and crinkled. 'Start again. Try and play your violin like the harps in heaven, not like you're sweeping the floor.' Everyone laughs, but not me. Red blood creeps inside David's skin. Sometimes the nun's even rude to the whites.

We stand for so long my legs start paining. In the lucky bean tree, the boy weavers hurry like they've got no time left, and God in the Bible's coming to check their nests. They've got fire feathers on their throats, they flap and boast, 'Mine's the best! Mine's the best!' The girl weavers bubble and chat, they shake the lucky bean sacks. I've never, never seen the lucky beans burst, but I've seen falling stars. My pa always catches them with his eyes.

Nita's recorder is gold wood with dark streaks. She plays Go Tell it on the Mountain for us. She's lazy to practise, her fingers get stuck. The nun doesn't frown, maybe because Nita's pa's a policeman. Then the twins play Kum Ba Yah so slow, it's like they're playing for all the dead people next door. 'Kum Ba Yah, my Lord ...,' dead people sing in my head. I wipe my smile off with my hand. That's how me and Nita do it, we wipe our smiles clean.

But the nun's not looking, she's staring over the hedge.

His hair is shaggy with blonde flicks. His moustache is light brown with gold tips. He smiles with lots of teeth, like a pop star. The sun even shoots his eyes to silver.

The nun gets mixed up. Her frown sits where it always sits, but a shy smile springs on her lips.

The Truth Lady leans to her recorder machine, 'Not shy. Sex.'

'Sorry?'

'Nothing, kid. Carry on.'

The nun's smile's a shock to us. Like if Mary suddenly dropped her child.

The nun pushes her fingernails like she's trying to slide them off.

When I look again, he's gone. But the nun's still the nun. When it's the choir's turn, The Lord's My Shepherd bursts out of me. Mary's made of cement but I know it's her song. She's as strong as God, she's as light as the sun, *'My soul he doth restore again ...'* Green grass sways, the wind strokes her face. Some wagtails fly back on her cement head. I sway with the grass, I fill the whole sky, but the nun's roads dig deep between her eyes. She sticks her knobby finger on her lips. Her spit flies in the sun, 'Ssshh!'

I must sing soft. The nun's still the nun.

Oom Piet sings, 'Lekker fat! Lekker roast!'

He keeps his chickens alive to keep them fresh. He hangs them upside down to look like meat, like the cows at Os's Butchery, with no head and no hair. The chickens flap and tangle their upside down wings. They drop their feathers from the worry. They lose their voice from screaming for help, they go *crip, crip, crooo*. Their eyes are open, but all their blood's in their head. I think they're too dizzy to see.

I duck behind Johnny Walker's cigarette stall. I think I know why they call him that, I think maybe he was a drinker. There's a rich man's drink called Johnny Walker, Gustav's got some in the lounge. I stick my face against the glass of the bar. 'La-duuuma!' the men cheer to the roof. Bafana Bafana scored a goal on TV.

I can't see my pa.

Mannie the barman's stomach is so big, it looks like he's planted there forever. He's like a tree at the river, with bottles and bottles of drink in the mirror. He sees me. He shakes his head.

My heart gives me a small glad kick.

Nita shouts, 'Stella, come and play for a bit!'

I spring away from the glass.

'Hi Stella.' Nita's pa's got smooth cheeks and no hair on his arms. He's got a smooth black gun in a gun holder thing. If you look in his eyes, he knows everything. But today his smile's got sorry in it.

The Truth Lady says, 'Hey?'

'I think he saw me looking for my pa in the bar.'

Nita's pa's a police, but he drives like a skollie for us. We hold tight to the bars in the back of his van. He swerves around the curves. The engine cries, *hiiiim* up the hill, then *wa-haa* when he slows. Nita's recorder falls, it bangs on the metal. I grab it, but I miss.

I spring. The van stops, we slide on our backs. I hold the recorder up high.

Nita crawls out, but she doesn't want it. She doesn't even love it.

Nita's ma's got a red skirt on, and a white shirt with rumples instead of sleeves. 'Hello mad things.' She walks straight past my nose with a fat, dripping koeksuster on a tissue. Nita's pa pulls her through the window, he kisses her so hard that their lips squash flat. She laughs like *she's* going fast around a curve. Nita's pa gobbles the whole koeksuster, he sucks his fingers while he drives. Nita's ma shakes her head, but seeds pop in her eyes, like the lucky bean seeds that I never see.

Nita's greedy like her pa, she sticks the whole koeksuster in her cheek, so it leaks. I pick pieces off mine and suck on the sweet, sweet pieces. It's warm and crunchy, each little bit bursts with delicious syrup. Nita's got a beautiful black stove with silver knobs. If we had electricity, Pa would get us one, I know. I feel like a fat, happy hummingbird with drunk, syrup eyes.

'Po-oppie, po-oppie, hoekom is jou hare so lank?'

I pull the elastic right up to my bum, so Nita's got to jump high up to her ribs.

'Po-ppie ...'

Nita's ma calls her from the house, 'Nita, come and get dressed, my love.' Nita's ma bends her head like a bird, 'Ni-ta.' I stand on the elastic so Nita's got to stop. I push her like a car that won't go, right up to her ma, to make her ma laugh.

There's a Xhosa song like running gold at the dump. The singing lady scratches through dead vegetables. She's got a pink skirt on, like inside a protea. When I close my eyes, there are Xhosas in the clouds, listening with me. She puts two brown cauliflowers in her sack. Her little girl climbs over foamy old potatoes. She holds up a pink plastic arm to her ma. The little girl kicks the rubbish with her shoes, the plastic is peeling in front, like mine.

Ma doesn't want me at the dump. It's dirty, she says, and it looks like you're desperate. It's full of shack people with no ground to grow things. The dump stinks like vomit and car tyres burning. Black smoke climbs the mountain whichever way the wind blows. But you can get lucky at the dump. Pa got our Diamond tape recorder there. I know because I asked him, 'Where did you get it, Pa?'

'Never mind,' he said.

And Pa doesn't lie, only about wine.

I try some old koki pens on paper. I pull a magazine stuck in a chair spring. Nearly Ninety! it says. It's got Mister Mandela's white hair and his white birthday grin. It's the Truth that we missed! It's wavy from water, but it's fine inside. I lift up a smashed painting of a white horse. I look for more Truths, but I find white hair and pink skin, instead. The doll's eyelids sag. It's got one arm missing. I slide one eye up. It's a sparkling blue marble. I push the circle in her stomach with my thumb. 'Ma-maa,' she cries.

'Mamaa!' The Xhosa girl points with the lost arm. The Xhosa song gets lost in the sky. Her ma talks soft and sorry to her daughter. I climb over the rubbish. 'Have it,' I say.

The lady prays her hands together, she dips her head like a dove. 'Enkosi,' she says.

I wish I could say, 'Thank you for your running gold song.'

I open the Truth. There's a white lady in a black, shining suit doing a new exercise in every picture. Big, red words say, SAVE YOUR HEART at the top.

I've found a way to save Mevrou!

My heart flaps like the magazine. I run off the tar, past the next door farm. Marais' apple trees burst with white blossoms, his bee hives buzz just like a noisy bar. At our Nooitgedacht gateposts, I swerve into the bush. Black butterflies fly off some hairy pink petals.

The Truth Lady says, 'Hang on. Nooitgedacht. What does that mean?'

'Never thought,' I say.

'Or …' she grins. She digs with her ink, *Nooitgedacht – Who would have thought?*

I wake up the sleeping air in the bush. A black and yellow tortoise climbs up a tuft. The robins complain, '*Seeee.*' The ducks on the dam slide like they're on skates. I run into my forest, straight past the stream near the ant eaten tree.

'Mevrou! Mevrou! Look what I found.'

'What now, mein kind?'

I push the bathroom door. Mevrou's big white skin runs with water. Blue veins crawl all over her legs. I flap the magazine, 'Something to save your heart!'

'Ooh.' Water from her hair rains *tiktik* on the book.

I pull the Truth away, I shake it. 'So you don't drop dead.' Mevrou's too big, the doctor said.

She slaps her hips so that her white fat shakes. 'I've lost some, haven't I?'

I shake my head, 'Uh uh.'

Mevrou laughs like I told the best joke in the world. Mevrou's like that, she always laughs when she shouldn't.

'Where have you been?' Ma's green eyes are cracked and cold in the smoke. I stutter a bit because of the green glass. I tell her about the exercises I found.

Ma asks, 'Did you see your pa in the village?'

I talk fast, 'No Ma, I looked.' The smoke blows away, I get stuck in the cold. 'On my life, Ma. I didn't.'

Ma turns away, she rubs her eyes. I hope, I really hope it's only smoke.

I tell the Truth Lady, 'I used to lie to Ma.'

Her black eyebrows kiss.

'Ma used to ask, Did you see your pa in the bar? I said, No, Ma.'

If I told her the truth she would take us to my ouma with the big arms and the Bible. We would never, never see my pa.

I wait for Pa in my tree. I tap my bottles to Akon. '*Convict, Convict …*' I listen to Radio Five now, not KFM. All the grade sevens do, because it's cool. But some of the Radio Five music is stupid. Some of the ladies can't even sing, and some of the men rap about titties and bums. It's rude, like they're doing it in front of you. But Akon sounds nice, even when he swears, 'Shit.' His voice is kind and brown, like a acorn.

Pa's very late.

Ma pokes the potatoes and ducks away from the smoke. Akon sings how he hates the rain. His voice is warm like a acorn, but Ma's stick pokes in my heart. Where is Pa?

I bang my bottles to show I'm not worried. I pray to God, not the one the nun loves.

Grace's already dirty after her bath. She rolls a gem squash, she slides on her bum. My chickens stay away.

I tell the Truth Lady, 'They are Amy and Bonny and Sonya.'

'Hey?'

'My chickens. That's their names.'

When Gracie was born, Pa gave up drinking. He sold beans and baby marrows outside the bar. He came home with milk powder and pork sausages in plastic. Ma put the milk powder away. She said she was happy, so there was milk in her titties for the day and the night.

Ma said she always had milk for me when I was a baby. She said I sucked like a vacuum cleaner. That made me laugh.

I tell the Truth Lady, 'We haven't got one, but Mevrou's got a strong German one. Its name is Bosch.'

Gracie was just a bunch of thin sticks. She came out light brown like Ma, not black like me and Pa. She couldn't even suck properly. I wasn't jealous of Grace then, she was just sleeping bread. Ma put her in a crate and covered her up. We joked that she would rise in the sun and we'd eat her for supper. Me and Ma sang, '*Brown girl in the ring, tra la la la la …*' Ma danced in the cabbages with her arms snaky, up near her ears. Sand fell down from her clicking fingers.

She said when her ma went to Bible group, she and her sisters danced in a ring. She said their shack shook full of five girls. She still didn't hug me, but sometimes she rubbed me between my wing bones. Ma's eyes were full of green sun, because my pa was a proper husband.

The Truth Lady says, 'Can you tell me about the trouble?'

Last Christmas, Pa came staggering with nothing in his hands. Gracie sucked and sucked for nothing all night. She cried and cried until her voice died. On Christmas day, Ma spoke slow and freezing, 'Frank, hear me. You will never see your children again. This is your last, last chance.'

Pa knew she was talking the truth. He knew from her ice voice and the green glass in her eyes. Ma pointed at me,

'And you.' I pressed my back against my tree. My fingers got a electric shock on the bark. 'This is your last chance too. I'm tired of your lies.'

We sell our veggies to Dora, now, at the Algemene Handelaar. Now Pa can't get thirsty outside the bar. Ma doesn't sing like she used to, she hardly even talks.

The Truth Lady says, 'The *other* trouble, Stella.'

The far rock goes sharp, it cuts the sun thin. It balances on the mountain blade. The road is a empty river of sand.
Where is Pa?

Gracie tries to walk to the hut. She turns her little feet out funny, not flat like they should be. She sticks her arms out, like someone's got her hands. She forces her legs forwards like something's stuck on her unkles.
The Truth Lady says, '*Ankles.*'
I hold my breath in case she tips over and smashes on her face.

The Truth Lady sighs, 'Can you get on with the story?'
'Huh?'
'The one for the judge?'

I see the car first. It's light green like veld grass, it bounces like a boat. The engine sounds like a long fart, *bbipppp*. Black smoke shoots out of the back pipe. It makes clouds in the apples, it bounces through our gateposts.
There are two men inside, one's dark and one's white.
When it gets to my tree, I see who the black man is.
The Truth Lady says, 'Who?'

'Pa!'

Akon sings, '*Oh daddy oh daddy ohhh …*'

Pa stands nice and straight. But Ma lifts her chin and sniffs. Pa laughs, 'Nothing, man.' The white man's got a brown moustache with lots of teeth underneath.

It's the man at the hedge who made the nun smile!

His eyes are light blue like bird eggs.

The Truth Lady says, 'Hey?'

'Starlings' eggs,' I say.

The silver metal on his chest is a big, fat cross. Red cigarettes stick out of his shirt pocket. They say Lucky Strike.

Grace pulls herself up on Pa's pants. Her mouth hangs open so her spit dribbles. Gracie's not used to white people, like I am. Pa says to Ma, 'Nancy, this is Jerry.'

The man stares at Ma like she's the full moon. 'Wow …' He shakes Ma's hand. Ma ruks it back like it's made of flames.

The Truth Lady says, 'Ha! A strike!'

'What?'

She laughs, 'Never mind.'

He sees me in my tree, 'It's a angel!' he says.

Even Pa looks surprised. That's *his* name for me.

Pa says, 'You should hear her sing.'

'Aah.' The man stares at my sparkling bottles. 'A musician.'

Something bursts in me like the lucky bean seeds. I rest inside his smooth, blue eyes.

Pa says, 'Jerry's looking for farm work.'

Ma's smiles like sour milk, 'Here? The only thing that grows here is slangbos.'

'And gateposts,' I say.

But Pa doesn't laugh. He says, 'Not for long.' My pa is sober, but he skips like a grade one. He calls Jerry, 'Come!'

Jerry swings Gracie off the ground. I wait for her to scream, but she grabs his sleeve, she jig jigs on his hip. She points at the sky and shows off her only word, 'Papapapa.'

Pa kicks some baby tomatoes by mistake. Ma bends down to get them. 'Everyone else grows apples,' Pa says. 'Not us.' He points at our rows of strong, green leaves, We're going to grow vegetables. We've got the sand for the potatoes, we've got water for the lettuce. Have you seen, now potatoes are forty five rand a bag!'

Jerry stares at the giant spinach next to Ma's knees. 'Bea-u-tiful.'

The Truth Lady dips her head, she whispers, 'The *spinach?* I don't think so.'

'Sorry?'

She says, 'Nothing, kid. Carry on.'

Pa spins. He points up the hill. 'You see that field? He said he'll sell it. It's two hectares. It's enough.'

'It's definite?' Jerry says.

Pa nods, proud. 'He said he'll sign when the papers come. We'll take the twenty thousand to the Land Bank, we'll get a loan for eighty.'

Up at the canal, the cut up sun turns the mountain rock pink.

Jerry stares at the slangbos. He points at the little white house waiting for us, 'Maybe he'll throw that cottage in.'

Pa grins, 'That's the dream.'

It feels like Jerry knows us.

He guessed our dreams about the house.

He saw me in my tree and said, 'Ah, a musician.'

It's like he can see in our hearts and find our old smiles.

Ma picks all the babies tonight, baby lettuce, baby carrots, baby green pepper. The potatoes are burnt, she forgot about them. She burns her fingertips on the black skin. She only puts the white insides on our plates. I tell Pa about my news. 'I'm going to save Mevrou's heart.'

He laughs, 'Hemel, Stella. That's a job!'

But Jerry listens, serious. It's like he also knows how much I love Mevrou.

Jerry's got thick, sweet cream for our tea. Ooh, it's delicious, it's name is Nestlé Condensed Milk. Jerry's cup has got Jesus with three sheep eating. It says, Christ is Among Us. He stabs two holes in the tin, he blows it in our cups. He says to me, 'Here, have a whole spoon.'

'Ooh, it's delicious!'

Gracie cries, jealous. She throws her bottle in the sand. Jerry feeds her a whole spoon too. She grabs his shirt like she's drowning, she shouts, 'Pa-pa-pa!'

Ma's old laugh bubbles up to her mouth. She washes the sand off the bottle teat.

Kutussh, Jerry lights a Lucky Strike. His hair has got fire flicks in it.

'Frank?' Ma points at Gracie's soft lips gone to sleep. Pa puts a little kiss where Gracie's nose dips. He carries her careful to the hut.

Ma asks Jerry, 'Are you from Cape Town?'

'Uh-uh.' Smoke pours through his smile, 'Hermanus.'

Ma says, 'Oh, I have a sister there.'

'Actually, outside Hermanus. Hemel-en-Aarde. Do you know anyone there?'

Ma shakes her head. Pa comes back and sits like a ghost. At night when he's not drinking, he goes quiet and shiny like he's got a fever.

'Is your family there?' Ma asks.

Jerry nods, 'My mom and dad.'

There's a secret question under my tree. You can hear it in the *ssrr* of the smoke and the *pikk* of the burning sticks. Why is he here?

Jerry hears it, he says, 'My wife left me. I had a bit of a nervous breakdown. My mom and dad said, Why don't you just drift for a bit? Take a break and find out what the Lord Jesus wants for you.' He sucks his cigarette. There's smoky love in his voice. 'They're good people, my folks.'

Ma doesn't ask about his nervous breakdown. I guess what it means. It's when your nerves can't go. It's like they're broken down on the side of the road.

Jerry twists his cigarette dead in the sand. 'Tell you what, Stella?'

I tell the Truth Lady, 'It's the first time that Jerry ever said my name.'

She nods, she checks her watch, 'Carry on.'

Jerry says, 'There's a box on my back seat. Get it for me please, man?'

It's a long wooden box the size of a bottle. I don't want to take it, it might be wine. I walk very slow. I put it far from his feet. Jerry's teeth flash in the firelight. He stretches to fetch it, he puts it on his knees. He snaps one buckle. His eyes smile wrinkly at the sides. He snaps the other one, he looks straight at me.

If it's a bottle of drink, Ma had better stop him.

He lifts the lid.

It puts treasure in my eyes. It turns the fire gold into silver. It makes silver veins on the leaves on my tree. It's the shiniest thing that I've ever seen, shinier than the silver pot when Ma scrubs it.

Pa blocks the silver light. 'Is it a trumpet?'

'A flute.'

Jerry nods at me. 'What must I play?'

It jumps out of my mouth, 'You Light Up My Life.'

Jerry hums the chorus. 'That one?'

Pa smiles his dimples. 'It was our wedding song.'

Ma looks young suddenly, like in her wedding photo.

Pa says, 'Nancy sang it when we got married at the dam.'

Jerry starts playing a long, silver song. Each note is true, the way it was made. His pale, long fingers float the notes. His fingertips are flat. Maybe the flute did that. Pa sits with Ma, and do you know what?

The Truth Lady says, 'What?'

'She tangles her arm into Pa's, it's true. Then do you know what?'

'Mm?'

'Pa kissed Ma on the side of her eye, and she didn't go stiff like a stick insect.'

I stare to make sure. Ma smiles her old smile from when I was in grade one. She hugs my pa's arm against her titties.

Jerry plays all the love that made Ma keep me, not kill me. He plays all the love that made Ma and Pa marry when my ouma said no. Ma's sisters sneaked to the dam for the wedding and Ma wore a pink skirt from Miladys. Pa bought a suit that was nearly new. They sold the suit later to buy me nappies. All that love, Jerry plays it.

I think God sent us someone like Jesus. His nerves broke down and his wife left him, but he brought us delicious condensed milk and flute music. He plays a silver song that loves us through our trouble, singing things you can't see, only feel in your chest.

The Truth Lady digs with her ink, *Shiny Christian.* She thinks, then she writes, *Sweet healing mission.*

Jerry slept at the fire. His …

The Truth Lady says, 'Wait! Is this a new day?'
I nod.
'When you start a new day, just *say*.'
'I'll bang on the tub.'
'Hey?'
I bang with a soft fist, dimm, *dimm*.
'Okay.'

I bang louder, *BOOMM*, *BOOMM*.

Jerry's head is wet. He's got man perfume on. Liquorice and cigarette smoke floats off his clothes. He's in blue jeans and a blue shirt, with shiny buttons. His brown shoes are flat in the front like his fingers. He's got a razor with a engine. His mirror has got pink flowers on the side. He sits on his car and buzzes his chin smooth. He snips his moustache with a tiny scissors. He even snips a hair growing in his nose. He sees me in his mirror, watching on the branch. He winks at me in his silver glass.

Pa's got a sharp piece of mirror stuck at the tap. He shaves with soap and his old plastic razor.

I say, 'Pa, you look like the cat that ate the cream.'

That makes them all laugh, but I know what it means. Mevrou explained. It said in the Truth, She arrived with him at church, looking like the cat that ate the cream. It was about this lady who made her husband come back. She said if he didn't come back and love her again, she was going to tell the police he didn't pay his taxes, and she was going to poison his race horses. He had race horses.

The Truth Lady says, 'Stella, go on.'

I follow Jerry and Pa to the sand, but Ma says, 'No, Stella. You'll be late for school.'

Jerry turns back.

'I won't, Ma. I'm fast.'

Ma points to the village.

'*Please*, Ma.'

Jerry waits with his smooth face.

Ma shakes her head and turns to the hut, but I see her mouth smiling up at the sides.

Prriip, prriip, the crust of the sand squeaks under my shoes. The birds are mixing their morning songs. The bush songs get sweeter and sweeter, like the jam doughnuts at

Dora's. First the icing sugar bursts up your nose, then you get the jam in the middle.

Suddenly their songs turn into crazy screams. 'WATCH OUT!' they shout. A black eagle floats in the clean sky. It stares down its beak, it bombs into the bush, *VOOSH*. The eagle sweeps up with a thin, twisting snake.

I shout, 'Pa!'

It's not the mother snake, she's fatter than that. The birds shout and clap. They all hate snakes.

I dive off the road.

Pa follows, but Jerry's shoes dig in the sand. 'No!' His face is as white as old bones. 'You won't catch me in there.'

Pa says, 'Man, it's just mole snakes and house snakes.' He laughs, 'Mostly.'

The eagle glides to the canal with its whipping, twisting snake. That flying snake makes Jerry shout, 'I kill snakes. I don't even wait to see what kind. I *kill* them!'

Jerry's very scared, so we go on the road.

Me and Pa love snakes. Pa's only ever killed one. It was a cobra, to save us, when I was small. I heard Ma whisper, 'Frank.'

She said louder, 'Frank.'

She screamed, 'FRANK!' to wake him.

Pa jumped up like there were skollies attacking.

Its shining yellow body curled above our door wood. It was as fat as my leg, it gripped strong and still.

'Jesus Christ!' Pa said. Pa never swears about Jesus!

Ma sunk me behind the cupboard. Pa ran right under the snake. He ran back with the spade. He smashed it to the floor, it landed *fllupp!* It poured thick circles around its own tail. It rised up and spread its yellow neck. Hate burned in its black mirror eyes. Pa chopped the metal spade, I saw through the door. *Krit! Krit!* he chopped on the cement square. I shut my eyes, I smelled the cement spark.

'Jesus.' This time Pa sounded sorry.

Flik flak flik.

I stared through Ma's legs. The snake's head sat alone on its own. Purple blood splashed all over Pa's toes. Its yellow body banged, *flik flak.*

'Papa!'

'It's okay,' Pa said. 'It's brain is dead.'

The snake with no head twisted and hit.

'Mamie!'

Ma said, 'It's okay. It's just its nerves.'

When its nerves were dead, Pa showed me its small head. He showed me the brown patches and said, 'This one's a cobra. Sometimes it's more brown, sometimes it's a copper colour like this. Be very, very careful my angel, this one kills. One little bite and you'll die in two hours.'

I started to cry, but Pa didn't hug me. 'The poison locks your throat so you can't breathe. You'll choke to death, Stella. Make sure you never *never* make a mistake.'

Pa didn't hug me, and he swore 'Jesus Christ.'

That made me know. Don't go near cobras.

A bush cutter chain curls like a huge, rusted snake. A old plough hooks its claws in the bush. Jerry asks, 'What's all this stuff lying around?'

Pa taps his brain. 'Old Eddie wasn't right.' Pa's dimples sink into deep lines. 'He was a salesman, not a farmer.'

'What did he sell?'

'Anything he could get cheap.'

Jerry looks furious, even with dead Eddie. He stares at the old telephone reel lying on its side. I think they left it here when the telephone was invented. Jerry asks, 'How did he die?'

'He promised someone a hundred proteas.' Pa points up to the canal. 'He was up there, counting the flowers.' Pa claps, *kapp!* Pa says, 'Like that! It was a stroke!'

The stroke shocks the lips off Jerry's teeth. He stumbles on, he zigs and zags his eyes on the ground. Pa bends down and pinches Jerry's leg. Jerry springs high, he runs in the air. 'Jurre!'

I tell the Truth Lady, 'That's a bad swear word. It's Afrikaans.'

'Bliksem!' Jerry punches Pa hard, but Pa can't stop laughing.

Mevrou's got opera music on loud. It's her favourite opera, Die Zauberflöte. Mozart wrote it, it means the Magic Flute.

The Truth Lady says, 'No!'

'It does, I promise.'

She shakes her head, 'That's insane.' Then she says, 'Don't stop.'

It's at the part where Prince Tamino is being chased by a snake. '*Zu Hülfe! Zu Hülfe!*' the three ladies sing.

The Truth Lady's eyebrows spring into her fringe, '*Really*, Stella?'

I nod. 'Mevrou's told me the story before.'

The Truth Lady stabs her page with her pen, *Magic Flute – Coincidence (Ghostly)?*

She says, 'And then?'

'Mevrou?' I shout.

Mevrou's frying a big pile of bacon for her and Gustav. I've had my porridge, but it makes me swallow spit. 'Mevrou!'

Hot bacon fat drips off her fork. 'Eina!' I lick my arm, but Mevrou doesn't even say sorry. Her big cheeks shiver, her eyes try to pop out. She drops her hot fork on the floor. She slips in hot fat. She grabs my head. She makes my neat hair a mess. She pulls herself to the dresser, just like a baby learning to walk. She snaps the three ladies off.

Jerry's eyes are dark like our sky after a cold, cold night. His silver cross is quiet. His buttons turn white on his blue shirt.

Mevrou squeezes the titty on top of her heart. She wobbles to the door.

Pa says, 'Mevrou Viljoen, this is Jerry.'

Mevrou hunts like a hawk inside Jerry's eyes.

Gustav comes down the stairs in shorts with cars on. His hair is fluffy like a chick. He's got titties like a girl's, his teats are pink. His legs are white like water lilies where his boots go.

Pa says, 'Gustav, this is Jerry. He's looking for farm work.'

Gustav just stares without saying hello.

Jerry's so funny! He throws his arms in the air like he's getting arrested. He turns in a circle with a big joking smile.

I've never heard this rough voice of Mevrou's. 'What's a white man doing looking for farm work?'

Jerry's smile falls off, but it climbs back on. 'What's a lovely lady like you doing in the kitchen?'

Mevrou hunts like a hawk.

Jerry stops the joke. 'No, man. I've just … I've had a bit of a hard time lately.'

I know what he means. He means his broken down nerves and his wife.

Mevrou asks, 'Where are you from?'

'He's from Hemel-en-Aarde,' I say. 'He plays the flute.'

'Only for our church.' Jerry looks through the door at Mevrou's smoking stove. 'My mom bakes the cakes and I play the hymns.'

Mevrou doesn't even trust Jerry's *mother*. I pull Mevrou's hand like I'm flushing a chain. 'The *nun* even likes him.'

Jerry's surprised. Then he smiles, 'Oh-hh, yes. I always stop at the church first when I get to a new town.'

The bacon makes a burnt stink. Mevrou picks the fork off the floor. She starts to wash it.

Pa asks Gustav, 'What do you say? He can help with the apples.'

I bite my laugh inside my lips. What apples? Gustav walks up the stairs on his white feet. My laugh leaks out between my teeth.

Pa warns, 'Ste-lla.'

Mevrou keeps washing the fork, so it's me who takes the burnt pan off the ring.

Gustav's hair is wet and flat on top. He pulls a shirt over his titties. He slides his lily foot into his long army boot. They're his oupa's boots from the world war. His ouma and oupa got burnt in Hamburg. Mevrou says the firebomb was so big, it sucked people off the pavements. It turned the tar into flames and cooked people in their homes. Gustav straps on his oupa's old sword. He stands up straight. He nods to Pa, 'We'll see about your Jerry.'

Gustav said yes!

Jerry can stay!

I race fast across Mevrou's smooth grass. 'La-duuuma!' I shout, up to the sky.

The Truth Lady asks, 'The boots and the sword. Where are they?'

I see a pink sword tip. I stick my thumbs in my eyes to make those green flashes. 'Maybe at the house?'

She writes, *Boots+Sword. Get a photo.*

Thik-thuk, thik-thuk, Gustav's boots bang the sand. I run backwards to watch him play his farming game. Pa calls it that because Gustav always says, 'Come Frank, let's get this place ready for apples.' Then Gustav grows fences, or gateposts instead. The apple prices have dropped a lot, but Pa says Gustav's stuck in his pa's dream. Pa laughs at Gustav, but he feels sorry for him. Pa said to me once, 'Look at anyone who is lazy, Stella. Lazy people are scared people. Think about it, lazy is never just *lazy*.'

I tell the Truth Lady, 'Pa always makes me think about things.'

The Truth Lady nods. 'Go on.'

Pa is patient with Gustav, like he's playing with Grace. But Jerry's skin is cross and stiff. He chews his moustache on its gold tips. I try to show Jerry it's only a game. 'Show us your sword, Gustav. Show us your sword!'

Gustav asks Pa, 'Must I Frank?', like it's a war.

Pa nods.

Shlee-eek. Gustav's sword flashes like diamonds in the sun. Its crooked cross glows black on the handle.

The Truth Lady gasps, she slashes, *Swastika!*

Gustav holds it high, so its tip pricks the sky. *Slatch! Slatch! Slatch!* Gustav slices some green reeds to pieces. Jerry stares like Gustav's a idiot. I laugh until his eyes smile crinkly at the sides.

Pa sends me to school. 'You better run before the nun burns you up.'

I skip nearly all the way to the tar, singing, '*Don't you wish your girlfriend was hot like me …*' that song on Radio 5.

I bang the metal, *BOOMM BOOMM.*
'New day,' I say.

We practise our God songs for the concert. The nun only loves God music, she thinks cool music makes us want to do sex. But some of the sex songs make me ashamed, and some of the break up songs make me scared for Ma and Pa. Nita and me wish we went to the poor coloured school. They've got sixty in a class and not enough desks, but you can listen to any music you want. They have all their classes in Afrikaans, and the girls play soccer and swear. I don't want to swear, I just want to listen to cool music at school.

They're not scared of God at the coloured school. Nita says the children pinch and tease in morning prayer, and no one writes essays for punishment. We had to write three pages of essay when the nun caught us singing Natasha's song, '*I wanna have your babies …*' The nun even phoned Nita's pa. Nita's pa pretended he was cross with Nita, but when he put the phone down he laughed. Pa also laughed when I told him. The nun didn't phone Pa because we don't have a phone. And she didn't phone Mevrou because she thinks Mevrou only pays for my fees.

The Truth Lady says, 'Oh yes?'

'Ma always says, Be nice to Mevrou, she's very good to us, but I'm nice to Mevrou because she's like my ouma.'

My pa's ma ran away when he was only two, and my Caledon ouma didn't want me to live. When I was in Ma's stomach, my ouma said, 'Just wait. One day you'll come crawling with your child of sin.'

That's me.

In my essay I wrote, I don't really want to have babies, I just love that song. I don't have a boyfriend, I'm only eleven.

I say to the Truth Lady, 'Because it was last year.'

I wrote, I can't help it that Natasha said that in her song, and she's also sorry. She says sorry in the song, if you listen you'll hear how she says she wants to keep her lips buttoned up, but it bursts out of her. I love the tune more than the words. I know I'm too young for making sex. I'm sorry.

The Truth Lady says, 'Okay, what next?'

I sing with the choir, 'O *come all ye faithful, joyful and triumphant …*'

The nun pulls her mouth like a dog's bum. She waves at me like she's trying to stop the Worcester taxi. I don't mind today, we've got Jerry at home.

I ask the Truth Lady, 'And guess what happens while we're singing?'

'What?'

'Lucky beans shoot out! It's like someone spat them!'

I catch them flying with my own eyes. Red beans land on Mary's head, some land on her baby. Some get hooked in the nun's veil.

Me and Nita watch them all day. I pick one off David's head in line.

'What are you doing?' he asks, but he stands dead still.

'I'm helping you.'

His hair is as silky as the reeds at the river.

I stop.

The Truth Lady says, 'No need to be shy with *me*, kid. I've been married twice.'

'It had electricity in it.'

Like the wall next to my desk, when I stroke it with my fingertips.

I'm brave today from the lucky bean burst. Everyone walks quietly past the nun, they go soft down the stairs in the fire escape. Then they crash through the sunbeam, they run. I take my bag slowly off the hook.

I ask the Truth Lady, 'Do you know sometimes you get a drum in your throat?'

She nods.

I follow the nun down the stairs. When she gets to the sunbeam, I say, 'Sister Beatrice?'

Her titty bumps into my cheek. I take a breath. I let the drums ask, 'Please can I sing my own song at the concert?'

She digs her claws into my shoulder bone. She pushes me out of the fire escape. 'No Stella. You must sing with the choir.'

I beg her to see. 'Sister Bea …'

'Only the Musicians are doing solos.'

When Nita goes to Dora's to buy bubblegum, I press my nose hard on the glass of the bar. I can't see my pa, but I'm still furious.

I walk to the stinky bins at the back. A pile of silver papsaks climb up each other. They stink of sour wine, but they're fat from *vrot* air. I jump on one hard because of the nun. I jump with two feet, *PAPP!* I explode another one, *PAPP!!* Mannie opens the back door of the bar. My bombs are so loud I can't hear what he says. Nita runs and jumps on a papsak. *PAPP!* She acts like she's also cross, but she's not. Her pa's a police, so she doesn't care. Nita never, never gets in trouble.

Me and Nita stop at the video shop. There's a vampire wolf there with dirty dog fur. Its eyes are white lights, its yellow fangs are smeared with blood. The writing says, Salvation, in dripping red blood. Me and Nita stare. Nita points at the red letters, 'What's that?'

I've heard the nun say about salvation. She thinks Jesus saved us with his blood. I pat the vampire's dirty fur. I say, 'It's the nun's little doggie.'

Nita laughs so hard, I've got to bang her on her back.

Ma's humming with the green squash, '*Don't kill the world …*'

That's a Boney M song! It was on Ma's tape, the one that I cut.

The Truth Lady jerks, '*Who cut? What?*'

'You can tell the judge. *I* broke Ma's tape. It was me.'

Boney M made Ma homesick for Caledon. It made her shout to Pa, 'I'll take the children to my ma!' That's my ouma with a mean God like the nun's.

'I cut that song with my scissors, it was me.'

The Truth Lady nods, 'Alright, alright. Carry on.'

I give Grace a kiss. She wants some more, but her chin is full of spit from her new teeth peeping. 'Mama,' Grace says.

'Ma!' I shout. 'Grace said *Mama*!'

Ma stops humming, she smiles. 'I know.'

I forget about the nun and the solo. My sister's got two words, not one. And my ma is humming in the sun.

The Truth Lady asks, 'What about the men?'

Gustav's in his jean shorts, planning with his hands. Pa holds a gum pole. He nods and nods like that's his job. Jerry squeezes, squeezes a rusted wire puller. He squeezes the metal, his teeth are bare like a dog. The fence wire whines under its breath, *see-eeee* … Suddenly it stops. *Dukk!* The puller snaps loose.

Gustav sings, 'Hoo hooo,' like a mad owl in the day. Pa claps Jerry hard on the back, but Jerry's frown still pulls like a wire puller.

'Hi!' I wave. Jerry's face snaps loose. Pa gets those proud eyes he gets when he sees me.

I go my forest way. *Splutch splutch* I walk through splashy grass from the underground stream. It's a broken water vein in the earth, it bubbles from the deep near the ant eaten tree. The roots of the beefwood still grab at the air. The ants attacked them, Pa said. He said it took years, then the wind came one day and teared the tree out. The roots still look surprised to be in the light. They coil from the trunk like snaky wood tails. I crawl over them into the dark cave. It smells like mice poo and mud inside. Lumps of wasp nest hang from the roof. The mother waits at the back on a big vein. She shines in the dark like black liquorice. She's a huge, sweet house snake, she can't hurt me. She flicks her tongue to see if I'm mean. I talk to her sweet, like Pa talks to me. 'Sorry, my girl, I just came to see if you've laid your babies.'

She tries to taste if I'm dangerous.

'It's okay, my girl.'

I look everywhere for eggs, but there's only tangled wood and old shreds of spiders' webs. I crawl back into the sun.

I spring over Eddie's traps on the path. Pa snapped them shut after Sheek got choked. Sheek was Ma's dog, when I was still young.

The Truth Lady sighs. 'As in rich Arab sheik?'

I shrug. 'Sheek.'

Pa was the one who found him dying. He ran to Gustav to ask for a gun, but Gustav has only got one sword. Mevrou phoned Nita's pa to shoot Sheek, so Sheek wouldn't suffer. Pa said it was the first living thing that Nita's pa ever shot. He vomited in the bush. Pa cried on the side. Gustav waited on the road, far away. Nita's pa asked Gustav later, 'What are those death traps doing in the bush?' Gustav lifted his chin, he stuck his arms straight. 'My father was a hunter.'

Pa and Nita's pa looked at each other quick. Pa said they nearly burst from thinking the same thing. Ja, like he was a apple farmer too.

I asked Pa, once, 'What did you do with Sheek when he was dead?' Pa took me to Sheek's trap on the path. Its long, sharp teeth were locked together. Pa pointed in the green. 'He's in there, buried deep.' I climbed in the bushes to look for the grave. There was a circle of thin grass in the middle. There were tiny white disas growing wild. I felt like a small chick in a huge bird's nest.

'Pa!'

'Ja?'

'Sheek has got flowers.' I picked a little white disa and crawled out.

I took the flower home to Ma, but she looked like a egg eater with a egg in its neck. All she said was, 'Watch out for snakes.'

The Truth Lady sags like she's falling to sleep.

I was three when we had Sheek. All I remember is that he was big and brown, and he licked my face wet.

I show the Truth Lady, 'I've got a scar on my cheek where his tooth hooked my skin.'

Ma said it was a accident. She said Sheek was beautiful, he never hurt things on purpose. He loved Ma's chicks so much, he licked them to death. Ma said she woke up and there he was, with a wet, dead chick between his paws. It was a heart attack, she said. Ma would love to get a dog, I know, but Pa says she won't because she loves them too much. Ma had to leave her first dog in Caledon because of me. Then her next dog, Sheek got strangled in the trap.

That last time that Pa got stuck in the bar, I asked, 'Is your first dog dead now, Ma?'

Ma nodded. She bit her lips like she was biting bad memory from the inside. 'Dogs are just heartbreak.'

'Why don't you get a new dog, Ma?'

Ma stared at our hut and our fire place and our washing line. She said it angry, like I was Pa, 'We can't go to Caledon with a dog. And we can't leave it here with your *father*.'

I climbed my tree and hung on my branch. I waited and waited for Pa to come and stagger.

I don't like dogs anyway, I like chickens.

It's lucky that Pa shut the traps. I don't mean for Sheek, I mean for the animals that hide on our farm. I've seen duiker buck in my forest. They flash their white tails, they spin their pretty legs. One Sunday I saw a caracal cat drinking at the river. It had black make up on its eyes, it had sharp ears with black feathers on the tips. It hissed and it spat, it showed its white fangs. It jumped off the rock. It landed soft, like the ground was a cloud. It lashed away like lightning. It didn't expect a girl at the river.

I told Pa, but I didn't tell my ma. I knew what she would say, 'Watch out for snakes.'

The Truth Lady says, 'Stella, can you stick to the story?'
'Huh?'
'You know.'

Ma's humming at home. Gustav's paying everyone to play the farming game, and guess what Mevrou's doing?

The Truth Lady says, 'What?'

'Star jumps on the grass! It's true!'

Mevrou's decided to try. She really, really wants to save her heart now. The ground goes *Bom! Bom!* I'm telling the truth, Mevrou shakes the earth! Her white gladiolus flowers shiver in their bed. Her skirt is tucked in her undies, her blue worms crawl. The three cherubs don't watch. They pee water from their winkies, instead.

The Truth Lady asks, 'How old was Mevrou?'

'Seventy three.'

Mevrou counts, 'One … Two … Three … Ooop!' She giggles. She hurries back to the house. 'Eeee,' I hear her laughing in there. She comes back out. 'I nearly had a accident.' The star jumps made her pee, you see.

Bom! The fat flaps off her arms, it makes a shaky wave at her unkles.

The Truth Lady says, '*Ankles.*'

I hope she's not breaking any more veins.

In the next exercise, the Save Your Heart lady lies down on the ground and jumps up with a smile. Mevrou tries it, but she gets stuck. 'Oof,' her face is dark red, like vrot watermelon. She struggles up, 'Oo-of.'

She wants to live, she wants to make her heart strong. Mevrou has really decided to try.

'Read to me,' Mevrou pants.

I turn the page. I read, 'I Sent Them to Heaven. Interview with a family murderer.'

I ask the Truth Lady, 'Did you write it?'

She nods, her black eyes shine.

Me and Mevrou stare at a red man with red cheeks and a white bandage on his head. He leans on his chair with his huge hands on his knees. It feels like he's going to fall on top of me. He's wearing jean shorts like Gustav, with no shoes on his feet.

The Truth Lady says, 'Believe me, that guy didn't need shoes where he wanted to be.'

There's a small photo of a scared lady with straight hair. It says, Koos's wife, Delene was about to leave him.

Koos's big toes are curled up, I think they're disabled. But I think Delene was going to leave him because of the drink. He's got that brandy sunburn the white men get at the Vyeboom Hotel. There's half a nurse behind the murderer, the camera cut her off.

I turn the page. There are two beds with bright red blood on the sheets. The white pillows are nearly all red. They are terrible, terrible beds.

The Truth Lady shakes her head, 'I remember those beds.'

On the same page, there's a drawing of a brain. It looks like sponges stuffed in a head. A silver bullet floats on a red arrow, it points in the mouth and out of the neck. That's where the bullet shot through their heads.

Mevrou drops on her stomach again. 'Oof.' Little pools of water hang under her eyes. A drop dangles off the tip of her nose. I read loud because Mevrou's ears are old.

'The killer is furious. I *hate* these doctors. I *hate* this hospital. They watch me all day and all night. They effed up my plan.' (I know what it says, but it's got those two stars, so I say effed instead.)

Mevrou makes a squeak.

'My wife and my daughters are waiting for me. I must go to them.

Where are they? The questions are in slanty writing.

'In heaven.'

Mevrou's giggle wobbles her stomach.

'*What about the neighbour who tried to help?*

I'm sorry about her. She should have stayed away. My wife promised to obey me, no matter what. She was mine. My children were mine. They were from my own body. My own …

The monster struggles to keep the tears in. He punches his knee.

She was going to leave me for a stupid doos. (It's also got two stars but I know what it says). She was going to run off with my whole life!

Were you punishing her?

No. No. Not punishment. I was going to go with them.'

Mevrou snorts like a pig.

'The monster sobs in a wave of self pity. When he is calm again, he says, I'm a good hunter. I shot my girls through the head with my hunting rifle. My little one, Milly, only woke for one second. My wife watched, but not for long. I told her, Don't worry, Delene, I'm coming, too. Then I shot her through the head.

He wipes his face with his murdering hands. He points at the nurse who is guarding him. They can't watch me forever.'

Mevrou grabs the Truth, she holds it up to her eyes. She laughs at the murderer on the chair. She wipes the pools, but laughing tears fill them. I don't know why Mevrou laughs at other people's trouble.

'Why are you laughing?' I ask.

Mevrou points at the brandy man. 'Just look at him. He's a beast.'

But Mevrou didn't laugh at Beauty and the Beast. When I was small, she read all of Gustav's fairy tales to me. Beauty and the Beast, Rapunzel, Rumpelstiltskin.

I tell the Truth Lady, 'I know how to spell it.'

She nods. 'Go on.'

Mevrou never laughed at fairy tale trouble. She only thinks true trouble is funny.

The Truth Lady sinks to her recorder machine, 'Slipping and sliding away from the truth ...' She thinks. 'Scrubbing the sink in case of Salmonella.'

'What's Salmonella?'

'It sounds like a fairy ...' She crinkles up her nose. Hairy black tunnels go up her nose bones. 'But it's a disease from old meat. Mostly old chicken.' She says, 'What next?'

Jerry and Pa buy chicken wings and bread. Ma takes the Spar bag from Pa. She leans close and sniffs. 'I see Jerry kept you good.'

I walk after Pa, I've got to tell him. 'Pa, a Rawsonville farmer shot his whole family *and* the lady next door.'

'No!'

'Dead.'

'A white man?'

I nod. 'In their beds.'

Usually Pa laughs at the Afrikaans farmers, but now he stops on the cement square. He stares in the air.

'Pig,' Ma says.

I say, 'He shot them like buck.'

'What?' Jerry asks from the car.

'It was a hunting gun.'

Ma stands with the bread. 'How do you know?'

'I read it in the Truth. He shot himself too, but he missed his own brains.'

Ma puts the bread high where the chickens can't steal it.

I say to Jerry, 'I think those guns are too long to aim at your face.'

Jerry nods like he knows.

I say, 'He said he sent them all to heaven.'

Pa mumbles like he does when the radio talks about murder and rape. Everyone's upset, not laughing like

Mevrou, so I tell them the worst part. 'The pillows were full of blood.'

'Oh God,' Ma's voice cracks like a egg.

'Shame,' Pa says.

'Shame for *who*?' Ma's angry with Pa instead of the brandy man.

'Shame for all of them.'

I whisper to Jerry at his car, 'I think he was drunk.' I say it soft, so Pa can't hear, because that's like saying he could kill us when he drinks.

Pa gets glad later, without even wine. When we're eating our chicken wings, he says to Ma, 'Guess who's going to be Marais' new son-in-law?'

'Who?'

Pa pokes his chicken wing at Jerry. Jerry lifts his lip like a dog, but Pa teases, 'Hettie smaaks him.'

'Don't talk crap, man.'

Jerry swears at Pa!

Ma asks, 'Oh? When's the wedding?'

'Frank's talking crap!'

Jerry swears two times, but my pa just laughs. They're good, teasing friends, Pa and Jerry.

Later, Jerry plays a slow, pretty song. 'For you, Nancy. It's from Frankie.' Pa tries to sing, but he only knows the chorus. '*Lady in red* …' Ma smiles at her knees, like she's too shy to lift her eyes. '*Lady in red* …' It makes me think of the red pillows and the mad, brandy man. But the notes are so pretty, they sound like true love.

I bang, *BOOMM BOOMM*.

The Truth Lady jumps, 'Hey?'

'New day.'

In the morning, my chickens argue loud in the bush. Ma's in the garden catching the snails that stayed too late, and Jerry's brushing his teeth at the tap. There's a pale shirt shape on his bare skin. He's got muscle bumps up his back, just like my pa.

Pa's feeding Grace porridge on the chopping block. She eats so fast, she makes Pa laugh. She swallows quick, then opens her mouth like a chick. Me and Ma saved Amy like that. The dog from Bergsig came and ate Amy's mother. Me and Ma fed the hatched chicks with a match stick. I fed them too much and the porridge squeezed through their nose. I panicked and blew it out with my mouth. But when Gracie's had enough, she shuts her mouth tight. She smacks the spoon hard, away from her face.

Most of our chickens just die of old age. Ma breaks their necks gentle, that's what she says. We even ate Bennie, our rooster, with curry rice. He was tough as a tyre. Ma used lots of garlic and Messaris red spice. I'm glad he was tough, that means he was ready to die. He couldn't make chicks and he was walking all stiff. Ma asked me first, 'Is he ready, do you think?'

'Yes.'

Pa said, 'Bennie can go home.' Pa thinks the same as the sad killer. Pa says dying is just going to God.

After we ate Bennie, I looked at the sky. 'It's far to God's, Pa, I can't even *hear* him.' I was still young.

Pa said, 'God is inside you. That's where he is.'

I listened hard in the morning. I heard Bennie shout inside my ears, '*Aar-ar-ar-ar-Rooo!*'

I tell the Truth Lady, 'I was still young, but it was the truth.'

'Mm. Carry on.'

My hens are screeching like it's a emergency. I crawl in the bush to see what's wrong.

It's a snake, that's what!

A beautiful brown egg eater, coiled around a egg. It flicks its tongue to check if it's fresh. It's got a small head and dark squares everywhere. The snake stretches its lips, it clicks its jaw loose. It covers the egg so its skin patterns stretch. I stick my head out. Pa's wiping Grace's face with a nappy.

'Pa!'

Pa comes to see.

'Sssh,' I say. It looks like the snake's choking, but its got spikes in its throat that crush the egg up. Gracie crawls after Pa. She grabs for my hens, she laughs like a evil child. Pa pulls her to him, he points at the snake. Gracie shuts up. We watch like it's our own special freaky show.

Ma laughs in our garden. Ma *never* laughs in the morning!

I peep between the leaves to see.

Jerry aims a snail at the silver coffee tin. *Shluk!* It smashes against the side. 'Stop it!' Ma says, but her teeth sparkle in her laugh.

I say to the Truth Lady, 'Do you know what he did?'

'What?'

'He put a slimy snail on his titty.'

'Urgh.'

It sways its slippery body out of its shell, it feels the air like it's climbing some stairs.

The Truth Lady says a secret to her machine. 'His nipple turned into small, hard bump.'

'How do you know?'

'Ag, just a guess.' She shrugs. 'And your Ma?'

'Ma giggled like the snail was tickling her own insides.'

Pa pulls me in so I don't miss the show. The snake sways this way and that. Its mouth is so wide I can see its air pipe. Forward and back, forward and back, it whips like it's attacking! Gracie digs her nails into my neck. The snake ducks its head. The shell shoots out, clean and white and crushed.

The snake only sees us when the show is over. It rubs its rough scales like a viper, *crrrrr*. Me and Pa laugh at its fake growl. It grips on the tree, it pulls its egg belly along the branch. Pa takes Grace so I can fetch the few eggs that the greedy snake left. 'Alright Amy, alright Bonny, alright Sonya,' I sing.

I tell the Truth Lady, 'When Jerry saw the eggs in my skirt, do you know what he did?'

'Ja?'

He puts his hand in his pocket. He pulls out three silver fives.

'Four omelettes please,' he says.

'What are omelettes?' I ask.

Jerry says, 'Ag, mixed up eggs in a pan.'

I take the money, I don't grab. 'Thank you Jerry.'

Fifteen rand for nothing! I didn't even *lay* the eggs.

I mix the eggs in a bowl, I stick the pan on the fire. I keep the coins in my hand while I cook omelettes. Ma has a little smile all the time. 'I know what *you're* going to do,' she says.

We pour my bottle of coppers out on the bed. Ma helps me count fifteen rand more. It's a heavy heap, it's nearly all of them. Now I've got thirty, thank you to Jerry.

I twist my money in a bread packet. I hold my pocket all day to keep it safe. I drop my lunch box on the ground at break by mistake. Adrian kicks it in the gutter. David shouts, 'Hey!' He cleans it on his leg and brings it to me. David's pa is the manager of Welgemoed, but David never never acts white and rich. Adrian talks high like me, 'David, David my love, please marry me!' I chase Adrian, but I stop after a few steps. I might lose my money, so I use words instead. '*You* can marry David if you want. It's *allowed*, you know.'

Adrian shuts up and stays away, because that's the same as saying he's gay.

I'm lucky on this day. There's a huge rooster flapping with Oom Piet's hens. His red rubber crown is hanging down, he's only got a few tail feathers left. His body is dirty brown, like dead leaves full of dust. He jerks his head this way and that, like a upside down police, looking for skollies on the street.

'The rooster please, Oom.'

'Forty rand for the breeders,' says Oom Piet.

I feel so upset, it hurts my chest. I want the upside down rooster in charge of the street. He'll make beautiful chicks.

'I've only got thirty.'

Oom Piet shakes his head.

I untwist my packet, I try and choose a hen. The rooster's still trying to fly himself right, he cools the half dead hens with his wings. It's Nita who says, 'Oom, can't she have ten rand off the rooster?'

Nita's my best, best friend. She knows, even though she's never even *seen* my chickens. She's never even come to my house.

The Truth Lady asks, 'Why?'

'I think they've seen Pa zigging and zagging on the road. I think they think I've got a bad home.'

Nita's pa comes in his yellow van. I think that's why Oom Piet grabs the rooster. I think that's why he unhooks its feet. The rooster twists its head and stabs his hand. Oom Piet swears, 'Poophol!' and that's probably why the rooster kaks on him. I grab its tied feet, I swing it up. I let it fly in one place. 'Thank you,' I say in the flapping wind.

I shut its wings and stick it on my hip. Nita's pa laughs through his window glass. He gets out, he opens the back for Nita.

Nita runs to him, 'Pa, there's a white man staying with them and he gave her fifteen rand and she had fifteen rand and Oom Piet said …'

'A white man?'

'It's Jerry who plays the flute. Oom Piet said …'

'Staying where?'

'Pa …'

'Ja?'

'He sleeps at their fire.'

Loud questions shout in Nita's pa's eyes. But I wave and walk away with my rooster. I carry it on my hip, like I carry my sister.

At Os's Butchery, three men in white suits carry dead sheep. Os's truck steams from white ice, the men wear white gloves made from rubber. The sheep hang on hooks in the freezing steam, with no head and no hooves and no coat. Someone's written purple words on their skin, maybe their name from when they were living. Inside, Os the butcher slaps a raw leg on a scale. It slides off the tray like it's trying one last time to get away. I say to my rooster, 'You see? You're lucky you're free.'

My rooster jerks and blows up, but it doesn't bite. It gets hotter and hotter because it can't flap. 'Wait, wait. We're nearly home,' I say. I sing it that old song Pa taught me when I was small. It's about this man who goes to jail and when he comes out, everyone forgives him and loves him again. '*The green, green grass of ho-ome* …' The song cools the rooster. He sits still, he turns his head. Like now he knows that maybe he's lucky.

The Truth Lady asks, 'Can you tell me something else?'
'What?'
A neat frown cuts her face, like it's made with a blade. '*Anything* else.'

Shupp.
'Hey?'
'Pa slapped cement on some new gateposts.'
'*More* gateposts?'
I nod. 'More.'
Gustav was pointing, planning apples with his hands.
'And Jerry?'
Jerry was up at the dam, fetching water for cement.

He dropped his bucket. 'Fuck.' But I'll say eff to the judge. He stared at the blisters.

'Wait, kid. How do you know?'

'Mevrou.'

'*Hey?*'

'Mevrou showed me all the things that I missed.'

'You mean ...?'

I nod. 'All the things I didn't see.'

The Truth Lady stares. '*Really?*'

A bee flew past his ear, *vuzuzz*. Jerry ducked like it was a helicopter, come to cut off his head.

The Truth Lady sighs. 'Listen kid, I need ...'

Water rushed at our hut. Ma dropped her dress on the lavender at the tap.

The Truth Lady says, 'Stella?'

'All he saw was Ma's bare arm.'

'Ja?'

He tipped his bucket with his foot.

I say to the Truth Lady, 'That's all I want to say.'

The Truth Lady sneaks to her machine, 'His mouth hung so wide that the wind dried inside it.'

The apples are silent in their rows. Marais sprayed something stinky to chase the birds away.

My school bag is rubbing my shoulder skin, but I don't care today, I sing to my rooster about his new home. I think of chicks as soft as dandelions running around the hut.

The Truth Lady says, 'Stella! What happened with Jerry?'

Something drums in the earth, I feel it in my feet. Hettie gallops past on her huge muscle horse.

The Truth Lady says, 'Hettie?'

'The big girl next door.'

It's a big American Saddler with a shining orange bum. 'Ea-sy,' she says. She rips the silver bar across its lips like a saw.

The Truth Lady frowns, 'Stella?'

'Ea-sy' Jerry said, just like Hettie.

The Truth Lady says, 'Yes?'

I can't carry on.

'Was Nancy naked?' she asks.

'No! Ma still had her panties and bra.'

'Ja?'

'Hey!' Ma rukked her wet dress on her skin.

'Jesus.' Jerry said.

Ma's voice was a slap, 'What!'

I stop.

The Truth Lady asks, 'And?'

'He stroked her strap.'

'Her *strap*?'

I nod. 'Tell the judge. He didn't touch her skin.'

Hettie's purple tracksuit flaps, her big purple legs stick straight in her stirrups. Pa says sometimes Afrikaners like to be American.

My rooster wants to race, he kicks his tied feet. I've got to sing him the Green Grass chorus again.

The Truth Lady asks, 'Did you bust them?'

'Huh?'

'What did you see?'

Jerry's pouring a bucket of water. Ma's dress is wet. Her eyes look strange, like Oom Piet's hen, when he did that trick for us. He stuck it on its side, he drew a white line on the tar. It fell to sleep, with its eyes wide and bright.

The Truth Lady says, 'Wow,' but it's like she's not surprised.

Ma's wet dress makes me worried, but I show her the rooster. 'Look Ma. We can make babies.'

I hold the rooster down. Ma crouches and cuts the rope with a knife. My rooster flaps a rooster storm. He stabs Amy and Bonny and Sonya with his beak. He's ashamed, I think, because they saw his tied feet.

'Hey!' I chase him.

Ma's strange. She's wearing a wet dress. She's got a funny, gentle smile for my dirty, dusty bully.

The Truth Lady smiles like a girl vampire. She writes, *Pied Piper. Hypnotised with his eyes.*

All afternoon the rooster charges our hens. Later he even dives for Pa's feet. 'He doesn't like men,' I try to explain. My rooster won't even let the hens eat. He wants everything for him. My old rooster, Bennie was like a sweet hen compared to him. I tell Pa, 'I'll be surprised if he even lets them lay eggs!'

Pa laughs. He loves my jokes. 'Why don't you call him Mugabe?' he asks.

We know about Robert Mugabe from the radio. All the Zimbabweans are hungry, but Mugabe goes shopping on jet planes. He took the white farms away, now everyone's starving.

Jerry teases Pa, he points at Mugabe. 'What's the bet you can't pick up a hen in front of him?'

Pa catches Amy. Mugabe slashes at Pa's unkles.

The Truth Lady says, '*Ankles*.'

Pa drops Amy, he hop hops away. Amy cries, she's terrified.

'Shame!' I say.

Jerry grabs Amy as she rushes past. He grips her tight between his knees. Mugabe runs at him, ready to strike, but Jerry shouts, 'Voetsek!' He kicks with his shoe.

'Hey!' I shout.

Lucky he misses. Jerry laughs with shiny, long teeth. Mugabe shakes his head. Furious air fluffs his feathers. Jerry strokes Amy hard with his hand. 'What you going to give me, Frankie?'

Pa says, 'I would buy you a bottle …'

Ma goes stiff like the thorn tree.

'But I can't. So … I'll sing you a song later.'

'I'll sing with him,' I say. I don't want Jerry to think that Pa's cheap.

Ma smiles and rubs me between my wing bones, 'It's only a joke.' Ma loves her new, big family with the extra man and the rooster.

Jerry bought lamb chops for us! Ooh, they're delicious. I keep my bones, I chew on the ends. Pa plays with Grace, he throws her up high. Ma only lets him do it when he's sober. Grace sticks her fists in her mouth. She laughs like a bunch of sweet berries bursting. Usually Ma leaves the dishes to soak, but tonight she scrubs the pot until it shines like treasure.

Jerry opens his flute box.

I throw my lamb bones into the night.

Jerry plays a song that I've never heard.

'*Michelle, my bell* …,' Pa sings from the hut. It sounds like a laughing, longing song. I store it in my body, even in my bones. I even forget to help my pa with his bet.

'Sho!' I say, when the song stops.

'It's the Beatles,' Jerry says.

The Beatles are very, very old, but Jerry plays them so cool.

'You should make a CD,' I say.

Jerry looks like I pulled him under water.

The Truth Lady says, 'You mean …?'

'Tell the judge, he wanted to cry.'

'*Really?*' she says, like it's a lie.

Then he plays another song for me, a lekker fast song. His fingers flick like little birds fixing their nest. Pa sings from inside, '*Dum diddy di dum dum* …'

I laugh at the silly song. Even Grace giggles.

At the end, I clap, I say, 'How do you do that?'

Jerry taps his heart. 'It's in my body.'

I stare at his chest, where he touched. 'Me too.'

Jerry nods. 'You and me are the same.'

I ask the Truth Lady, 'Did you know that your heart can catch light?'

'Uhh…' She shrugs.

Even my ribs catch fire like dry, happy twigs. That's when I tell Jerry about the nun. 'The nun won't let me sing a song for our concert. Only the instruments get solos.'

He says, 'She *should* let you sing!'

Jerry's *also* angry with the nun!

Jerry understands everything!

'It's nice with you here, Jerry.'

His eyes are surprised, so I explain. 'We're all happy again.' I say very soft, 'Pa's not drinking, so Ma won't take us away to Caledon.'

We watch my ma dry her hands at the hut. She strokes her hair neat. Jerry picks up his flute and do you know what he plays?

The Truth Lady shrugs.

The Green Grass song! He plays it like the end of sadness, like a man out of jail that everyone still loves.

The song makes Pa carry Grace to the door. It makes him look at Ma with proud, brown love. It makes him kiss Gracie's feet underneath.

The Truth Lady says, 'Stella. Can you tell me more trouble?'

'Just now. It's coming.'

I hit with my fist, *BOOMM BOOMM*.

In the morning, Pa watches me fight with my hair. I stretch it and hurt it, but it still stands wild.

Pa laughs, 'Leave it, my angel. It looks like a halo.'

'Huh?'

'You know in the paintings the Catholics make?'

Pa means the bubbles that float around their heads. I laugh and laugh about a black halo. 'The angels are white, Pa.'

Ma comes to look, she says, 'Come home early from Mevrou. I'll braid your hair for you.'

Ma wants to braid my hair again! The last time she did it, Gracie was just a bunch of thin twigs. And Pa went to the bar for one quick drink. When my braids got old, Ma said, 'Take them out, or you'll lose all your hair', but I could hear she didn't care.

Now Ma wants to me to look beautiful again.

The nun slaps a big book open, *flupp*. She lifts it up for us to see. A teared strip falls out, it floats next to Nita. The nun shows us a octopus lady with lots of arms. She's shiny and brown, she smiles inside and out. She makes us all laugh.

'Stop!' The nun turns us to stone with her eyes. 'Hindus don't know Christ. They have chosen evil gods like *this* one to replace him.'

I slide my shoe on the teared paper. I drop my pencil, I pray it doesn't smash the lead. I bend under my desk and pick it up with the paper. Devil Worship, it says in the nun's fountain pen.

That's rude to say about the octopus lady! It's rude about all her clever arms and her smile. It's rude to the people who love her like God.

I crush the paper up, I squash it in my pocket.

KFM plays old Mango Groove songs. Ma lies a blanket under my tree, she gives Grace clean pots to bang and fill with sand. Her fingers press cool and clever in my hair. I turn my nose to her wrist and sniff. Ma smells like rain and fresh red pepper. Her fingers are kind and perfect and quick, it feels like she's got many, many fingers on many, many hands. It feels like she loves me like when I was small. Grace climbs inside the big pot. She sits like a fat chicken with her feet sticking out. She tries to get out, but her bum is stuck. She starts to cry. Me and Ma laugh, but that makes her cry more. Even Mugabe comes to see. He goes for her toes, but I stop him with my shout, 'Hey!'

I don't move my head. Mugabe chases the hens instead. He listens to me, that cheeky rooster. I'm the only one that he loves.

Ma pulls Grace out of the pot. I say, 'Remember when we used to bake her in the crate?'

I don't move my head, but Ma laughs a lot.

Grace comes to kiss me with her spitty gums. Ma's many, many hands turn back to only two. She makes Grace a bottle, even though the milk is only for the night. Gracie lies in the sand and sucks. Me and Ma talk.

'Ma, I wish I had all of you.'

'What do you mean?'

'I wish I had your green eyes and your soft hair and your nice light skin. I wanted your colours, but Grace got them instead.'

'Stella!'

'It's true. I wish I didn't have so much of Pa.'

She touches one of the new bumps on my chest. '*These* aren't from Pa.'

I giggle and hug my arms over them. It's true. I do have something of Ma's.

Ma says, 'And your skin is beautiful and smooth.'

'It's so dark, Ma.'

'It shines like someone took the night and polished it.'

I giggle.

'And you've got lovely dimples.'

'What's so good about dimples?'

The real truth is I like my dimples. Sometimes Nita sticks her fingers in them. Sometimes she says, 'These are so cute.'

Ma says, 'They make people want to smile, even when they're cross.' That's when I know Ma's forgiven Pa, like the man in the song who came home from jail.

When she's finished, I run to the mirror in the hut.

I look like a woman. About fifteen. My skin looks as smooth as a black brinjal. And my dimples, I think they look a bit …

I stop.

The Truth Lady says, 'I told you, Stella. There's no need to be shy with *me*.'

'Sexy.'

After supper, Jerry spoils my ma. He says, 'Sit back and relax. I'll serve you, my lady.' Ma sits with her legs under her like a Hindu. Jerry puts the kettle on the fire. I go to Pa, in the hut. He's lying with Grace against his chest.

'Pa?'

Gracie snaps off her bottle teat, she sits up wide awake. Pa pulls her back, 'Sleep baby.'

I sit and wait against the bed. Grace falls to sleep after seven breaths. Pa wipes the milk off her chin, he pulls the blanket up. I give him the teared paper. He smoothes it out and stares at the words. 'It says Devil Worship,' I whisper, because he can't read. I tell him what the nun said about the octopus lady.

Pa asks, 'Who loves to worry about the devil? The nun or the octopus lady?'

I think of her many hands and her smile. 'Not the octopus lady.'

'So who's worshipping the devil?'

I'm shocked. 'The nun?'

I think for a bit. 'But Pa, you said you don't believe in the devil.'

'The devil's not real. If he was real, where would he live?'

I say what Pa always says to me. 'Because there's no such thing as hell.'

Pa nods. He says, 'The devil's just a bad dream, see?' He rubs a circle on my forehead with his thumb.

I say, 'Now I feel sorry for the nun.'

Pa smiles. 'I like your hair.'

Jerry makes delicious condensed milk tea. He drinks from his Jesus cup with the sheep. Then he asks Ma, 'What must I play?'

Ma thinks and thinks. 'I can't think.'

So I think of one of my favourite songs. I ask, 'Can you play, To the Left?'

Jerry can even play Beyoncé! He plays it bouncy on his flute like a pop song. He plays it like Beyoncé would even love! I sing it sexy with my braids, I dance and I waggle my finger at Pa. Ma laughs so much that her eyes even leak. It's a break up song, but Beyoncé sings it strong. It's funny, not sad, and Ma's forgiven Pa.

I drum the metal, *BOOMM BOOMM.*

I feel Ma's fingertips in my hair all day at school. Everyone says, 'Shoo. Smart.' David can't stop staring because I look like fifteen.

The Truth Lady says, 'Stella, you said …'

On the way home, I feel so cool I sing that song I heard on Radio 5 with the fish nets and the night dress, and the drums that go *dut! dut! dut!* in your chest.

The Truth Lady says, 'Stella, what about …'

Wee-up!

'Hey?'

'It's the sound of a siren, cut up.'

'On the farm?'

'Far away on the tar.'

He ripped his cross out of the hairs on his chest.

The Truth Lady says, 'Who?'

He tuned his car radio with a red line that slides. He shoved the volume right to the top.

'How do you know?'

'Mevrou.'

It was Christian Radio. I know the song from the man who sells CDs outside Pep. *'The treasure of youuu.'* It's a tune that catches you.

Marais and his men are working far away at the top, so I sing extra loud to the apple trees and the bees. A car screams *zzeeeeeee* like a grand prix on TV. Jerry's wheels slide wild. They spray a swerve of sand, they burn a smoking curve. Jerry's green car speeds straight at me! I spring over the ditch before I die! His tyres lock up, his car slides to me. Red dust rushes up over us. 'Junne!' I say. Jerry shoves the door open on my side. His eyes are desperate blue lights. 'Tell him I'm family.'

'What?'

A police van comes speeding through the dust. Jerry throws a huge packet of Bubbles off the seat. He shouts like smashed gravel. 'Get in!'

I get in the car, I twist to the back.

Nita's pa jumps out of his van. He marches in the sand. Jerry says, 'Tell him I'm family. I'll give you my flute.'

The pretty wood box sits on the back seat.

A squeezing hope starts hissing in my head. It makes me light, it lifts me up, even though I'm sitting. It feels like I'm turning into a angel. I'll tell the judge the truth. I'll tell him it was joy.

Nita's pa's buckle hits *clak* on Jerry's side. His hand covers the top of his gun. Jerry opens his window a little bit. Nita's pa breathes like a dragon through the gap. 'Why didn't you stop?'

'Did you want *me*?'

He's got a long ditch from his nose, just like Nita. His eyes stare like furious black bullets. Jerry hits his forehead with his hand, 'Sorry, man. *Jus*, I'm dof.' Jerry laughs so real, it must be true. 'I was trying to get out of your way!'

Nita's pa looks trusting at me, 'Stella, how do you know this man?'

Jerry gives me a snarly smile. His teeth are packed tight and yellow today. I can see that his gums are melting low down. I forget to take a breath. 'He's family,' I say, without any air.

Jerry smiles his tight teeth. Nita's pa stares at my arm next to Jerry's. Jerry's skin is like porridge with margarine mixed in it. His freckles are like sugar sprinkled on top. My skin is dark like polished night, just like Ma said.

'Family?'

I nod.

'But he's white!'

Jerry laughs again, but this time it's fake like on stage. 'No man, *Gustav's* family.'

Nita's pa looks like he's doing sums in his head. 'Then why are you sleeping at Frank's fire?'

Jerry's ears go red like the berries that the stink bugs love.

'Wouldn't you? Have you seen Frank's *wife?*' Jerry laughs, but no one gets his joke. Nita's pa jerks like someone punched his chin. 'Can I see your ID please.'

Jerry opens the little door near my knees. 'Shit. It's not here. I must have left it …'

'Driver's licence then.' Nita's pa's lips are stiff. His fingers creep further down his black gun.

'*That* I can do.' Jerry starts scratching in his door.

Nita's pa says, 'I take it as my job to watch Nooitgedacht.'

Nita's pa tries to stare through Jerry's skin. 'A woman phoned me from Joburg years and years ago. A young ou attacked her. He pushed her down the stairs.'

Jerry's ears are very big, they stick right through his hair! Jerry keeps scratching. 'Where's the bloody thing?'

Nita's pa says, 'She was from a orphanage.'

Jerry's lost licence is making him pant.

'She was scared he would come back and hurt her worse. She said, Watch out, he might come to Nooitgedacht.'

Jerry tries to smile, but it falls straight off.

'Since then I watch for funny ous. I look after Mevrou Viljoen.'

Jerry asks, 'Did you get the guy's name?'

Suddenly Nita's pa is like a mongoose with a snake. 'Why do you ask?' His eyes are cold, black magic, guessing when to strike.

'Ag, Stella.' Jerry stretches to the back seat. He drops the wood box on my dress. 'You go home so long.'

The flute is on my knees.

It's *mine*, Jerry said!

Hope hisses and sings, even after my lie. I should feel terrible, but I don't, I feel pure. I'll tell the judge, I felt like a angel who was laughing and drunk.

I say to the Truth Lady, 'You can tell him if you want.'

I unsnap the buckles. I breathe in, in, until I'm dizzy. I lift the lid a tiny bit. Silver light sneaks out, it makes a snaky flash on the window.

Jerry shuts the box hard, he nearly crushes my fingers. He shoves me out, 'Go!' It's the voice with smashed stones.

I leave my school bag on the floor. I go.

I breathe in too much, I get too light. There's a rushing sound like I'm flying. I open the box, I let the light flash. I shut it again. I hear it in my head. It's not wind, it's falling water. It's the same sound as the waterfall in the kloof. Me and Pa go to see it when the sun melts the snow. It rushes like a huge, wild audience clapping. I lift the flute out, I grip it tight. I run through the gateposts. It's too beautiful to look at, now that it's mine. I hold it up to the sun, I run. 'Mamie! Mamie!'

The Truth Lady digs in her page, *Silver flute – Get a photo?*

It's funny, I don't shout for Pa. My pa would be the gladdest, but it's Ma I want to show.

My ma's like me, she can't look at it for long. My new flashing flute burns tears in her eyes. I blow a screeching note, *Pheee!*

Ma strokes it like it's alive. Pa taps it careful, like it's wild. He points at the sky, '*Someone's* looking after you.'

It's the first treasure that my family's ever, ever had.

Jerry's car stops under my tree. Ma says 'Thank you, Jerry, thank you,' with her glowing, green eyes. Pa nods very proud, like Jerry's a president who came in his Datsun.

Jerry grabs my hand too tight, he hurts my fingers.

'Eina,' I say.

He pants, 'No point, hey ...' He grabs the handle of our metal tub, he drags it right to the *here*, to the thorn tree. He drops it down, *dumm*. '... if you can't play.' He sits on the tub and pats the metal, *dimm dimm*. He tries to take my flute, but my fingers won't let go. Jerry rips it away. He makes his mouth tight like the nun's. 'Make your mouth go like so ...'

The flute sings clear and sweet. I nearly snatch it back. I make my lips thin, I squeeze it against my cheek. It comes out squeaky like a boy's breaking voice.

'Try again. Blow *across* the hole. Sideways, not deep.'

I twist my lips, I blow sideways, not deep. This time the flute sings smooth and sweet.

'Good!'

Joy bangs my heart, hot and strong. Jerry tries to take it, but I hang on. 'I'll teach you C,' he says.

His fingertips block three holes on the top, his thumb chokes the one underneath. He blows a smooth, shiny note through the silver.

I stretch my fingers until they do the splits. Eina. Jerry pulls hard on my pointing finger. He puts it on the pedal. 'Blow.'

It comes out squeaky, like a fright.

Jerry presses the flute deeper in my cheek. 'Across the hole.' This time it blows pretty and deep. 'Very nice!' he says.

The waterfall starts again. I keep my fingers still. I blow and blow the same beautiful C. Jerry pulls the flute from my lips.

'We didn't see him.'

I've got a breath ready.

He says, 'If they ask, we didn't see that policeman.'

'Why?'

'We lied to him, Stella. They stick you in jail for lying to the cops!'

My lie rolls onto me like a mountain.

'We'll go *straight* to jail, both of us.'

Shrrrreet, Ma tears some paper, she crushes it up. She stuffs it between some cold, waiting logs.

I whisper, 'Why did you make me lie?'

Jerry strokes the flute with his finger. 'I didn't *make* you. You wanted the flute.'

'Why did you say you were family?

Jerry laughs a ugly laugh. It sounds like wet earthworms, deep in the ground. 'Ag, if you think about it, we're all God's family, man.'

He spits it like punishment, 'Stella, we didn't see the cop. Otherwise, you can say goodbye to your family.' He watches Ma's flames catch on the paper.

He forces my fingers. This time my marriage finger has to stretch. Eina.

'That's A. Blow.'

I blow the new note.

Jerry's teeth at the side look sharp when he smiles. He nods. 'Nice and pure.'

After supper, Ma asks him, 'Play, Don't Kill the World for me.'

I hug my flute box. Ma laughs like she's never, never had a worry. 'He'll give it back, Stellatjie.' That's her old name for me, it means small Stella. I open the box, I let Jerry take it.

He plays it like *I* would, if I knew how. He plays it like a begging prayer. I close my eyes and imagine it's me blowing the notes. When I open them, it's like Jerry's rocked us to sleep. Ma's eyes are shut, she's swaying. Pa's eyes are closed too, I think he's praying.

At the end of the song, I take my flute back. I'm glad about Ma swaying and Pa praying, but I don't want Jerry to think that it's his.

I lie with my flute box next to my head. *Don't kill the world* plays in my brain. The flames of the fire go *cricka crack*. I don't think of Nita's pa again.

I say to the Truth Lady, 'Tell the judge. I don't think of him. I just fall to sleep.'

Chigachigachiga knocks against our bricks. I roll to my knees.

My tree is stuck in bright, yellow light. Its thick veins stick out. My wine bottles look guilty and scared. The engine drops to soft. A door slams, *klatt*. Two black boots march through the bright light. It's a uniform like his, and a blue police cap. But it's a short man with short legs that rub together, *shrik shrik*. His skin shines white. It's Oom Roos who sometimes rides with Nita's pa.

I slide under the bed. I scrape my back, I shove to the wall. I hang as tight as I can to the leg of the bed. Pa says, 'Wat die donner?'

Oom Roos shines a torch in Jerry's eyes.

Jerry's face gets screwed and confused. 'Say again?' His hair sticks up like Mugabe's crown. One side of his moustache curls up, not down. Ma and Pa stumble out of the hut. Gracie sits on her bum and starts to whine. I lock my fingers together to make them extra strong.

Oom Roos says, 'We found his van just off the tar. Did you see him today?' Everyone shakes their head. I shake my own head under the bed.

'Strange,' Jerry says.

Oom Roos sighs. Gracie crawls to Ma and Pa, 'Pa pa-aa.' Oom Roos swings his light. She cries even more, her nappy drags in the sand. Then he swings his light right in my eyes. I shut them hard, I see dark red. I lock tight to the leg of the bed. My muscles shake, there's a splash inside my head. It sounds like water, but I know its blood.

The light slips off my eyes.

Chigachiga … gggrooom. The police van drives up the road to Mevrou's.

Pa lights a candle, *shika*. My baby sister *skoffels* and kicks. She sucks, *ssee ssee* on her empty bottle. Ma sinks on the bed, the wood makes tiny splits. Pa makes millions of little cracks.

'Come, Stella,' Pa says. The wood cries quietly. I let a little bit of candlelight into my eyes. Pa looks like a upside down black clown. 'Come, my angel, go back to sleep.'

I creep out and crawl under my blanket. I touch my flute box. Pa blows the candle out, *thip*.

When everyone is sleeping, Mugabe kicks his claws on the cement. He spies in the door. He comes right inside and climbs on my foot. His claws grip through the blanket, just like I gripped on Ma's and Pa's bed. It's like Mugabe knows he's bad, and he also doesn't want to go to jail.

The Truth Lady looks up suddenly, 'Ah, *thanks!*'

Ma gives us red Kool Aid in two cups. She gives us bread with tomato, one piece each.

I say to the Truth Lady, 'Sorry there's no Rama.'

But the Truth Lady's too busy testing her machine. My last words come out much squeakier than me.

'Is that me?'

She nods, 'Carry on.'

I drum, *BOOMM BOOMM*.

I forget about Oom Roos who came with his torch.

I say to the Truth Lady, 'It sounds like a lie, but it's true.'

I've got a box of silver in my bag. It should be heavy to carry, but *it* carries *me*. Even my legs feel light underneath. Even my feet feel glad under that.

Nita comes to school very late. Her face is stiff like a statue. She's got a blue line down the back of her head. Someone's made her parting with a blue pen.

I whisper, 'What's wrong?'

Nita turns to me, her eyes beg for help, 'My pa is lost.' When she blinks, tiny tears slip out. The nun catches us, but she doesn't say, 'Sssh.'

I remember my lie for a terrible bit. But I forget again, it's true.

My flute shines in my heart. Today, I can see how nice the nun really is. She really wants us to know our maths. The sun shines her skin young through the window. It shines her black habit to fuzzy grey. Today her eyes look like kind milk. I write a note to Nita. 'He gave me his flute. I'll show you at break.' I make like I'm stretching, I stick it in her collar. Nita waits, then she makes like she's itchy. Nita's smile usually takes up all the space in her face. But when she turns her head, it's just a little pinch. That's when I start to feel sick. I write another note, 'Your pa will come back.' But her pigtails stay still.

Today is strange. Nita lies her head on her desk and the nun says nothing. When the nun says, 'Get your spelling books out,' Nita doesn't move. Simon with the pimples points at Nita's blue parting. 'Shut up,' I say, but he hasn't said a thing.

'Stella, I take it you are far ahead with your English and you don't need to be here today.'

'No, Sister.'

'Get on the bench.'

You feel stupid on the bench. Everyone stares, especially the boys. My skin starts to cook, I can nearly hear the sizzle. Their eyes can see my shirt is too tight. Please God don't let any buttons pop. Tarryn, the best at maths, stares at my broken shoes. I stare back at hers. They're old and wrinkly, but they're not broken yet. Mine are peeling from old age, and my one strap flaps. Underneath they're melted from David's fire in grade five. He made a tiny fire with a magnifying glass. The other boys fed it dry leaves. When I saw the nun coming, I ran and stamped it. My shoes melted a bit underneath. I showed my pa later, but not my ma.

I tell the Truth Lady, 'I think that's when David started to like me.'

'I see.'

David tries to help, he stares at the board. I stare back at the others, but there are too many eyes. Pa's funny face comes into my mind. I know what he would say. 'All it means, my angel, is that you're much, much more interesting than the nun.' But the buttons near my bumps are stretching too tight. I suck my chest in. If I was on stage, I would breathe deep. I wouldn't worry about popping. I would swell up my lungs and play a perfect song.

I dream so hard, I don't see their eyes. I even hear Jerry's words that he said last night.

The Truth Lady says, 'Which words?'

'Nice and pure,' I say. 'Remember?'

At lunch I lift my beautiful flute out.

'Wow,' Nita says, but she sounds like she's dead.

Another day she would have squeezed me. She would have skipped all around, maybe tripped on the roots of the lucky bean tree. She always stuck her foot in the loop of the root and fell over on purpose. Nita guesses things about me, like me and trees.

Some children come close and wait for me to play.

I stare at the flute. It's got every song you need in the world. *I've* got them too, they're in the tip of my fingers and the tip of my tongue. But they can't come.

'Come on, play!' big Amanda says. Her pink lips look hungry.

Tarryn frowns like she's adding up my stupid wishes.

I don't know what to do. When I look at Nita, she's awake again. Her fists are squeezed pale, she waits for me to play.

I put my fingers in the place to play A.

Someone rips the flute out of my hand. 'Ha-ha-ha!'

David jumps on the bench. He blows it ugly, *barp-peep, durrr*. He's trying to save me, but Nita doesn't see. She drags on his pants. She pulls him off the bench and tries to snatch it back. David's much, much taller. He holds up my flute like the torch in New York. The children all laugh, the small ones come to stare. Nita's gone mad. I can see her bottom teeth and all the white in her eyes. She springs on the bench, she hooks her nails in David's face. She scrapes them down his neck and hangs from her claws. David's white shirt rips. The children roar from the war. David spins away, but he's got bleeding red streaks. Nita chases him, but the nun shouts, 'Stop! Stop! Stop!'

She stares at the blood on David's face. She stares at my silver flute in the air. 'Who does that belong to?'

'Me.'

The nun stares at me like I'm a robber. She gives it back to me slow, like her arm doesn't want to. We wait for her to burn Nita with horrible God words. But she takes Nita's hand. Her face is soft, like someone's nice ouma. 'Come child. Come with me. You're upset today.'

Nita and me have been friends since grade one. We were the same size until I stretched tall like Pa. Nita stayed small like her ma, with her ma's fluffy curls. She's got her ma's caterpillar eyebrows and her tiny hands. She's got her pa's strong round eyes and his long, curly lips. You should see the size of her smiles. And you should see her usually, she talks a lot. But today she bends forwards, over her feet. She pushes up the hill, she doesn't speak. There's trouble in her head, I can nearly hear it screech. I can nearly hear her beg, 'Please, please, please.' She stares at David's blood under her nails. We push up the hill. Now my bag is very heavy. It's full of silver guilt. We push past the brick houses painted all the colours you can get, bright purple and bright yellow, the same as the bright plastic buckets at Pep. All the houses have got lounges with soft sofas inside. They've got a nice warm shower with electricity. They've got a toilet inside, I know from Nita's house.

Nita's as quiet as the mountain rock at the top. Only the wind lives there, and the black hawks. The fynbos tries to crawl there, but the mountain shakes it off. Only the dump smoke floats there without asking. Even the rain asks, 'Can I rain down?' Even the snow asks, 'Can I drop softly, just for one week?' I know it's dumb, but I pray to the quiet blue rock at the top, 'Please, please bring Nita's pa back.'

It's terrible to see your friend turn into a violent tiger. I don't pray to God, I can't. He saw what I did yesterday.

Nita calls, 'Ma?'
Nita's ma doesn't answer.
'Ma-a?'

Nita panics. 'Ma!'

Her ma's in her bedroom. The curtains are closed, it's nearly like night. Her back curves in the mirror. Her hands lie loose, facing the roof. The telephone looks huge and as pale as a snail. Nita's ma sags like the ant eaten tree, before the wind teared it. It looked like it was sighing and paining in the sun.

'Ma?'

Nita's ma springs out of her skin. She stares at the phone like it's ringing.

'Have you heard anything?'

Nita's ma says nothing. The phone listens, too.

The room is too dark. The phone is too big and quiet in the mirror. Nita's ma is too bent, her roots eaten up by selfish ants.

'Bye Nita. See you tomorrow.'

I run out of the gate, far away from my friend and her sad ma in the mirror.

I say to the Truth Lady, 'There were nine police.'

'What?'

One looks like Thabo Mbeki, but he's not. He's got black soft eyes and a moustache like grass.

There's a white, thin one with a bent nose past the tar. He presses his hands together like a praying mantis. I think he's even turning light green.

There's another black man with big cheeks like a bum. He touches a tyre swerve in the sand.

I bend my eyes to the ground, I walk past like a brown mouse in a emergency.

There are more of them! I try not to look, but my eyes want to count. … seven, eight, *nine* policemen. And five yellow vans parked on the sand.

The Truth Lady shakes her head, 'Amazing.'

They look like we did in grade six, when we did Nature Studies. We drew beetles and dandelions and spider's cocoons. I even found the trail of a snake. They click their cameras, they crouch. They scratch in their hair under their hat. They press the grass flat. Sometimes they stroke it, like it's a cat. I creep past a Indian one. His hair shines black, his backbone makes little bumps through his clothes. There are Indians in Worcester. They sell silky dresses with gold threads that makes everyone look rich like a emperor.

The Truth Lady says, 'What else, Stella?'

A sad coloured man holds his police hat in his hand. He asks a white man with itching red freckles, 'You say his marriage was okay?'

Mevrou's busy tying a steak up with string. I watch her tie the knot. I say 'Look what I've got.'

Mevrou's fingers curl like claws on her heart. 'He gave you his flute?' She stares at my flute like it's a snake. I hug it tight against my bumps. 'Forever?' she says.

I nod.

Mevrou sighs. Her skin goes loose, like she suddenly shrunk. 'Detective Booysen, is he still missing?'

I nod. My flute keeps me strong.

She asks, 'Do you think he ran off?'

'Hey?'

Mevrou shrugs. 'It's hard to believe.' She looks far away through the window. 'A good man like that.' She sounds dizzy from the distance, 'So true.' She pours meat juice in the spaces in the ice tray. She puts it in the freezer.

I ask, 'Why are you making brown ice?'

'Oh,' she waves, like she's dreaming, 'For meat gravy, later.'

Pa says, 'Shoo, they work *hard* when a police gets in trouble.'

Jerry laughs, 'And the ou probably just went on holiday.'

Ma asks, 'Do you really think so?'

Jerry shrugs. 'Maybe his nerves needed a break.'

Ma and Pa shut up, because that's how Jerry came to us.

The thorn tree is painted orange from the flames. Jerry shows me a brand new note. 'Blow.'

I breathe deep, but I don't blow.

I hear Nita's pa's buckle go *clak* on the car glass. I ask, 'Do you really think Nita's pa went away on holiday?'

Jerry nods. 'Blow.'

'But he didn't say goodbye to Nita.'

Jerry checks the hut. Pa's inside, folding a nappy like a kite.

Tuk tuk, Ma taps milk powder into Grace's bottle. Jerry's eyes stick into mine like thorns. 'Listen, Stella. It's *horrible* in jail.'

I rub my eyes to get the thorns out.

Jerry's blue eyes are silver, like a mirror. He chews on a piece of his moustache. 'You feel worse than a dog.'

'Did you go to jail?'

Fire flames shiver inside his mirror eyes. 'They locked my mother up all the time.'

'Your ma? Why?'

There are sore tears in Jerry's voice, they make tiny cracks. But the fire keeps his blind eyes dry.

'She was brown. That's all. I was white.'

'Your mother is coloured?'

'The cops kept picking her up. They thought she'd stolen me from my whities. She had to tell *lies* to make them let her go.'

'What lies?'

'She had to say I was a albino.'

The Truth Lady snorts.

'What?' I ask.

'Nothing! Carry on.'

I've seen albinos in the Truth, I think they're born with no skin. They wear black glasses and a hat, like Michael Jackson.

I stare at the tiny fires in Jerry's eyes.

I hear her voice first, it sings in my ears. '*Somewhere over the rainbow …*'

I see a little boy lying on a sticky floor. His tears are dirty and dry on his face. His little white hand holds his ma's through the bars. The sad lady sings him the rainbow song. She looks like Mary at school, but she's made of real skin. And she's not pale like cement, she's brown like me.

I rub Jerry's hand on the upside down tub. 'Sorry,' I say.

He shocks his hand away.

He forces my fingers back on the flute. He teaches me B again.

Then D, E and F. He makes me play them one by one. Then he makes me blow every note that I know.

When I stop, the fire stops its explosions. Pa stands at the door, I think he loves me even more. Grace hangs on Pa's leg, her mouth hangs round. Ma pinches the bottle teat shut with her fingers. She shakes Gracie's milk, *shik shik shik*. But her eyes stroke us, soft. They say, Thank you, thank you, thanks.

Nita's not at school ...
The Truth Lady says, 'Wait.'

She bangs with her hand, *BOOMM BOOMM.*

Nita's not at school. Scabby red tracks run down David's face, but the sun in the hall shines his teeth white. His smile is naughty, it says, Hey, I'm okay. We make the air cross on our forehead and our two bumps. We say, 'In the name of the Father and the Son and the Holy Spirit.' But I'm not a real Catholic, I've never seen the Holy Ghost. The nun prays deep, like she's alone, on her own. 'Dear Lord, comfort our Nita in Swellendam with her gran. Help Nita and her family to see that we are only mortals, born sinful. Only *you* can cleanse us. Only *you* can decide what is right. Help them to trust in your wise decisions ...'

The nun thinks God did it!

She prays, 'Help us all to remember that we are small and weak. We must accept your place for us in your holy plans.'

The nun thinks God made Nita's pa disappear! I stick my fingers in my ears, I take them out. I break the nun's terrible prayer into pieces, 'never be ... understand ... justice.'

The nun is mad. I'll have to ask Pa.

Mugabe's picking cooked mielies off my plate. Gracie tries it, she thinks she's a rooster. Pa pulls her away, Mugabe might bite her.

'Pa?'

'Yes?'

The wrong question comes out. 'When can we get a dog?'

I'm as surprised as my pa.

'You want a dog?'

I shrug. I ask another wrong question. 'And when are we getting our land?'

'The papers are coming now now.' He looks to our field, like some papers might blow in.

'Pa?'

'Mm?'

'The nun thinks God made Nita's pa disappear.'

'Ai, that nun!'

'Did he?' I ask.

'Never!'

'How do you know?'

'God is just love. He doesn't make sore pain.'

'Where do the bad things come from, then?'

'From people, their mad part.'

I lied to Nita's pa, now he's gone, like the Holy Ghost.

'Why do they listen to their mad part, Pa?'

Pa rests his chin on Gracie's head.

'They're …' Pa stops like it hurts. 'Just greedy for something.' Pa swallows and shuts his eyes. 'They *think* they need things.'

A big temper blows through me! 'They *do* need things, Pa!'

Pa hunts in my eyes to see what I mean. He rubs the bottom of my ear between his fingers. Mugabe watches him with a evil look. Pa puts a tired kiss on my eye. Mugabe flaps at him, but he doesn't bite. I think he nearly likes my pa.

Jerry makes me play all the notes I know. I blow them right the first time. Jerry gets proud eyes like Pa, he even gives me a little hug from the side. Jerry's full of love, his God part is strong. I think he just doesn't like policemen.

I ask, 'Did you lie to Nita's pa because of your ma?'

The skin next to his eyes pulls tight. It pulls the blue sparkle right out.

'Because they stuck her in jail all the time?'

Jerry nods. He watches to see that no one's listening.

Ma's busy giving Gracie to Pa. Pa takes Grace. He slides his hand down Ma's back. He touches my ma's bum! Gracie laughs and hangs on Pa's face. She pulls his cheeks right off his teeth, 'Papapa.'

'Why are you white?' I whisper to Jerry.

He jerks his head, 'Hey?'

'If your mother is brown, then ...'

I can nearly hear a machine grinding in his head. His eyes want to crush me. 'Shit happens,' he says.

It's like *I* made shit happen.

I shut up. Mugabe struts near us, but he won't come near the grinding.

I practise careful because I'm scared. What if Jerry goes away? And what if he takes the flute with him?

But the flute smooths his fury. I play perfect notes, over and over.

Afterwards I ask, 'Jerry, can you teach me a song for the concert?'

'When?'

My voice squeaks in my ears, 'Two more weeks.'

His eyebrows jump up. I sit shy and scared. But Jerry's eyes catch hot, happy sparks. He grins. 'What are you going to play?'

I press my face hard into his arm. It smells of man perfume and the metal smell from his fury. My words are hot floating air, 'Amazing Grace.'

I drum, *BOOMM BOOMM*.

Nita's still not at school. I go alone to the staff room and knock on the door. Miss Duncan and Mrs Frith are eating yellow cake. I go alone to the nun at her hot tea tank. The tank goes, *dup, dup dup*, like a hot monster kicking.

'Sister Beatrice?' I keep my eyes off the tank. 'Please can I play my flute at the concert?'

No kicks against her lips. It cuts new lines into her mouth. After a long, long time she says, 'It had better be good enough.'

'I'm still practising.'

'I want to hear it.'

'Can I show you on Monday?'

'Be ready on Monday, or the answer is *no*.'

My legs try to run, but I force them to walk out of the door.

The nun said yes! I can play a solo!

I've got one week to get good enough for the nun.

I *can* get good enough. I'm a Musician.

I just don't know how.

I play my notes in the air all the way home. I don't even care if the cars laugh. Tonight I will learn my concert song.

The men are at the dam where the river rushes in. Gustav's leg hairs look like a orange horse in the sun.

His sword sits in its holder against his leg. Gustav's white tummy creeps out of his shorts. He points his finger like a gun, 'That one on top. Ja. Good!'

Jerry holds a huge, mountain boulder. His long jeans are wet, his shirt is missing. His shoulders are boiled pink from the sun. His silver cross looks jumping hot. Muscles pop in his back as he staggers with the rock. My pa packs small stones in the cracks. Pa grins his dimples when he sees me. His wobbly drunk face is gone, and the yellow clouds in his eyes. He looks young today, like in his wedding photo. Pa's cool and young, now that Jerry's come.

Please God, let Jerry stay. Don't let Gustav chase him away.

Little green kites follow me through the trees. I step over a tortoise, the ones that are in trouble. It's got old black hills and yellow stripes down its slopes. There are hardly any left, Pa said.

'It's okay, it's okay,' I say.

A new orange erica grows right through Sheek's trap. I step over it. I sit. I play all my notes a few times over. The last time is perfect. The kites come and listen. Some sunbirds leave their lilies, they fly close to my notes. It's like the birds have been waiting for my call. They've heard me banging my bottles. They thought I was just a clumsy child. But I've got a bird voice now. Tonight I'll learn a real song. 'I'll play it for you,' I say, 'even before the nun.'

The Truth Lady turns, she stares at my tree. 'Who hung them, kid? You never said.'

'Pa hung them up when Gracie was tiny.'

He bought a whole reel of red ribbon from the co-op.

I asked, 'How much did it cost, Pa?'

'Haai, that's a secret.'

'Was it more than the sausages?'

Ma tapped my mouth, 'Shhh.'

Ma cooked the sausages and Pa got empty green bottles from behind the outhouse. Autumn Harvest Crackling.

I hopped like a crazy, lucky girl. The baby was sleeping in the crate, I had a whole roll of shiny red ribbon, and my teeth were getting ready to go *puck*, through the sausage skin. Pa poured water in the bottles at the tap. I tapped them with a fork, I said, 'A little bit more,' or, 'Take a bit out.'

Pa sniffed at a bottle. He saw me stare, scared.

'Sies,' he said. He tied the red ribbon to their necks, instead.

The Truth Lady says, 'Thanks Stella. Carry on.'

Pa climbed my tree! He was the first person except me. Pa turned my tree into sparkling glass. The sun flashed and spun as I tapped and tapped my own new notes. By the night I could play a whole tune.

I say to the Truth Lady, 'I'm not boasting, it's just the truth.'

'Stella?'

I played Dancing Queen, that's a Abba song. I sang to make the notes grow long, because glass notes don't stay in the air.

The Truth Lady says, 'That's enough, kid. Can we get back to the story?'

I splash through the underground leak. I hang on a thick, twisty root, I lean in to see. My eyes flash sun patterns. Those white balls are just sun tricks, I think. I blink my eyes lots of times to see in the dark.

There she is in the roof, hanging a long loop.

The mother snake is thin again! I blink at the white balls.

They're eggs! The mother snake has laid her babies!

I count thirteen white eggs in the ant eaten tree!

I run all the way back to the men. I run past Jerry, still boiling hot with rocks. Pa's picking up stones where the river dropped them. 'She's laid her eggs, Pa. Thirteen!'

Pa claps, 'Sweet!'

Pa understands, don't say the word snake, because Jerry hates snakes. I creep past Jerry with my snake secret. He rests a huge boulder on his leg. His leg shakes underneath, but he's casual, like he's Samson. He stares at Gustav. 'Why don't we start clearing the slangbos?' He picks the boulder up. He forces his shoulders up to a shrug. He smiles, 'I'd like to see you farming.' He stumbles with the rock, he drops it, *bakk!* into a gap.

Jerry lies with his bare back against it. His ribs stick out like pale piano notes. He smiles with his one eye shut for the sun.

The Truth Lady whispers, 'Mmm. Sexy and cute.'

I hope they make friends. I really, really wish.

'Hiya child,' Mevrou's got Les Miserables on loud. '*Luvly ladies* ….' It's the part where Cosette's ma is a whore at the harbour. It's a CD but I can see it. There are blue boats and black tractor tyres on the sides. There are ladies in see through dresses like teared butterflies. The other whore girls wear crooked lipstick. They laugh like a man. But Cosette's ma has got green eyes like Ma, and Ma's shining curls. Her skin is brown like the Nesquik Mevrou makes me in winter. They sing in cockney, Mevrou told me before. '*Luvly ladies …*'

The Truth Lady sighs, 'What else, Stella?'

'Nita went to Hout Bay once. She said they tie tractor tyres on the walls so the boats don't smash them.'

'Stella. The *story*.'

Mevrou's got smooth long pieces of meat on her board.

She shouts, 'Pig's neck.'

But I can't see any bones to hold its head up. Gustav's collars soak in bubbles in the sink. His shirts hang out with no bones in them either. There's a flutter flutter from somewhere in a gutter. Maybe some birds followed me here. On the CD, Cosette's ma's got the purest voice of them all. She's selling her own hair to get money for her daughter.

I tell the Truth Lady, 'Mevrou cuts the long pieces of meat so they fall open into fat hearts.' I pat her leg to tell her what the nun said. Instead I ask, 'Where are the bones?'

Mevrou grabs a handful of fat under her chin. She stretches it out so it looks like dough. Mevrou is much too fat for her heart. She laughs at my worry. She cuts the music off with her knife. She washes her hands. 'Come and read to me while I torture myself.'

'It's going to fix you.'

'It's going to kill me,' she jokes.

'You're doing good.'

'No, I'm not, I'm doing *well*.'

'Well. I'm also doing well.'

'Hmm?'

The shyness makes my tongue as thick as pig's neck. 'I'm going to play a song for our concert.'

'What?'

'Jerry's going to teach me. I already know five notes.'

Mevrou strokes my braids. 'Very good.' But she stares at my flute like it's a snake. And Mevrou also doesn't love snakes.

Outside, I play Mevrou my five notes.

'Gut getan!'

She lies flat like the lady in the Truth, but her stomach sticks up like a huge ant hill. Mevrou lifts her head, but her ant hill starts to shake. She falls back laughing, but I can see that it's sore.

I check. The lady in the cat suit has a smile on her face. Her knees are bent. 'Bend your knees,' I say.

Mevrou tries it, but her legs keep lifting. Her skirt flaps up so her legs are all bare. Her wriggly blue veins crawl everywhere. It's those little blue worms that are the problem, I think. The blood's got to climb around those little bends.

I pull her skirt down. I sit on her feet. 'Try now,' I say.

Her chin digs in, her red skin rumples. She opens her mouth to catch extra air. Slowly, slowly, she comes up all the way!

'Gut getan!' I say. I grab my flute and blow some notes.

Mevrou's got red patches and purple spills on her skin, but she sat up exactly like the Save Your Heart lady.

Mevrou's too busy doing torture to see the starling ma. She flies over us with sticks in her beak, through the small window in Mevrou's roof. Her coat is so black you can see rainbows in it. She's got a bright yellow ring around her eyes. She shouts, '*Squee-air*!' to her husband, 'Hurry up, come and help!'

But I can't see him anywhere.

I look away to keep her hiding place safe. But Mevrou never looks up at the sky, anyway. She's always got her head down, unfreezing meat in plastic in the sink. She pours the blood out and chases it onto a plate. She sticks knives into it, and garlic and spices. Sometimes I see whole onions going into the bum. She's always chasing meat or cutting wet potatoes. I told Mevrou, 'You should eat colourful things. Pa says colour gives you new batteries.'

I used to bring her carrots and broccoli and baby butternuts. But Mevrou didn't listen. They got dry and shrunk under the sink.

The Truth Lady says, 'Stella. What else?'

Mevrou squeezes all the way two more times. She makes a fart. She doesn't say sorry.

'Read to me,' she pants.

I read a heading in the Truth, 'Gay Abandoned.'

Mevrou's laugh starts snorting out.

'We thought Danny was just a late developer. He had girl friends, but no *girl*friends, do you know what I mean? We raised him by the Bible. We taught him about sin. When he was sixteen, he started camping with his friend. They put a tent in our garden on the weekends. We thought it was just boys playing boys' games.

Didn't you think he was a little bit old for those games?

I ask the Truth Lady, 'Did you write it?'

'No, not this one.'

I read, 'I told you, Danny grew up slowly. One night, I went to take them some sausage rolls to eat. What I saw shocked me to hell. I found them lying together with nothing on! They were lying like man and wife after ... a good time in bed. I ran to the house and called my husband. He flipped. He dragged Danny into the house. The boy, Niels, ran home. We asked Danny, What the hell are you doing? My husband flipped into a rage. He dragged Danny into the garage and locked him in the freezer.

How big was the freezer?

It was big. We used to keep half a springbok in there when my brother went hunting.'

Mevrou's laugh blows her flat on her back. She lies on the grass like she's been shot.

'*How long did you leave him?*

I said, Leave him for ten minutes, but Pete said a couple of hours will sort him out.

So, how long did you leave him?

Two hours and ten minutes. Danny nearly died. We are so sorry. We told the judge, we are so, so sorry.'

Mevrou tries to get up, but she's laughing too much. She falls flat again, her tears run the wrong way.

I don't know *why* she thinks it's funny. It's hot here in the sun, but it's cruel and terrible, the way they froze him.

'Why is it funny?' I ask.

I always ask her that. Maybe I'll know when I'm old.

Mevrou rolls on her side, she goes 'Heee, heee,' like she's crying. She hangs over the book. Danny's ma and pa have got guilty eyes. The white freezer's outside, someone carried it to the grass. Mevrou points at the freezer and starts laughing again.

'Shame,' I say for frozen Danny.

Mevrou waves her hands. She rubs her tears in her skin. 'Ag, these people.'

'What?'

'They ask for it.'

'Why?'

'Telling the whole world their secrets.'

She goes, 'Heee,' again, like Danny's a joke.

I see him squashed in the ice box, shivering and pale. He waits for his pa, trapped in the dark. Danny makes me think of Nita's ma. The mirror made two bent ladies, waiting on the bed. The phone was cold and pale.

I get scared in my stomach, I ask, 'Isn't it *good* to tell the truth?'

Mevrou's grey eyes dry up. She sniffs. She sits up and stares at Eddie's white flowers. 'Ja, Stella. Ja, the truth is good.'

But Mevrou sounds angry, like I spoilt her fun.

The Truth Lady says suddenly, 'Wait, kid. I need a pee.'

I point at the out house. 'It's a long drop. Sorry.'

The Truth Lady looks around at the slangbos. 'Never mind. Carry on.'

I only have to learn two more notes on my flute! G and C2. They're also real stretchers, but my fingers are loose.

Then Jerry says, 'Watch.'

He plays the first part of Amazing Grace. I stare carefully.

I say, 'Play it again.'

It's my turn to try. The silver metal feels as soft as hen's feathers tonight. '*A-ma-zi-ing Grace, how sweet, the sound, tha-at saved, a-a wretch, li-ike meeeee.*'

My flute knows the song! Even my fingers! These notes are all mine!

'Very *nice*!' Jerry's face is amazed.

Ma claps at the hut. It wakes Gracie up, but Pa pats her back. He doesn't speak but the candle flickers on his big grin.

'Can I learn the next part now?'

'No. Get that part slick first.'

'I've only got …'

'I know you've only got until Monday. Get that slick first.'

I play it over and over, about twenty times. Jerry holds his head in his hands. He stares at his feet. The fire makes his blonde streaks melt like hot honey.

The Truth Lady says, 'You loved Jerry.'

I nod.

He listens so hard, he nods in time with my song. I play it over and over until Jerry says, 'Okay, that's enough. Give your poor mother's ears a break.'

Pa walks out, 'No, man, play it again, Stella. One more.'

Ma slaps Pa's shin, so I know that Pa's teasing.

I laugh a little bit, it must be boring for them. Only me and Jerry are real Musicians.

Wait for the real night.

The people all laugh when Pa walks drunk on the tar. They laugh when he falls. They pay him with wine to tell his drunk stories.

But on the night, I'll play my flute to the coloureds and the whites. Even the ones who own farms. I know my pa. He'll feel proud of himself, because I'm his child.

Jerry stands up.

'Jerry?'

He sits back on the tub.

'Sorry I made you cross. I was just worried.'

'What?'

'After Nita's pa.'

'Stella!'

'Ja?'

'What have you got to be worried about?' He sounds sick of me.

'*You* know.'

'Stella!'

'Ja?'

'You know what I worried about when *I* was your age?'

'What?'

'That my mother was *dead*.' His voice is violent, like *he* killed her. The night crushes my chest. I can't move from his news. Then I remember what he said when he first came.

'But you said she makes cakes.'

'She hung herself in the fire escape.'

He looks into the dark like there are stairs.

I can see them too. They're not clean, like at school, they're sticky and black. The fire escape sign is cracked. Her hands and her feet are swelled and black. One shoe dangles off her foot. A pretty blue scarf sways from her head, full of the bluebells that burst at night. The air up the stairs blows the blue flowers flat, it presses her long, grey dress against her legs. She looks so, so sorry, even in her sleep.

It's the brown lady. But this time she's not singing.

This time she's dead, and swinging.

The Truth Lady digs, *Death on the dirty stairs! Check!*

Our fire burns up the fire escape and the sad lady hanging, but I hear something under the hot, hissing wood. It's a little boy crying like his heart's in thin, hurt pieces. He cries like thin glass, not like a donkey. Jenny from the coloured school got crushed by a tractor. At her funeral, her mother cried like a donkey.

Jerry's mouth jerks into funny cuts. His words come out cut and crooked. 'So don't talk to me about worry.'

The hanging lady is the worst thing that I've ever seen. Why didn't God stop her?

'Did you pray to God when you were small?'

Jerry coughs up the glass. He laughs. 'One thing about God, Stella. He's a snob. He couldn't care less about people like us.'

'But did you pray?'

'Till I was fucking blue in the face.' I'll say effing to the judge.

It pains inside from the picture I saw. God should have stopped her. Maybe he tried. Maybe she didn't listen.

Jerry thinks that God's far away, not inside us.

I want to tell Jerry where God lives, but I can see he hates God, so I shut up.

The Truth Lady starts to rock. She still needs a pee.
I ask, 'Must I stop?'
She says, 'Nn-uh. Go on.'

I bang, *BOOMM BOOMM.*

The stairs at school are like the ones from last night. They are dark, with sun stripes from a thin, high window. A white sign says FIRE ESCAPE in red letters. When I hang up my bag the air sways above my head. I can feel the soft trouble of a dead body. I wait for the children to run through the sunbeam. I look up slowly.

There's nothing there, just two naughty sparrows hopping on a ledge.

Jerry lied about his mother making cakes.

I go down the stairs. When I get to the door, I check again for the lady. But those two naughty birds just fly over my head.

I run out with them, into the sun.

In Religious Studies, the nun reads the Beatitudes to us. 'Blessed are the poor in spirit, because theirs is the kingdom of heaven. Blessed are those who mourn, for they will be comforted …'

I stick my hand up. 'What does it mean, poor in spirit?'

'Stella, don't interrupt.'

Maybe it means people who sin. Maybe God also blesses people who lie.

The nun reads the rest of the Beatitudes. When she's finished she says, 'Remember, the Beatitudes are the only way to happiness.' But she looks cross, like it's punishment. 'The way to pure bliss.'

She takes us to the hall to practise where to stand. We've been practising with Mary, but the real concert's in the hall, in case it rains. The nun sticks the choir in lines from small to tall. She digs her fingers in the children. She pushes them rough, like she does with her books. Sometimes I watch her getting ready for lessons. She hooks her nail in a book, she throws it open. She flicks the pages, *slick*, *slick*, *s-lick*. When she finds her place, she presses it down. The book stretches wide, the backbone goes, *cruck*. She tears strips of scrap paper, *srrip*, *srrip*, like skin off the side of your nail. The spike of her fountain pen scratches the paper. She sticks a strip in the book and slams it shut. She's rough like that, pushing us. When she finds the right place on stage for a child, she presses, *cruck*, *crack*, I can nearly hear their back. When she gets to me, she looks at my empty hands. 'Is it ready yet?'

'Nearly.'

Her fingers dig deep into my meat. She pushes me towards the choir, 'We're running out of time.' I dig my shoes into the wood. 'You said I could show you on Monday.'

She stops and she sighs, like she's suffering. She frowns like a hundred year old nun. She looks up to the roof where the miggies have made lots of tiny poo dots. She pulls me sideways, 'You can take Nita's place.'

She puts me between David and the Kum Bah Ya twins!

David jerks up straight. The pocket of his shirt touches my shoulder, *crr*. There's electricity in it.

I'm with the Musicians, where Nita's supposed to be!

At the back of the hall, Jesus is being stabbed in a painting. There's a big silver sword deep in his side. You can see the brown fist of the person who did it. Jesus is falling, he looks down to the ground with his long eyelashes. He is white from the torture, as white as Mevrou's legs under her dress. The sky is blue like our own sky. The blue sky makes the stabbing beautiful. The brown fist makes it bad.

But David's breath is cool on my neck. His pocket goes *crrr* against my uniform. I've got a beautiful flute in a box. I've got a place on stage with the Musicians. I'm going to play on stage with a real audience. Everyone will hear my Amazing Grace.

Jerry teaches me the second part of the song. '*I-I once, wa-as lost, but now, am found, wa-as blind, bu-ut now, I seeee.*'

I want to try the whole song, but Jerry says, 'No. Get that part slick.' I complain with my face, but Jerry says, 'Get it slick.'

Jerry says very loud and slow, so I know, 'Musicians know how to wait.' Ma walks past with a thin, long stick. She swings to us, but she doesn't interrupt. She goes to poke the bottle teats that are boiling in a tin.

I drum, *BOOMM BOOMM.*

I practise and practise until the second part is slick. The next day I call the birds in the forest, 'Come and listen.' Some swallows and kites follow me to Mevrou's. I call her out of the kitchen, 'Come and listen.'

I play Amazing Grace on her grass.

The forest stops its singing. The starling in the roof watches through the glass. My flute song makes Mevrou whisper, 'O, mein kind …' It's like she's nearly scared, 'You have a wonderful talent.'

That makes me heavy and hot in my heart. Talent feels like something that you carry in a box.

Later, I play the whole song for Jerry.

I play it sweet and graceful, like it was meant. My song makes them all quiet, even baby Grace.

Jerry says, 'That's my girl,' like I'm his real daughter. 'Play it again.'

I play it again and do you know what?

The Truth Lady shakes her head. She crosses her legs.

'My ma starts to sing! She sings three verses of Amazing Grace. I don't get one note wrong. I'm not lying. It's true.'

My fingers love the soft, silver notes. Grace giggles every time Ma sings her name. Ma's voice sinks in my bones, gentle and strong. It makes my soft meat sore, it makes me feel too much.

That's when I guess about the nun. She doesn't want my songs in her body. That's why she says, 'Shhhh.'

But I *love* Ma's singing. I like the sore feeling, it's like when me and Nita laugh too much at break. We feel beaten up in the stomach, we wish we could stay beaten up all day.

At the end of the song, Pa says, 'You see where your voice comes from, Stella?' He tells Jerry, 'My mother, too. She sang like a angel.'

Pa never *never* talks about his ma!

Ma and Pa forget to say how I played, but Ma sang for us and Pa said that about his mother. Jerry said, 'That's my girl,' like I'm his daughter.

This is the best day of my life. Or maybe it was the day I got my flute.

I say to the Truth Lady, 'Tell the judge. I don't know which one.'

I hit the upside down tub, *BOOMM BOOMM*.

On Saturday, Mugabe's with me in the bush, counting the eggs like a shopkeeper. The egg eater sneaked in again yesterday. Mugabe's furious about the crushed, sucked shells. He stamps his foot and barks, his red rubber crown shakes with hate. His mean eyes shout, 'How dare he? How dare he?'

You should see Mugabe now. He's got shiny tail feathers, like a black fountain. He's got bright new reds and goldy yellows, he wears them like a new coat from Cape Town. He's not one bit shy about the teared rubber on his head. He thinks it's like a beautiful crown, not like the red lungs inside a fish. Mugabe thinks he's a beautiful singer, but he can only crow when he's straightened his pipe. 'What? What?' What?' he stretches his neck. Then he blows, worse than a police siren. He's not at all shy about his legs. They're like thick, dry twigs. I know the English word, it's called *camouflage*. But Mugabe's twigs can't be for hiding in trees. He can hardly fly! He's too busy anyway, bossing us on the ground. He's bossier than Gustav, with his mean eyes that say, 'How dare you? How dare you?'

Today Mugabe hates that egg eater.

'Stop shouting Mugabe. There are enough eggs.'

That's when a car growls *grrrrr*, past my head.

Pa hurries up from the garden, he rubs his bare chest. The sprinklers spray a bright rainbow behind him. Pa blinks at the white post office van. He runs in the hut and comes out with the white shirt he wears to school things. He does the buttons up, but he can't do one sleeve. His fingers are shaking, I don't think it's the drink.

Ma comes from the hut, she does his button up.

Oom Samuel from the Post Office leaves his engine on. He holds a board through the window, with a pen on a string. He stares hard at Jerry on the chopping block, drinking his tea. I hear his question in my head, 'What's a white man doing at Frank's place?'

Oom Samuel says to Pa, 'I haven't seen you in the village.' But I know he means the bar.

Pa smiles shaky. 'Gustav's farming at the moment.'

'Ohhh.' Oom Samuel sucks his smile back into his mouth. Everyone knows about Gustav's dream apples.

Pa's pen is shaking. Ma whispers, 'Must I sign?' Pa shakes his head, he bites his lip. He writes FRANK RODRIGUES too slow and too big. He writes it right across the next block. I want to say, 'Write smaller, Pa,' but I shut up. When Pa grew up, there were no schools for children like me.

Mugabe charges after Oom Samuel's van. Then he struts back to us like *he* spun up the dust. We all squeeze around the big, white envelope. Ma hangs on Pa's arm like her legs are useless. Pa slides the paper out. Everyone leans to see. Gracie pulls on Ma's skirt so her panties stick out. I fix Ma's clothes, I take Grace away. I pull Pa's thumb off the black letters. Gracie grabs a corner of the page, she crushes it like she's just caught a chicken. 'Grace!' I shout. I force her fingers off one by one. Grace grabs again, but I swing her away. Jerry takes her and sticks her on his hip. Gracie smiles suddenly like a small gold angel. She touches his moustache gentle, like it's a porcupine that might prick. Pa strokes the paper smooth on his thigh. He keeps staring at the words. Ma tries to read for him. 'South African De ...'

Ma gets stuck, so I finish it. '... partment of Land Affairs.' I practise the next words soft, then I say, 'Land Redistribution for Agricultural Development.'

Ma's legs are weak, but her green eyes are as strong as the lily pads at the dam.

Pa carries the paper like it might fall and break.

I run around my tree like a laughing, crazy girl. Our happy dreams make the air soft and ticklish. I peep inside the hut. The contract is on the bed. Ma bends her head over Pa's hands. She goes, *kit, kit* with the nail clipper. She clips Pa's nails, she talks soft to him. 'If he says no again, say, Gustav I've lived on this farm all my life. And my father before me …'

'No, he might think I'm fighting for land rights.'

'What will you say then?'

'I'll say, Gustav, we've been friends all our life. It's only a small piece. '

'Okay.'

Ma dusts Pa's face with her own hands. Pa picks up the contract. He gives Ma a hard kiss.

I tell the Truth Lady, 'It gives them flat lips.'

Outside, Pa says to Jerry, 'Wish me luck.'

Jerry claps Pa hard on the back. Pa nearly falls over, he laughs, 'Lucky. Not *dead*!'

Say yes. Say yes, I beg in my head.

I let Gracie stick small stones in my hair, I don't care. Ma goes to the garden. She sits with her legs straight, like baby Grace. Sometimes she stares up at the sky. Jerry shaves his chin with his electric thing. He watches my ma. He watches the empty road to Mevrou's. His mirror dangles on a string, it makes bright flashes on his Datsun. His eyes burn something grey, maybe that's how he prays.

Maybe Jerry's also begging in his head, 'Say yes, Gustav, say yes.'

The Truth Lady dips, she whispers, 'Maybe, just *maybe*, he was swearing a blue streak.'

Pa comes home with empty hands and gold in his eyes. He looks full of miracles, like if you were a cripple, he could fix your legs. Ma runs up from the garden. 'What did he say?'

Pa grins like he's God's mad, happy son. 'He said, Of course! He said, I *told* you last year I would sell you that land. He put the papers on the table, then he said, Go and get Jerry. We must burn the slangbos. We must start on your piece.'

But Ma's worry won't go. 'When will he sign?'

'I asked him, When can we have the papers back? He said, You can post them next week. But now we must burn!' Pa shakes his head, 'He's mad, that man. He's *glad* for us.' Pa holds Ma's face in his two hands, 'It's happening, my love.'

Pa called Ma 'love' in front of everyone!

Then Jerry and Pa go up to Gustav, and guess what?

The Truth Lady says, 'What?'

They start on our field! It *is* happening!

Grey smoke charges high up to the sky. The blue sky sweeps it clear like it was never there. Me and Ma walk up the road to watch. Pa stands like a fire tamer, pouring water around the flames. Gustav shouts, 'Deeper Jerry! It's not good enough to chop off the top!'

The Truth Lady asks, 'Even after Jerry, you know … acted like Samson?'

'Huh?'

'With the rock.'

'Ja.'

Jerry hacks with a axe, digging deep. He springs away from a sand frog, and a desperate, hot mouse. I think his eyes are seeing snake stripes.

Ma pulls me away, 'Come! Let's go and sell vegetables.'

Something's happened to Ma.

She *never* goes to the village! She used to sell from the barrow when I was in grade one. But when Pa came home drunk, she said no, no, no. She won't sit at the stalls. She said if she *looked* at the bar she would get sick. Ma never goes off Nooitgedacht. She never, never even gets friends.

On Saturdays, I usually watch Music Mix. But today I make my old clothes look new. I put on my strap top from when I was ten. It's got pink and white squares, it shows my stomach skin. I put on my old red skirt, with my jeans underneath. Penny, whose Ma sews, got dressed at school last week. She put her skirt on over her jeans. I laughed because I thought she was just being silly. She said, 'Don't be a skaap. It's the style in the city.'

Ma says, 'You look cool. I've seen how they do that.'

'Where Ma?'

'In the posters at Pep.'

My ma knows much, much more than I think.

Ma walks the wheelbarrow of green beans next to me. She says, 'It's okay, Stella. When we've got our land, we'll pay a big truck to fetch the vegetables. We'll have big orders from all the Spars everywhere.'

I carry Grace on my back, I sing on the way. And do you know what?

The Truth Lady says, 'What?' She shivers her legs on the metal.

'Ma sings again. And, guess what? She even knows the words from Radio 5.'

We sing Amy Winehouse, her bad rehab song. '*No, no, no!*'

Ma laughs after those three nos. She laughs again when I say, 'You and me should make a CD.'

My ma's much more lovely than Amy Winehouse. Amy's thin, with tall, koeksuster hair. Ma's soft, brown dress crosses in the front. Her skin shines like Pa's eyes with the new gold inside. You can see the dip between Ma's titties, like the singers on TV. Her eyes are greener than Beyoncé's, that's the truth.

The Truth Lady jiggles her knees, like she *really* needs a pee. 'Then what?'

When we get to the tar, Grace gets too heavy. I give her to Ma, I walk the wheelbarrow. I hit a stone, the wheelbarrow tips. A whole lot of green beans pour to the ground. Ma doesn't frown, she doesn't even shout.

'What have you got there?' someone calls from Vermaaklikheid. It's Tannie Sandré who knows my ma from Caledon. We pick up the spilt beans, then do you know what?

The Truth Lady asks, 'What?'

'Ma walks the wheelbarrow right up to the house!'

Ma *never* visits people in Vyeboom, but here she is in her shining gold skin. The big boy next door waves straight at me. He knows me from the road, when I was eleven. I helped him to drag his dead dog off the tar. I lift my hand quick, because he's sixteen with skating shoes.

Tannie Sandré's got silky white hens! They glitter in the sun like they've been washed in Jik and brushed for hours. A big black dog lies on its side. I walk behind Ma in case it's violent. Tannie's husband is fixing a soccer ball with glue. His two little boys watch like he's a doctor at a operation. Gracie stares from Ma's back. She smiles at the boys. Ma says, 'See the woof?'

Grace laughs at the lying down dog. 'Woof,' she says.

Tannie Sandré knows my ma's sister. She says, 'Rita was asking about you when I was in Caledon. But I never see you in the village, so I had nothing to say.'

Ma just smiles.

Tannie Sandré sounds cross. 'And I haven't seen Frank!' I know what she means. She hasn't seen Pa zigging and zagging on the tar. She misses laughing at him from her stoep. Ma lets it all sweep away, like the sky and the smoke.

Tannie Sandré points at Nooitgedacht. 'It's the first time I've seen them burning.'

Ma nods at our smoke. 'Slangbos.'

I want to say, 'Tannie Sandré, it's my Ma and Pa's land!' but I shut up and watch the silkies scratch the sand. They look like angel's hens in heaven. One walks over the black dog's back. The dog lifts its head, it stares with yellow eyes. I hide behind Ma, but the dog drops its head, 'Uff.' Tannie Sandré's smile stretches her question, 'So what, Gustav's actually farming?'

'You never know,' Ma says. 'People can change.'

But I know she means my pa.

She bends to the black dog, she scratches its ears. She strokes her hand over its big, bumpy stomach. It opens its yellow eyes, but it doesn't growl. I reach very slow, I touch a white silkie. It's as soft as a dandelion.

Tannie Sandré asks Ma, 'Do you want a puppy when they come?' Ma's eyes flash like a match. 'Maybe,' she says, but I know she means yes.

That's when I know, we're all staying home.

There's no more Caledon, and no more heartbreak.

Ma leaves a big pile of green beans for a present. The beans are so perfect, it looks like we polished them. Ma says, 'Send my love to my sisters.'

'*And* your Ma,' Tannie Sandré corrects Ma, like the nun corrects us. Ma just shrugs. She leaves the perfect green beans.

We sit between Oom Piet and Johnny Walker at the stalls. The man who sells CDs blasts songs outside Pep. It's mostly God songs and old songs, like *Wake me up before you go go* ... Ma's too shy to sing with me, but she sells green beans as fast as Johnny Walker's cigarettes.

I ask Ma, 'Why's his name Johnny Walker? Does he drink a lot?'

'What?'

'Gustav's got Johnny Walker whisky in the lounge.'

Ma laughs, 'No man, it's just a joke. Johnny won the walking race in Cape Town eight years in a row.'

Ma knows much, much more than I thought.

Men come from the bar with pap knees from the drink.

'It's not my pa in there,' I say soft to Ma.

Ma laughs, she says, 'It's not *my* Frank.'

Ma still loves Pa, that's why she said it.

We watch a lady shouting outside. Her man sticks his arms up like she's the police. He keeps his drunk legs wide to balance. She *ruks* money from his pocket, she shouts the bar down, 'What must we eat, hey? What must we eat?' She swears terrible things, I won't tell the judge. The man's got sorry eyes just like Pa, when the drunk jokes are over. The wife spits at his feet. She walks on stiff, furious legs to the Algemene Handelaar.

Tarryn from school comes past with a Pep packet. She stops to show me what she's got. She lifts the lid off a white box. They're shining, black school shoes, the kind that I love! The ones with the silver buckle, and the leaf holes in the toes. I hate her for a splitting second. I want those shoes even more than I want white silkies. My words come out jealous, 'Cool shoes.'

Gracie's white dungarees get filthy in the street. She whines, she's tired, so Ma ties her on her back. I feed the upside down chickens with bread. The way they gobble makes me glad. If they were very, very scared, they wouldn't eat, would they?

I find out the truth.
It happens to me.

The CD man has taken all his songs home. I'm standing with Ma, chewing white, fresh bread. A yellow van stops at the stop sign near us. It's Oom Roos, the police who shined his torch at us. His flicker is on, but he doesn't drive left. He stares at us instead. His eyes sit on the steering wheel.

The Truth Lady says, 'Hey?'

'Oom Roos is very short.'

The bread swells as big as a brick in my pipe.

Clippa, clippa, clippa, goes his flicker, right through the cars and the noise of the bar.

My eyes go blurry. I really can't swallow.

Ma looks see through in the sun. She's like a just landed butterfly, ready to fly up with my sister.

I grab Gracie's sleeping hand. She rubs her sore gums on Ma, but her eyes stay shut.

Oom Roos drives towards us.

I can't breathe through the bread. Blood swells in my head.

Oom Roos doesn't stop. His pink mouth smiles.

He waves at Ma as he passes.

It was my beautiful Ma, not me, he was watching! It was Ma's Beyoncé eyes and her shining skin!

The Truth Lady says, 'Wait. Hang on. Stop!'

She flicks her red switch. She drops her book on the tub.

She runs in the toilet with her black pen. She slams the door, *dagg!* She pees like a tap turned on the hardest.

The Truth Lady bumps the door open, she nearly falls out.

I point to our tap. 'Do you want to wash?'

She goes to the tap, then she comes back.

'Where were we?' she asks.

But her pen's not wet. I think she should have washed it.

I bang the metal, *BOOMM BOOMM.*

It's Monday. It's nearly my turn to show the nun. I stand in Nita's place, where Mary's skirt ends. I grip my flute hard so my knuckles sting. The birds have got used to David's Silent Night, but there's a mother up there who's furious with the wind. It rocked two of her eggs out and exploded their yolks. '*Chack! Chack!*' she shouts. David's violin stops.

My breath turns cold, even though it's summer. I shut my eyes. Inside my flute, it glows round and smooth. The sun shines pretty stripes. I suck air up from the tips of my lungs. I stretch my fingers long. I blow my breath nice and easy, just like Jerry said. I open my eyes, I blow perfect notes.

They are Amazing Grace.

My air strokes through me, my fingers touch the song. I know it's beautiful, because of the bliss. I'm a light, shining song that floats in the sky. I know it's beautiful because the nun looks sick. My music is hurting her insides, I think.

Afterwards, the nun is silent. She looks up at the sky past the lucky bean tree. Her own God says, 'Dear Nun, you must be happy with *that*.'

The nun nods, 'Good.'

She means it was beautiful, I know. My song stroked in her body, it shined in the sky. One thing about the nun, she never, never lies.

She asks, 'Who taught you, Stella?'

'Oom Jerry.'

'Is he a real uncle?'

I shake my head. 'No. He's white.'

Hungry questions bite inside her eyes. She watches me quiet, like I'm a white child. The twins play Kum Ba

Yah like someone just died, but my heart shines inside me sweet, like a whole river of gold syrup.

When the nun lets us go, the children push close to me and my flute. They say things that aren't words. 'Yeesh.' 'Shoo.'

David lifts my flute careful out of my hands. Today there's no Nita to scratch him. He sticks his eye to the mouth, he stares into it. 'Did you find it in here?'

'What?'

'The song.'

A laughing bliss comes up in me. The others laugh, too. They all want to ask, 'How did you learn so fast?' They don't say it, but I hear the words flutter in the playground.

The Truth Lady says, 'Stella, can you skip all this stuff?'

'Huh?'

'Can you tell me some trouble?'

I think for a bit. 'I'll have to make it night.'

'Right.'

We've got our own land. The nun looked sick from the bliss.

I sleep deep and happy with my sister.

In the night, Ma cries, 'No-o. No!'

I wake up in a shock.

Pa says, 'Ssh, the children.'

My eyelashes still touch. Ma's on her knees in the fluffy dark. 'Why-y-y? she cries.

Pa sounds like a desperate man. 'Something happened at the fire.'

'What?' Ma asks.

'I don't know.'

Ma hisses, 'You're making excuses!'

The Truth Lady says, 'Wait! What happened? What did I miss?'

Fire flames scream *ttsseee*, like sand in the wind. Jerry's blisters leaked, sweat dripped off his skin. The slangbos thorns cut the skin on his wrists.

The Truth Lady says, 'Oh, that day.'

Jerry swung a silver twig low through the smoke. It burst far away, it grew orange tongues.

'Did your pa see?'

'Uh uh. Only Mevrou.'

Gustav's finger stabbed. His spit flew in the sun, 'Jerry! Help Frank!'

Dooff! Jerry threw down his axe. He lifted his shirt, he wiped his eyes.

The Truth Lady sinks, 'He showed his six pack and his creamy stomach skin.'

He tapped a cigarette out of his box. He lit a match, *gutschh*. It made a new, baby flame. Jerry sucked his Lucky Strike.

He turned his face, he blew out his smoke. He pointed to Pa.

'What did he say?'

I shrug. 'Pa was too far.'

The Truth Lady hisses, 'Snake in the grass-s-s.'

'What?'

'No, nothing. Carry on.'

But she writes, excited, *Snake in the Grass. Good title?*

'Just wait,' Pa begs Ma. 'Gustav will change again.'

Ma's shadow is a black giant on the wall. It sways this way and that, its long arms wave, cross and crazy. Her shadow whispers hard in Afrikaans, 'Just wait. Just wait. I'm *sick* of the waiting! I've *waited* to trust you. I've waited and waited for you to come home *drunk!*'

'Not for a long time, Nance.'

Ma's shadow attacks Pa with its fists. I open my eyes wide.

Ma's punching Pa! She shakes her head like a metal singer, her titties shiver, shaking and crazy, her crying whisper is worse than a shout, 'What about all those years?'

Ma falls on the bed, she pulls the pillow over her head. She cries and cries into the sheet. She jerks like there's a small girl inside her, hitting on her bones.

Ma cries for ages. I block Gracie's ears in case she wakes.

I tell the Truth Lady, 'The brown lady comes again.'

'*Come* on. Really?'

I nod. 'The one who was singing. Not the dead one, swinging.'

She smiles at me from the corner of her jail. She lifts her many hands and wipes off my tears. The brown lady's the one who strokes my eyes closed.

'Aaaaaii!' My ma screams in my sleep! It's so loud I think it's me! I dive on her bed. Gracie starts screaming like someone just dropped her. That makes Ma stop. My heart bangs hard against my front teeth.

'Ma, what's wrong?' I hug my ma's head against my chest.

Ma's cold and jerky, she stares at the dark glass. Her breath gets caught like a broken zip. 'It's nothing. It's nothing. It's just my nerves.'

The Truth Lady asks, 'What *was* it, Stella?'

It was a man's head with a horrible flat nose.
Its wolf hair was sticky in the moonlight.
'A wolf?'
Its eyes were glowing stones.
The Truth Lady laughs.
I stare until she stops. I say, 'It was just like the vampire at Vim's Videos.'

I hit my fist, *BOOMM BOOMM.*

Everything's strange. Jerry is missing, but his car's still here. The sprinklers are on. Pa stares at the rainbows like they're rubbish, not sparkling spray. Ma's cotton threads are falling out of my hair.

I climb on Jerry's car, I catch his dangling mirror. My head looks half skollie, half smart. I try to fix it, but Gracie cries at the bumper.

'Don't make her cry,' Ma says from her bed. Ma's had a very bad night from her nerves. I lift Gracie up. She pulls my loose braids, she grabs for the mirror.

Everything's strange. I'm going to be late.

Jerry walks fast down the road towards us. I grab Grace off the car, I slide to the ground. Jerry's hair is blown back, his eyes have got two blue rainbows in them. 'No slangbos today! I'm moving in.'

Pa comes up from the garden. 'Moving in where?'

Jerry shakes his sleeping bag. Sand slaps my face.

'Into the cottage.'

Pa's face crumples into a surprise.

Grace sticks her foot on the tyre and cries.

Jerry throws his pillow in, he stamps to the tap.

Ma sits up in bed. Her eyes are dark holes full of nerves.

Jerry shouts from the tap, 'Just for a bit.' He comes back from the tap with his Christ is Among Us cup. 'I told Gustav I need somewhere to crash.' Jerry goes in our toilet, he takes our toilet paper. He flies the white paper tail to his car. 'I mean, you guys need your space.'

The Truth Lady says, 'Hang on. *When* did he ask Gustav?'

Ggggiii ggghhaa, Mevrou snored, like a pig talking.

The Truth Lady says, 'Hey?'

Her hair made long grey streaks on her pillow. Her mouth was so wide, the sun warmed her tongue. His forehead bumped the glass. The Truth Lady asks, 'What glass?'

Mevrou shut up, like she was the guard of Eddie's photograph.

'Ah.'

He creeped to the crack in Gustav's door.

Gustav was fast to sleep in his car shorts, those old, old cars that drived very slowly. His silver trophy shined on the table.

The Truth Lady bends her head, she whispers, 'He had a erection in his pyjama shorts.'

I know what a erection is.

I ask, 'How do you know?'

Her hair sticks to her cheeks. 'Ag, just a guess.'

She says, 'What then?'

Gustav bent over his legs, his teats touched his knees. Jerry stretched in the door, he yawned.

The Truth Lady whispers, 'Rude black hairs sneaked out of his jeans.' She asks, 'What did he say?'

'I think he told a ugly lie.'

'Like?'

'Ma and Pa fight, then they make sex in front of him.'

'Serious?'

The Truth Lady thinks. She sinks to her machine, 'Nice people, Jerry said. Just a different breed.'

She taps my leg with her pen, 'And then?'

Grace screams like she's being killed. There's blood on her mouth and blood on the bumper. Ma springs up in her nightie. 'Stella, man!'

Gracie screams the farm down. Blood smears on Ma's white nightie.

'It's not my fault,' I say.

Ma wipes Gracie's blood with her hand. Pa comes to see. 'Eina. It's just a hole, it's alright.'

'It's her new tooth, Pa.' I blame her tooth, because I should have stopped her.

Ma splashes Grace's mouth at the tap. Pink water splashes onto the cups, but I shut up. Grace's mouth is cut, and Jerry's going to live in our house instead of us.

Ma orders me, 'Get her a clean shirt.'

But Jerry's digging in Ma's basket of clean washing by our door. Pa's voice is desperate, like a hungry stomach. 'You know we want to buy that house.'

'Hey, it's not forever. And you need me there, Frank.'

Jerry untangles his pants. 'The problem with Gustav, he needs to grow up.' He throws the empty legs over his shoulder. 'I'll get him to farm for *him*, first. Then he'll relax.'

'What?'

'Gustav's stressed that you want to take over.'

'Hey?'

'He's mad. He thinks it's a land grab.'

Pa stares shocked.

'Stella!' Ma shouts.

Mugabe marches past on his morning march.

Jerry says, 'You just have to wait.'

Pa opens his hands. They're huge and empty. 'Nancy won't wait. It's too late.'

'Stella!'

I get a clean shirt for my sister.

I walk backwards, I watch.

Jerry's bum crack creeps out of his jeans. He scratches for something under his car seat.

Pa shakes his head violent, like he wants it off his neck.

The Truth Lady asks, 'What was it?'

'I couldn't see his hands. Only green car metal.'

Pa follows Jerry behind the outhouse. Jerry lifts the black plastic.

The Truth Lady asks, 'Could you see it, yet?'

I shake my head.

I help Ma pull Gracie's shirt over her head. We stretch the neck where her broken lip is.

The Truth Lady says, 'Stella?'

I push Gracie's tiny arm through her pink arm hole.

'Was it a bottle?' she asks.

I nod.

The Truth Lady bends, 'He lay a full green bottle on Frank's grave of empties.'

I say, 'He pulled a paper money from his pocket.'

'What colour?'

'I think it was pink.'

My ma's a angry knot. She attacks the wood, she doesn't feel it kick and spit. She stamps on the branches, she rips the thin ends up, *ku-takk!* Splinters fly into the soft under part of her arms. Pa waits on the chopping block, he waits for Ma's eyes. He needs one soft look, he begs her without words. But Ma only sees branches to break, branches to burn. She bends the green ones until they split. She tears them off their leaky bark. She makes a pile to let them die. Ma burns like a hell fire, if the Bible was right.

'Bye, Pa,' I say, but Pa doesn't listen. Only baby Grace waves as I walk away.

Marais' men are digging pig poo around the apple trees.

Marais pours Smarties onto his tongue. Oom Neville, the foreman, wipes his sweat with his sleeve. His eyebrows are brushed straight up to the sky.

He says, 'Hey Stella. How's your pa?'

'Okay,' I say, but it's soft, like a lie.

Marais tips the whole box, I can see in his mouth. All the nice Smartie colours have turned to brown mud.

Something's happened to the nun. She says, 'Stella, are you sick today?'

'No, Sister Beatrice.'

'Is everything alright at home?'

The others hang their mouth like their ears can't be working.

I nod very fast so the nun stops asking.

The Truth Lady says, 'Stella, can you leave the school stuff?'

'Huh?'

'Can you rather talk about Nooigedacht?'

Jerry sharpened a rusty panga to cut through snake meat, *shlik, shlik!* He slashed the long grass to the door.

Something's happened to the nun. She says, 'Stella, go and tell Miss Duncan that the grade one books have come.'

The Truth Lady sighs, 'Stella?'

The nun *never* sends me. She always asks Barry, he's our head boy. He's white and he's quiet and he never, never runs. He walks tall and sorry, like someone might hit him.

I forget about Ma's sobs and Grace's orange snot. I stare at the pile in front of the nun. I stand stuck, like a statue.

'Must I take the books?' I ask.

'Can you manage?'

I pick a pile up with one arm. I slide the other pile against my chest. One slips off the top, *shhlluf.* More readers drop, *shopp, shopp, shopp.* They lie on the floor like birds that have been shot.

The Truth Lady says, 'Stella, Nooitgedacht!'

The mattress dropped, *fuddh!*

Jerry bounced on his back.

Gustav's giggle nearly ran out of the door.

Jerry lay with his hands behind his head. 'So you'll bring me some DDT?'

The Truth Lady jerks, 'What?'

I say, 'DDT. I think Eddie had some in the shed.'

'*Really?* What next?'

Gustav tapped the leg of the bed, 'Here.' His cheek touched Jerry's shoe underneath. He glided to the window, he touched the ledge, 'And here.' He stroked the floor, across the door. 'No cobras will cross.'

The Truth Lady pants, she scratches in black, *No Cobras will cross.* She smiles, satisfied.

I stare at the books with their wide, spread wings. I feel wet sweat in my armpits. I hear my ma sob.

The nun says a strange excuse for me, 'You're trying to carry the world on your shoulders. David, go with her please?'

The nun sends David on a message with me!

We walk past the other classes. We can see their bent heads, we can feel the warm air from their working. David whispers to me, 'Walk slowly so we miss the grasshopper parts.' But I love Natural Science, especially the insects. I want to explain, but everything's too strange.

Johnny Walker looks over my head and not in my eyes. Even Oom Piet's chickens stare past me at the cars. Everything's strange, that's why I go and look. I creep to the bar. I put my face against the glass.

The Truth Lady asks, 'Ja?'

I don't want to say. It makes me pain everywhere to remember. I wish I could tell the judge, 'I don't want to say. Please can you guess.'

The Truth Lady says, '*Tell* it, Stella.'

Pa looks like he's been hung upside down. His face is swelled up and burnt dark from the bar. His head nods like it's too big for his neck. His dimples hang loose off his cheeks. Pa looks like he's been cooked in a pot. He stares at his hand. He picks up his glass, he waves it to his face. He stretches his lips, they suck a big sip. Pa chews his wine to keep it in. He's worse than a baby. He sways his big head to the TV. He laughs, mad and slow. He looks for someone to share his joke. He says something to Mannie, but Mannie looks away. My pa's all alone in his ugly world of wine.

Pa's a stupid baby.

And I'm just a ghost.

Mannie looks past me through the glass.

I walk slowly home. A frightened feeling falls through me, like a staircase of scared air. The police could take me now. I've got no father to stop them.

I don't want to go home, I want to fly far away from the fights and the lies. I want to float far away from our breaking dreams. But I'm as heavy as a dead dog, the one we dragged off the tar. The box in my bag crushes my backbone.

When I get to the bridge at Bergsig, Gustav drives past, excited and fast. I don't even wave. I feel like a stranger.

I force my legs around the bend. I walk slow past the grader at the gateposts. Ma's splitting a pumpkin with the axe. Her whole body looks like a chopper. She swings up straight. The sun sparks the axe. She swings down, *crruck!*

Ma drops the split pumpkin into the pot. She puts a new pumpkin on the stump.

Gracie crawls sleepy, out of the hut. Ma must have seen her, but she swings her axe up. She stares at the pumpkin like it's done something terrible.

'Mamie!' I shout.

Gracie reaches up.

'*MA!*' I run as fast as a car.

Ma forgets the evil pumpkin, she sees Gracie's soft meat. Her axe slides down between her titties.

I beat my fist in my heart to shut it up.

'Ai! That child!' Ma says.

Gracie stands up and staggers to me. I kneel in the sand. She flaps her hands like I've been gone too long, over the mountains and far away. Her feet are too slow, she falls on me, laughing.

'Was your pa in the bar?' Ma's question chops my head.

I can't tell the truth. It will cut us all up.

But Ma braided my hair and she sang Amazing Grace. She took Pa's kisses. She even clipped his nails.

Gracie hugs my neck.

I turn to Ma, I beg her to make it not true. 'Yes.'

Tears jump in her eyes like I pricked them. They're pretty by mistake, they shiver and stick.

Ma's voice is full of sore scratches, 'Stay here.' She drops the axe against the wall. She grabs Jerry's mirror and pulls it, violent. The string snaps, *dikk!* She marches up the road like a soldier in a war. The mirror makes flicking flashes on the sand. It flicks on the grass, it flicks in the bush. It makes pretty sparks by accident.

Ma leaves me with the split pumpkins and my little sister. Grace wants to play, but I'm heavy and dead. I wait under my tree, I let her crawl on me. She plays in the fire, she gets filthy from the ashes.

The Truth Lady asks, 'Where was your ma?'

Shupp. He slapped cement on his new, huge stairs.
Ma marched up the new, slashed path.
The mirror burnt a hot square on his shirt. Ma said, 'Do you think I don't know you when your face is flat?'
The Truth Lady giggles.
I stare until she stops.
'Sorry, go on.'
He stroked her on her wrists. 'I heard you crying, Nance. I was just worried.'
Ma started to sob.

Gracie staggers past the outhouse. I can see half of her digging down there.
I stare up at my dead, hanging bottles. There's something I miss deep in my stomach.
I miss banging my bottles. I miss lying to my mother.
I want to climb up and try it, but I'm too heavy.

The Truth Lady says, 'Stella, your ma. The mirror. Remember?'

Grace giggles by herself, like everything's fun.
I didn't see the scorpions.
'Scorpions?'
I nod. 'One raced to Grace with a fat, curled tail.'

Grace ripped her finger away. She picked up a bottle and threw it.

Klissh! Grace's breaking glass! I run down to the plastic and grab her hands. There are no cuts, just the scab on her lip from the car. Her eyes are big from the smash.

I shout, 'You're a naughty, naughty child!'

Grace makes shocked, sucky noises, her sore lip sticks out. I pick her up and let her cry on my hip. I don't say, 'Alright, Alright.' She hangs on my neck, she cries louder and louder. She cries a new word, 'My-na, my-na-a.'

I tell the Truth Lady, 'That means, 'Mine, mine.'

Then Mugabe also starts. He crows, 'Wake up! Wake up!' like a siren. Over and over, and it's not even morning.

Grace forgets I was cross, she tries to get back to the outhouse. I take her to the hut, I lock her in with me. Grace is quiet and good while I change my school dress. She crouches in the corner and scratches the paint. Gracie's quiet, like the wall is a interesting place. Then I hear her grunt, 'Uggh.'

'Ag, no, Grace!' She's doing a poo.

I change her nappy on the cement square. Sies.

I kneel down and hang her against my back. I tie the blanket over my bumps. I stand up with strong legs.

I do what Ma doesn't want me to do. I follow her with my baby sister.

The Truth Lady mumbles, 'God, at last.'

Gracie talks in babbly baby words on my back. Only the birds answer. My tongue is too heavy.

I see him from far, he's floating colours in the sun. It's Mevrou's lovely cloth, the one with Hamburg painted on it. The sun shines pretty colours across my ma's skin. Jerry floats it on a big, round table. His words blow to me. 'Don't move!' He copies Gustav, 'Or I'll cut you with my sword!'

Grace chats on my back, still dirty and black. She sticks her fingers in my ears. She pulls my loose braids.

Glass rattles, *ting-a-ting*, like it's riding on a truck.
The Truth Lady says, 'Hey?'
It was two cups of tea in Mevrou's white cups. He put a Marie biscuit on the saucers. They were also Mevrou's.
The Truth Lady asks, 'And your ma?'
Ma did a last, sad shiver. She dipped her biscuit too long, she dived to catch it.

When I'm past the pine trees, that's when I see!
My eyes are lying. I cry, 'No, no.'
The Truth Lady says, 'What, kid? What?'
Jerry's touching Ma's legs!
I rip Grace's hands away. My ears hear Ma say, 'When I said forever, I meant forever.'
Jerry says, 'I know.'
Ma says, 'I'm not the kind that says yes in front of the pastor, and then plays around.'
'I know.'
'But he broke his promises over and over.'
He nods like Doctor Phil, that's Oprah's boyfriend.
Suddenly Jerry starts to sing, '*You … light up my life …*'
It's Ma and Pa's wedding song!

I cut my bare feet on the burnt black spikes.

I want to run, but my legs drag.

My ma shuts his mouth, but he sings through her fingers.

Jerry's fingers slide up.

The Truth Lady says, '*Under* her dress?'

'Yes.'

He sings naked and deep.

I stop.

'And then?'

He ducks his head.

'Ja?'

He sticks his lips to her neck.

It can't be real. It's a ugly, violent lie.

He sings in a whisper. He's …

'Yes?'

'… eating Ma's skin.'

Ma …

'Ja?'

'… puts her own mouth on his.'

Jerry moans like a bull, he drags her to his lap. They press tight together, they melt through their clothes into one body.

I stand next to them, I watch from the top. Gracie sticks her knees into me, 'Mamama.'

Ma springs off his lap. She falls with her bum onto the box. She hides her face in her hands and cries like she's hurt. Jerry's eyes are far, far away, like he's drunk. They come back slow. He holds a biscuit to Grace. Grace grabs it and gobbles it in my ear. I sink down on my shivery legs. I untie the blanket, I let it drop. The wet biscuit squeezes out of Grace's mouth, but she goes on her toes and grabs for more. I stand up and stare at my mother's bent head. My heart is sore like it's caught in a door.

I turn and run in my peeling shoes. I run through the burnt spikes, through the black ash. Black dirt smears my legs, it messes my dress.

My ma is worse than my pa and his drink. She's much worse than Caledon.

My ma is making sex with Jerry.

I rip my flute out, I climb up my tree. I bang my bottles with it, harder and harder, with no tune and no song. I want to break up the world. I want the blue sky to shatter. I want it to rain giant splinters, the size of our house. I bang so hard, a bottle smashes, *KRRISH!* Broken glass rains down from my tree.

My own mother!

The broken bottle neck swings evil and sharp. Even Mugabe comes to see. 'Voetsek,' I say, like Jerry. I want to smash Ma off him, I want to cut her off his lap. She had her mouth open, eating him like a animal. *Mlup*, *mlup*, they made soft sticking sounds, making sex with their clothes on. I'm not stupid, I saw. Like that rude Fifty Cent song where he undoes her buttons and pulls her pants down just a little bit.

The Truth Lady nods.

'They would have done it, if I hadn't stopped them.'

I know what sex is.

When I was small I heard Ma sighing in the hut, 'Huh huhh huhh.'

I woke up, 'Ma, are you crying?'

Ma shut up. Their blanket kicked and shook. 'No baby. I'm ... singing.'

I giggled, 'Oh. You sound like a hadeda.'

I say to the Truth Lady, 'I'm older now. I'm not stupid like that!'

I bang the glass with no song and no tune.

'Stella, is that how you play the flute?' Jerry stands on the green splinters. He holds his hands high, so I can't cut his eyes. He can see that I'm trying to smash up the sky. *KRISSH!* Jerry springs back as the green glass shatters. The sharp bottle neck jumps high on its string. Jerry wipes the water from his eyes. He shakes the green glass out of his hair. 'Stella, I was just trying to make her stay.'

'You put your hands under her dress!'

He ate her tongue, too.

Jerry's shoulders sag. 'Sorry man.' He snaps the glass with his shoe.

I say it with hate, 'I'm going to *tell*.'

Jerry's face turns slowly to me. I can see his sharp bottom teeth. 'What are you going to tell?'

'I'm telling Pa what you did.'

'Do you want a divorce?'

KRISSSH! More glass explodes in my tree. Jerry dives to the side. 'Stella!'

'I'm telling about your lies!' I shout.

'What lies?'

'Your mother's *dead*. She doesn't bake cakes.'

Jerry's moustache jerks to a smile. He hangs his fingers in his belt. 'That was a joke. That hanging stuff.'

But I've seen the brown lady. I know it's true.

'I'm telling about Nita's pa.'

Smashed metal spins inside Jerry's eyes. 'Stella. You'll go with me.' I grip my legs on my branch. I bang on my bottles, 'I'M GOING TO TELL!'

'SHUT UP!'

I bang harder.

'Shut up, you FUCK!'

The eff word hits my chest.

I shut up, but now I know.

Jerry's here to smash things, not fix them up.

'Come down!' he roars.

I hit softer on my bottles. I grip with my legs.

Suddenly Jerry's hair springs closer to me.

He's climbing my tree!

I hold my flute tight and climb high, to the top. But Jerry keeps climbing up, up, up. A evil bottle neck twists near his eyes. He pants, 'I'll tell the police we *both* did it.'

I squeak like a just born bird, 'What?'

'I'll say we did something bad to Nita's dad.'

Some thrushes chirp to cheer me up, '*Chip chip chipirru.*'

Far away, Nita's ma tjanks like a puppy. I'll tell the judge I heard it, but not with my ears.

I ask Jerry, 'What did you do?'

'Tell the cops, and you'll find out. I'll say we *both* did it, you and me. We'll *both* go to jail. And Stella?'

Jerry's a metal monster that makes sex with my mother.

'It'll be *forever*,' he says.

Silent, dry crying starts in my ribs.

'You'll miss home so bad, you'll want to hang yourself. That's what happens. They *hang* themselves, they miss home so much.'

The Truth Lady scrapes a word on her page, *BLACKMAIL!*

I pick up the green glass in case of Grace. I shut up. When my ma comes near, I look at my feet. It's like *I* made sex with Jerry, not her.

When it's time to sleep, I see it again.
Ma's on his lap. Jerry sings the wedding song.
I smash my bottles loud in my mind. I see exploding glass on purpose. It feels like I'm sleeping with broken glass in my bed.

Pa comes home very, very late. He trips over my legs, he falls, *dukk!* against the bed. Pa stinks of vrot grapes. He crawls onto the bed, he drops his arm over Ma. Ma throws it back, it swings like it's cut off with a axe. Ma spits like the caracal I saw at the river. 'Don't touch me! *Out!* Sleep outside!' She doesn't even care if me and Grace hear.
Pa crawls to the door. He staggers out to the night.

'Stella, are you alright?' Ma shouts from the garden.
The Truth Lady shouts, 'She's fine! She's having fun!'
She says, '*Aren't* you, Stella?'

I bang, *BOOMM BOOMM.*

In the morning, Pa's curled like a chick that fell out of its nest. He slept in the dead fire, with no blanket or pillow. I think he's still drunk, he staggers to the tap. Ma waits until his head is wet. Pa comes up shocked, like it's winter. Ma's voice is much, much colder. It's so freezing cold, it gives me a horrible headache. 'Drink! Go drink in the village. But don't come home again.'
Pa's mouth freezes open.

'Yes,' she says. '*You* can go. Why must we?'

My life is cracked and shattered, not the sky. The sky is clear blue, but big storming pieces fly into me. When I was a baby, the northwester blowed the zinc roof off our hut.

I tell the Truth Lady, 'I didn't even know, Pa hid me in his shirt.'

But now there are zinc roofs flying everywhere.

Jerry tried to make sex with my ma. And he did something terrible to Nita's pa.

The nun is rude about us coloureds. After the Glory Be prayer, she says, 'As you know, the concert's in the hall, in case God brings bad weather.' She looks only at the brown children. 'We really don't have space for all your aunties and uncles and grannies,' she looks like she just bit into a brown apple, 'and the whole big family.'

She turns to us with our instruments. 'Only the Musicians may bring extra guests. They've been practising hard, and they are the stars.' Her eyes choose me. She tries a old, rusty smile.

I watch a shiny black beetle climb Mary's dress. Up, up, it slides. It disappears somewhere in her cement skirt. Mary smiles like she's ticklish, like from a man's hands.

Mary's smile starts the storming again. I don't stop for the chickens, I go straight to the bar. I lean hard against the glass, I don't care if it smashes. Pa's not there! The storm stops a while, but it stays dark inside.

I stare at the vampire with blood smears on his teeth. His evil eyes are glowing and white. They make my heart feel raw and soft and red. Vyeboom feels dangerous.

The Truth Lady says, 'One thing, Stella. You know the first day?'

'Hey?'

'When he made the nun flutter. What was he doing outside your school?'

'Fuck! Fuck! Fuck!' but I'll say Eff to the judge.

He kicked the grave stone, *Dugg!*

The Truth Lady says, 'Ahh.'

The grave stone cracked a thin, long crack.

He grinded the white petals with his running shoe.

The Truth Lady says, 'Cheap.'

'Huh?'

'His *cheap* running shoe.'

Ma's planting seeds in old egg trays. Grace crouches down, she talks to Ma's knees. She picks dropped seeds from the sand, she hangs on with one hand. She pushes Ma's dress up by mistake. Ma's bare leg looks just like the Fifty Cent song, '*Just a little bit ...*'

They would've done it, if I didn't stop them.

I think my ma's a slut.

I put my bag down quietly in the hut.

I look for the men, but I can't find them anywhere.

They're not at the dam. They're not at our field.

They're not on the road, planting gateposts.

I'm nearly at Mevrou's when I find them behind the shed. There's a old, red tractor growing in the long grass. Jerry sits on top with his shoes tucked under his bum. He looks through a box with engine pictures on it. Gustav stops the sun with his hand, he smiles at Jerry in his hand shadow, 'Found it?'

My pa sweats under the tractor lid. He wants to vomit, I can see, from drinking all day. His fingers are filthy from the engine. His face is yellow inside his black skin. Jerry gives Pa a silver part. He points to the engine that's too black for his hands. Pa wants to vomit, but he sticks his arms back into the tractor's black stomach.

I don't go to Mevrou's, I walk back down the road.

I take a short cut through the bush. I go quietly like a girl in the dark.

I try Jerry's door. He forgot to lock it.

There's no hurt man in the kitchen. The kitchen cupboard is tall and thin. I know it's dumb, but I think, Maybe Jerry tied Nita's pa's hands and feet.

I open it slowly.

There's no man inside, just a old, rusted tin, and the cups from their ugly tea party. His Jesus Christ cup is in the sink. I hate that cup. I don't want to be a sheep in a flock.

I tell the Truth Lady, 'I'm a human girl, not a dumb sheep.'

There's no one suffering in the bedroom. Just a lady in red pants lying on a red car. The poster says, Neptune Car Parts.

The Truth Lady says, 'Oh yes?'

Her titties are bare. Her big red lips look like red rubber. I think her red pants are plastic. She's got red shoes too, they're high and shiny. I think she's a slut.

I look in the toilet. There's no man there, just another white lady hanging on the door. Her titties are so giant, she's got to hold them in her hands.

The Truth Lady says, 'He sold car parts for years.'

'Huh?'

'I found out.' Her purple lips creep into a grin. 'He charmed all the girls at the Biltong stall next door.' She flicks through her book, *slik slik slik*. She reads, 'He broke all of their hearts one by one. He was careful to crush them to pieces.'

She smiles, 'Carry on.'

I go to Jerry's car. I stick my face against the glass. There's no man on the floor. I push the button at the back. The lid swings up. A pile of clothes tie together like they're just as scared as me. Broken Lucky Strikes spray tobacco everywhere. I roll the tangle away, my hand hits something hard. It's a bottle of wine, Pa's favourite. Autumn Harvest Crackling. There's something crinkly too, it's a bag of orange Bubbles. Maybe Jerry's feeding Nita's pa orange chips.

He's not in the forest. Jerry's too scared of snakes to take him there. I walk to the river anyway, to think. There are three red orchids wide open on the path. They're redder than the lady's plastic pants, even. They're supposed to come in Christmas, they've made a mistake.

I'm not glad about them, I am jealous.

They would burst open red, even if I was in jail. Even if I was crying and wishing I was dead. I kick their red heads off their stems.

I'm jealous because they're beautiful. But they've got nothing to do with me.

The birds follow me like I'm a dangerous stranger. They sing to each other, but not to me. I listen anyway, they can't stop me.

I wait with my face in a streak of sun. Robins and weavers try a clumsy chorus song. I don't hear the truth in their out of time song. I hear it in the quiet when the song stops.

Jerry said *forever*. Forever means murder.

You go to jail forever if you *kill* someone.

Jerry killed Nita's pa!

Nita's pa is *dead!* Not eating Marie biscuits, or orange Bubble chips.

I run to where the river pours into the dam. I crouch at the new wall of mountain rocks. I stare through the silver into the mud. Maybe Jerry threw him in. Maybe he's down there, tied to a rock.

But the dam is still. Slimy frogs with brown streaks blow out their cheeks. Two snotty eyes stick out of the water. It's a terrapin, waiting to kill. Swimmer bugs float on their backs like boats. Their legs are ugly, hairy oars. Two ducks float past without any children. Far away, on the bank, a mean man goose hisses, '*Hhhgggg.*'

I can't go home. My ma's a slut.

I can't go to Mevrou's, she laughs too much.

I walk through black butterflies, the way that I came. I step over one of Eddie's shut, rusted traps. Today it's not just Eddie's crazy game. It's a evil thing that made Sheek bleed to death. It made the beautiful brown buck meow like a cat.

I get to the mother snake's ripped over tree. Her old, dry skin hangs off a root. Her eggs are like lamps deep in the trunk. She's waiting at the back, a black, shiny strip. I give her time to see me with her tongue. Then I climb in to hide from Jerry's forever. The mother snake lets me stay with my scared, dark mind. It's peaceful in her hiding place, it's lit with white eggs. I wish I was one of them. The mother snake watches them the whole day and the whole night. I wish I had a mother like that.

It's too far for my ears, but I can hear Grace baby-talking at home. A little black lizard tickles my foot. I wriggle my toe. It snaps its tail, it whips like black lightning. I stare at the cramping tail on my skin. I stare at my brown hands. I don't want to leave home forever. I don't want to go to jail.

I *won't* go! *Never!*

I'll shut up so no one can take me away.

I bang the metal, *BOOMM BOOMM.*

I stay home and watch, I keep my ma good.

The Truth Lady asks, 'You said nothing about the kissing?'

'Uh uh.'

In my mind, I say, 'Don't you dare go and sit on his lap. Don't you dare go and kiss him again.' I don't say the words. I only stare.

'So?'

Ma's titties go dry so there's no milk for the day either. Grace lifts Ma's shirt and cries. Ma whispers, 'Uh-uh, leave.' She pulls her shirt down, like I'm just a stranger who shouldn't see. Ma's trembly like Pa, but hers is nerves. My eyes make her guilty. She can't tie the knot in Grace's blanket, her fingers keep slipping. The onions roll off Ma's chopping board. She's too slow to catch them.

Pa works in the day, but he's drunk in the night. I don't know where he gets it, we never see any wine. In the day, Pa's quiet and shivery. When it's dark, he throws his arms out and talks loud to the night. His words fall around like drunk people. Ma doesn't shout, she speaks soft, 'Shut up.'

My pa shuts up like a frightened child.

On Friday, Ma chops supper for us. Her knife slips. She drops it in the sand, she grabs her hand. Blood drips from her thumb, but I don't even go to see if it's deep. Ma leaves Gracie at the fire, she drip drips on the sand. She gets toilet paper, she wraps it and squeezes. She stands straight like a soldier, she stares at me in my tree. It's a warm, pink night, but she makes a ice wind, '*You* finish the supper, then. Get the broccoli in the pot!'

Ma thinks *I* made the knife cut her. She thinks I did it with my eyes.

Pa's cheeky that night. He says very slurry, 'I'm not drunk. I'm just in a good mood.'

'For what?' Ma asks.

Pa's story swaggers and sways like his legs. It's a funny story, but I can't laugh. It's about Smart Fanie, who owns Bergsig.

The Truth Lady asks, 'Smart Fanie?'

'That's Pa's name for him. He's got gold rings and gold chains, and a fast, red car. Its name is Porsche.'

Pa says in Afrikaans, 'He got so drunk, his wife locked him out. She screamed out of the window, Sleep with the apples!' Pa tells us with words that are wobbly and vrot. 'She locked him out like a dog. Smart Fanie got very, very cross. So he hooked his bush cutter up and got on his tractor. He cut her whole smart garden down to the ground.' Pa says in drunk Afrikaans, 'Pinkrose, witrose, geelrose, enigekleurrose.'

His wife watched through the window, she didn't touch the phone. She didn't want anyone to see her husband drunk. Pa talks up to my tree. 'See, my angel, it's also them.'

I want to laugh, but I can't.

Ma will hate me.

Ma's as sour as the wine at the bottom of the bottle.

I tried it once when I was small. I spat it out on my feet.

Pa laughed at me, he said, 'Don't touch that stuff, Stella. It's poison.'

'Why do you drink it, Pa?' I asked.

Pa used Ma's words, 'Because I'm a rubbish.'

It's the same, now. Ma wishes Pa would fall in the fire and burn up like rubbish. That's how she looks at him.

I sit quiet in my tree. I don't even play my left over bottles. I watch Ma through the door, she pats Grace to sleep. Pa's too drunk to help with the baby. I wish *I* could give Grace her bottle and pat her soft back. I miss my baby sister. I wish I could love her, but Ma's in the way.

Everything's changed.

Nothing's fun anymore, not even Music Mix.

The Truth Lady says, 'Stella, wait.'

She bangs with her hand, *BOOMM BOOMM.*

Gustav and me watch in the lounge. Today I sit far away from the sofa. He lied about our land, I don't love him like I used to. But we both love Rihanna, she's still our favourite. Her hair shines like pouring black water. Her black eyes are beautiful, like a caracal. Her brown legs sparkle all the way up. She's in a rich house, with her umbrella up. But then she turns naked and gets made into metal. I can see her silver titties, even her bum. Gustav sings, '*Ella-Ella*' with her, but I keep my mouth shut.

A monster called Marilyn comes on the screen. His eyes are black bruises. His lips are black red like he's been sucking blood. He's got black beads on his cheeks, sometimes they shine silver. He grinds and he growls like a men eating monster. His growl echoes deep inside my meat. He reaches to us, he begs us to touch him. He holds out his hands, they're sliced and bleeding.

Gustav laughs at Marilyn's begging, bleeding hands.

He's just like his ma.

I stand up and watch behind the sofa.

'What's wrong, girl?' Gustav asks, he laughs, 'It's just a video.'

I leave him with the growling devil, I run home to watch my ma.

Ma orders me like a slave, 'The twigs are finished. Go and fetch pine cones for tonight.' She speaks like I'm evil.

I drop prickly pine cones into a Spar packet. *Ggrroommm!* Two giant wheels roar past my head. It's a truck full of straw, with a little white fridge tied on top! The fridge gives me a sudden, bad dream in the day. I see Danny in the freezer, the boy from the Truth.

He's got Nita's pa's face, but it's blue.

I follow the truck all the way up the road. It turns to Jerry's house. I hurry through the bush to watch where it stops.

Jerry sends my pa up with his pointing finger. Pa climbs up the truck, he unties the rope. I think I can see his fingers shake. He slides the fridge to the edge. He jumps off the straw, but he lands on his back. The men laugh at Pa, stupid and collapsed. Pa pulls himself up, he picks up the fridge. His veins stick out like the bones in a wing. He sweats like it's raining. Straw sticks to his skin.

Pa walks with the fridge all the way to the men. He puts it down at Jerry's feet.

My pa is a slave.

He makes me ashamed.

Jerry orders him, 'Show the driver where to go.'

Peep-peep-peep, the truck reverses.

Pa walks too slow. The truck's going to crush him!

'Pa!' I shout from the bush.

Pa stares at the leaves, he thinks he's dreaming. But he walks his legs faster, out of the way. The truck roars through the burnt circle, it stops in our field. Pa climbs up. He shoves the straw, *thuk … thuk*.

I hate my pa for being a slave.

From far, the straw bales look like sheep eating. Jerry tips back on his feet, he sticks out his hips. 'So?' His eyebrow lifts like a thin, flying wing.

Gustav giggles at the fridge like it's a funny thing. Pink spreads inside his skin. He says, 'I like my whisky cold.'

I wait in the bush, I watch and listen.

Gustav and Jerry carry the fridge to the kitchen. They stick the plug in. The fridge starts to hum, *zzimmm*. It's bossy and new. Jerry puts a pink polony in, with a red, shiny wrapper.

'I love polony,' Gustav says.

I tell the Truth Lady, 'But I know it's a lie.'

'Why?'

'Mevrou always said, Don't ever eat that stuff. It's full of poisons, Stella, it's not even meat. It's just a cheap trick for the poor.'

The Truth Lady says, 'What then?'

Gustav says, 'I'll go and get some Johnny Walker.'

I don't go home, I watch Jerry in his kitchen.

He stares at the straw bales tied up in their string. He takes the old rusted tin to the sink. He sticks a orange screwdriver under the lid.

The Truth Lady sits straight. 'What was in it?'

I shrug.

'Did you see the label?'

'Uh uh, it was rusted.'

The Truth Lady says, 'Go slow, Stella. Tell me *everything*.'

He lies the lid upside down on the sink. He dips Mevrou's silver teaspoon into the tin. He drips brown drips into his new plastic tray. He turns on the tap. The pipes moan, *aaarr*. They're not used to working. They spit water in blasts, *bok bok bok-kk*. Jerry turns the tap to a trickle, he slides the tray under it. He puts it in the freezer, just like Mevrou did.

The Truth Lady asks, 'What was it, Stella? *Think.*'

I shrug. 'I don't think it was meat juice to make gravy.'

I hit with my fist, *BOOMM BOOMM*.

I'll tell the judge the truth, I still love my flute. I hurt it on the glass, I scratched ugly scrapes in the silver. While the others play their songs, I rub the scrapes with my spit. In the Jesus Christ picture, it's still a beautiful day. The sword in his side is still silver. The hand stabbing him is brown, the same skin as mine.

I rub the ugly scratches, 'Sorry,' I whisper.

We've got to write a essay for Afrikaans. Sometimes I'm the best in the class, but today …

The Truth Lady interrupts, 'Can you leave the school stuff?'

I stop and think. 'I'll try.'

Ma stands behind flapping nappies. Gracie is throwing the pegs at my hens.

In our field, Gustav runs around with a knife, cutting the strings of the straw. He grins like a goblin with bright red shorts. He kicks the bales like a bully, they collapse for the tractor. Pa digs the plough hooks into them. Pa bites his jaws like there's a hammer in his head. He looks sick like the tractor's grinding him to dry dust. I think Pa's got sour vomit in his throat. But he clamps it back, he spreads gold straw where it was just slangbos before.

The Truth Lady asks, 'And Jerry?'

'Jerry's still clean and fresh.'

'Oh yes?'

'He's got his own shower now, with pouring hot water.'

He waves his arms, 'This side, Frank!' The dirty dust tries to catch him, but he marches like Gustav, out of the cloud.

Mevrou's back from Eddie's grave. Her gladiolus bed has got bald spots in it. She's in her black dress with her white face powder. She bought the new Truth, so now we've got two.

I say to the Truth Lady, 'We kept the one to save her heart.'

Mevrou's black shoes sit like twins on the grass. Mevrou is cheating. The lady in the catsuit rides a invisible bicycle, upside down. But Mevrou's flat on her back, kicking her cracked heels to the sky. I don't tell her she's meant to be upside down. I don't want to see inside her dress. I didn't mind before, but now it's too ugly.

'Isn't that your smart dress?' I ask.

'Yes, but … I'm going to … wash it … anyway. Ughh …' *Dooff!* Her legs crash down like trees. She pants like Hettie's horse next door. Mevrou tells me again, 'I went to England with *one* dress.'

I tell the Truth Lady, 'That's ein kleid in German. She told me before.'

Mevrou lifts her head up, her white hair runs out of its bun. 'I was the same age as you.'

Mevrou talks like the British suddenly. Even her face is white like the British. 'My English was very weak. I was too scared to speak. Every time I opened my mouth, they knew I was German. They *hated* the Germans, Stella. They thought I was a dirty German who wore the same dress every day. But I had no choice! My bag was stolen on the train. One dress!'

I flick the dirt off my skirt. Mevrou says, 'I washed my dress every night, and in the morning I put it on wet.'

I told Nita all about Mevrou's wet dress. Nita asked, 'Why did she wash it so much? She must be a cleaning freak.' I didn't say, 'Ja, she is,' because I love Mevrou. Instead I told her how they stood in line for two potatoes. 'The line was as long as Vyeboom main road.'

'Like the voting,' Nita said.

I nodded. 'In Cape Town they slept in the line to see Celine Dion.' Celine Dion's not cool, I know, but I miss her songs on KFM.

Today Mevrou doesn't say about the fire bombs in Hamburg that burnt her Ma and Pa. Today she says that there were bombs in England too. The Germans sent planes without any pilots, they were called Doodlebugs, which sound cute, but they're not. Mevrou says everyone hid under the ground at night. They played records and told stories. But Mevrou sat alone on her own. She had no friends, only her big English dictionary. It's the one on her dresser, it looks like Mevrou got it from the dump. The rips are stuck with sticky tape. The edges are crushed, it's got Bible thin skin. It looks like dead moth wings, not paper. It looks like Mevrou rubbed the flying powder off with her fingers.

'Those bombs explode in your stomach, not just your ears. The sky falls down.' Now she lies on her back, she watches our clouds, 'But it's not blue, Stella. It's orange.' I'm not really listening. Mevrou's told me lots of times about the London Blitz. I think of the boys in grade one, how they run around the playground throwing pretend bombs, '*Eeee ... Pggghh! Digadigadigadig.*' They shoot each other's planes. They don't feel the ugly spit in the corner of their lips.

'Buildings and blood mix, Stella, did you know?'

'Huh?'

She shrugs, she stares at our blue sky.

The mother starling shouts, '*Chacker, chacker, chacker!*' The starling pa comes in his black and blue suit. He brings her a jerking worm that looks just like Mevrou's vein.

Ma used to shout at Pa like that, but now she's stopped. The waiting's much worse. It's worse than bombs, even.

It's like I'm waiting for Ma to go and kiss Jerry.

And Ma's waiting for Pa to fall in the fire.

I open the new Truth. I read to stop thinking about Ma and Pa.

'It was a green Ford with stripes on the side. The man gave the keys to my mother. He snatched my hand and said, Come, I'll buy you a Sprite.'

Mevrou blows though her mouth like a fart.

'My mother swapped me for a car.'

Mevrou's legs crash to the ground. Her stomach pumps up and down, like it's full of water. She rolls on her side and laughs nearly to death. She sits up to see the lady that the little girl grew into. She's a sad, white lady with her eyebrows drawn on. Mevrou pokes at the photo, she laughs close to my nose. She smells like salami, that's special German meat.

The Truth Lady says, 'Italian.'

'Sorry?'

'Never mind. Go on.'

Mevrou lies on the grass with her hair spread everywhere. I stare at the book to see what's so funny. The lady's got missing hair like the flower bed. Her eyebrows are drawn on with a pencil.

'What's funny?' I ask. My face is hot, but my voice has got Ma's ice wind in it.

'Ag, Stella.'

'If I told you my secrets, would you laugh?' I ask.

'No, Stella, of course not.' Mevrou reaches to me, but I move my bum away. I hate her today. I'll tell the judge, I hate Mevrou for laughing.

I go up on my shoulder bones like the lady in the Truth. I show Mevrou she's wrong. I ride a upside down bicycle, like she's supposed to, if her heart was strong.

Something bad's going to happen. Pa's not even trying to hide that he's drunk. Tonight he puts the radio on and dances. He still moves groovy, his feet shuffle the sand like a African. Pa's half Xhosa, you can see by his feet. He dances cool, even when he's so drunk that his mouth can't shut. Ma comes out of the hut. She still doesn't shout, but her voice is so frozen, if you licked it, your tongue would stick.

I tell the Truth Lady, 'That's what happened to Nita's cousin. She went to work with her ma and her tongue got stuck to a white lady's fridge.'

'Ouch.'

Ma makes the warm air burn like snow, 'Where did you get the wine?'

Pa's like a bad dog, he tries to sit. 'You said stay home ... I'm home. Hey, Stella?' Pa's eyes are so blurry he can't see me in the leaves. He throws his arms out, 'We're all staying home.'

But something bad's going to happen. Pa's already had his last, last chance.

Ma sleeps on her edge of the bed. I cuddle Gracie tight. Pa snores outside, as far as the mountains. When Pa used to snore inside the hut, Ma used to say before the sun came up, 'Frank, please lie on your side.' Pa rolled over and breathed nice and quiet. I miss Ma's sweet voice, when she was too sleepy to remember if he was bad, or what.

In the morning …
I stop.

I drum, *BOOMM BOOMM*.

In the morning, Mugabe screams at our window. I spring up with my heart flapping wild. Pa's snore didn't warn us that the sun was coming.

Outside, Pa's lying with his back in the sand. He was too drunk last night to even get a blanket. There's grey ash powder on his clothes, even up the hairs of his nose. If Pa wasn't snoring, he would look dead.

In the mornings, Mugabe thinks he's the boss of the world, like he owns the sky and the mountains and the cities I've never seen. Today he orders me to fetch the new, laid eggs. I let him pretend.

I put the eggs on the fire grill next to Pa's head. Pa's still snoring because no one's turned him over. I try Ma's sweet voice, 'Frank, please lie on your side.'

Pa rolls in the sand, he curls up like a baby with his hands between his knobby knees. It makes me so sad.

Then I see it.

The Truth Lady asks, 'What?'

My ears go hot. 'I don't want to tell the judge.'

'Spit it out, kid. What?'

'It's a big wet patch.'

'Hey?'

'Pa wet his pants.'

The Truth Lady sags, 'Oh.'

My Pa wet his pants. I don't know what to do.

Gracie staggers in her nappy. 'Myne,' she says. She drops down and crawls. She stretches her hand, she watches me, cheeky.

I say nothing.

Gracie grabs a egg, she squeezes, *cluck*. The shell snaps, the yolk bursts in her hand. Slimy yellow egg hangs in the sand. Gracie laughs a slippery egg laugh. Mugabe shouts, '*Craaaa!*' He beats with his wings, he stabs with his beak. I grab him and throw him hard to the sky. He scratches the air, he grabs on a bottom branch. He swears up there, '*Kak kak kak kak.*'

I say to the Truth Lady, 'It means, shit shit shit shit.'

'I know.'

I let Grace break every, every egg.

At school, we …

The Truth Lady interrupts, 'Can you miss the school stuff?'

I sigh. 'I'll try.'

After school, our whole field is glittering with straw. Far away, at the edge, Pa drags a big drum with knives stuck to it. It crushes the straw and punches it in. Jerry and Gustav stand and watch like two bosses.

Mevrou is flying foam everywhere. She scrubs the car like it's been bad, and she's scrubbing it good. Her skirt is wet, it sticks to her legs. Her rolled up sleeves stretch down wet. She says 'Hello,' but today she's not glad. Maybe she's cross because I haven't been coming. She says, 'The Truth's in the kitchen. Read while I work.'

Today I read, 'My lovely pets chewed the man's arm to twenty centimetres from his elbow. The maid should never have let the carpet cleaner in.'

The Truth Lady says, 'That's *mine*. I wrote it.'

'Oh.'

There are two black dogs with flat heads and robber's eyes. One hangs its pink tongue. The other one frowns like a wrinkly man at the camera. I see it in my mind. The sun shines through the curtains, like in Mevrou's lounge. The two black dogs lie down like lions, they crunch through the man's bones, *ggik*, *ggik*, *ggik*.

'So?' Mevrou looks like the frowny dog when I stop. I'm about to read more when Gustav shouts from the house, 'Man-n!' He bends over, he squeezes his soft, white stomach. His hair sticks up like strooiblommetjies. His teats are longer than you think. 'Listen! Just listen!'

We listen in the kitchen. Gustav moans, 'Aaarh. I've got a bad stomach. I haven't slept all night, now *listen* to them!'

The starlings screech like they're teasing. Gustav looks around crazy, he grabs at the air, 'Give me something. I'll get up there!'

'NO-O!'

It's me. We're all shocked. I'm like a men eating lion. My fingernails are sharp teeth inside my fists. Another roar is on its way. It makes me blind, 'NN ...'

Mevrou touches me with wet, fluttery fingers. 'Never mind,' she says. She touches Gustav, 'Go on, mein liebling.'

It's like she throws water on us.

She pulls Gustav's angry shoulder straight. 'Stella will sort them out.' Mevrou flutters Gustav towards the stairs. I'm still big enough to eat up the whole house, but she says, 'Stella's just the right size.'

Mevrou puts on Mozart to hide the starling shouts. She moves a big bowl of green apples off the dresser. She lies her old dictionary flat. 'Climb up,' she says. I climb up the shelf and balance on top. I push on the square in the roof. It lifts. Dust falls in my eyes, I cry it out. I sneeze. I creep in the shadows.

Ag, moeder. They are fat and fluffy. Pink skin shines through their hair, just like the lady who got swapped for a car. There are broken blue egg shells everywhere in their nest.

I stick my head back through the hole. I whisper, 'There are six little chicks!'

They are crumpled and untidy with wide yellow mouths. It looks like they've got no ma to dress them.

I look for their mother. She's not on the roof planks in the shadows. She's not on the shed. She's not with the cherubs. She must be out hunting.

Suddenly I get a sore shock in my chest.

It's terrible!

The Truth Lady begs, 'What?'

She's hanging in the fig tree next to the house. Her eyes are dead holes. Big pieces of meat are teared off her bones.

It's the Jackie Hanger! I've seen how Jackie Hangers eat their own friends. I've seen dry bird bones on Marais' fence. They bomb mice and lizards and other birds, Pa said. They stick them on a spike while they're still living. Sometimes they eat them, sometimes they let them rot. Sometimes they're just showing off for the girls.

I slam the window shut. I've got to bang it three times so it can lock. Gustav shouts something furious. But what if the Jackie Hanger comes back for the babies?

Mevrou stands on her tippy toes like a fat Christmas angel. She holds up some mielie porridge and a matchstick. I hang upside down, 'Thanks.'

I stick the match gentle down their throats. I've done it before, me and Ma did it with Amy. I hum with Mozart to calm them. They're greedy and squeaky, they swallow the stick. Just when I think they'll never shut up, they get calm and happy and fat.

Gustav should shut up. How would he feel if his mother got eaten by a Jackie Hanger? Imagine she was hanging there half gobbled and ripped?

I leave the chicks in the roof. They can die from heart attack if you take them from their home. Pa said.

The Truth Lady says, 'Do you want to stretch your legs?'

'No thanks.'

But the Truth Lady's walking creaky to her car.

I go for a fast pee. I think, 'Don't forget, don't forget.'

The Truth Lady smells sweet and fresh. Her teeth are a cage, she slurs, 'Want one?'

It's the peppermints with the sticky stuff in the middle.

I drum on the tub, *BOOMM BOOMM.*

I carry on talking with stuck together teeth.
After my chicks …

'Wait!'

The Truth Lady flicks her red switch.

She digs some sweet out of her teeth.

'Okay. Go.'

I get birds' wings in my stomach about our concert. We practise one last time in the hall. This time, when I play Amazing Grace to the school, I hear my own ma singing it, like the first time I played. She sings it sweet and free and forgiven, like the green grass man who came out of jail.

After my turn, I stare at poor Jesus falling with the sword. Today I see that his thick twisty hair is like mine, even though he's white. I think I can see light, light wings in the blue air around him. They must be angel wings, waiting to fly his spirit away. Pa says that your body is just like your clothes. Pa knows because his ma ran away when he was only two. But Pa told me one day, his ma stayed with him, every second, every day.

'How can she be in two places?' I asked.

Pa said, 'Your spirit can leave its clothes and go anywhere that it wants to.'

'Even when you're alive?'

Pa nodded. 'Even when you're dead.'

'How do you know?'

'My father said.'

I don't know why, but my chicks make me excited about our concert. When I …

The Truth Lady says, '*Forget school*, Stella. We haven't got time.'

I sigh. '*Fine.*'

Marais' apple trees have dropped their flowers on the floor. The new apples are only tiny hard balls.

I drop my bag at the hut. Ma's washing some perfect green peppers at the tap. They're sparkling and fat, they shine like green glass. Grace kneels in the wet mud. She licks a green pepper like it's a ice cream.

Pa's the slave again. His spade goes, *chup chup chup*, he digs a long ditch. Jerry's clothes are still clean, like he's been drinking tea, maybe with somebody's mother. There's a whole lot of irrigation pipes on the grass. Gustav stares at a pile of silver irrigation things. He picks one up and turns it in his fingers. Suddenly he gets the same sore face from the kitchen. He drops the silver part on the grass. He bends like he's bowing to a audience, but he's not. Eina. Shame.

My chicks are as noisy as the grade ones. I feed them and say, 'Don't worry, don't worry,' about their mother. How would *I* feel if I had no ma at home?

PAGG! I look through the window. *PUGG!* Jerry's Datsun shoots another bullet from its pipe. Jerry waits behind his dusty glass. Gustav walks in slow. He talks like he's sore. 'I need to wash. Jerry's taking me to the doctor.'

Mevrou says, '*Gott sei dank.* At last.'

When the green car is gone, I drop onto the dresser.

Mevrou says angry, 'I've told him go to the doctor, how many times? But no, he waits for *Jerry*. Really, Stella, every day it's, *Jerry* says forget apples, let's grow vegetables. *Jerry* says potatoes are forty five rand a bag …'

I just say, 'I can't stay today.' I go home to my own ma as quick as I can.

Ma's busy …

The Truth Lady interrupts, 'Wait Stella. Did the doctor talk to the cops?'

I nod.

'Tell me quick?'

Jerry held Gustav under his armpit.

He looked worried to the doctor. 'You know what worries me? Gustav's been using DDT.'

The Truth Lady dives to see in my eyes, 'DDT?'

'Yes.'

She digs with her ink, *Google DDT.*

Gustav waved, weak. 'Ag, all the farmers use it.'

The doctor pinched the bump of his own stomach, 'The problem with that stuff, it hides in the fat. You can't see it in the blood.'

The Truth Lady grins, '*Shit!*'

'What?'

'Go on!'

Gustav bent over from a big, terrible pain.

Jerry gripped his shoulder.

The doctor said, 'Shame.'

The Truth Lady breathes fast, 'DDT's bad stuff, isn't it?'

'Ja. We learned in Nature Studies.'

'What?'

It's a insect killer, it's not allowed anymore. It kills all living things, even birds that sing.'

'And humans?'

'It gives them cancer.'

'Aha!'

'It makes birds' eggs too thin, so the chicks can't grow if their home is broken.'

The Truth Lady slaps my knee, 'Thanks, kid. Carry on.'

Ma's busy bathing Grace in the tub.

'Hi Mamie.'

That's all I say, but Ma's green eyes go like soft grass. Her back goes soft, like a plant. She knows I like her again.

I play Amazing Grace in my tree. Ma smiles up at me. When she tries to wash Grace's face, Grace fights with the cloth like Ma's trying to kill her. She splashes to catch her pink star fish. Ma's got to hold her up by one wing, or else she will drown.

'Ma?'

'Ja?' Ma sounds careful, like I might ask for help with my maths.

'Ma? Don't you love Pa anymore?'

Ma jerks like I swore. She lets Grace go, she ruks up straight. Grace's wash cloth wets her leg. She doesn't care, there's green hate in her eyes that could blow trees over.

'You must love him, Ma. You *must*,' I beg her in the storm.

Ma rips the washing off the line. She cracks our clothes, *crukk!* like a thunder crack. She leaves Grace all alone in the water.

It's dangerous, so I climb down and wash my little sister.

The Truth Lady says, 'Hey.'
She asks me, 'New day?'
I nod.

She bangs, *BOOMM BOOMM.*

The next day, Pa's voice shouts down from the sky, 'Stel-la!'

I stare everywhere.

'Stel-la!'

I see him small and waving, up at the canal. I climb down my tree, I run up the hill through the fynbos. The big hairy proteas are like pink animals on the hill. Sugarbirds and green sunbirds hop all over them. Pa showed me the proteas a long time ago. He joked, 'Look, Stella, they're hiding in the bush. They don't know that Eddie's dead.' Eddie used to cut them and sell them in Worcester.

When I get to the top, Pa's up on his toes, staring into a square of still water. 'He's stuck.'

I try to go close, but Pa's arm shoots. Pa smells like vrot fruit.

Suddenly a head rises over the wall. Its eyes are popping, its neck is spread wide like a terrible kite. A cobra!

'Pa!'

Its black eyes are silver in the bright sunlight. Its skin is dirty yellow, like inside a cigarette. Its scales are wet. It glips in the air, higher and higher. It sways to the back, it sways to the side. It feels like it's creeping out of a bad dream. One little bite and I'll die in two hours. I'll first feel a tickle in my lips. Then I won't be able to swallow my own spit. My muscles won't work, not even my tongue. I'll get strangled, Pa said. The poison will choke my throat.

But the wall is too steep, the cobra can't stick. It crashes back, *splussh!* It twists and swims. A dead rat rolls in the dark water. The cobra doesn't want it, it climbs the wet wall.

Me and Pa crouch, the canal runs, *ssshrrrr*.

The snake's head rises up, it flicks its tongue. It falls back, *splussh*, over and over. Slower and slower.

Me and Pa get brave. We go right to the wall and stare at the snake. Pa says, 'He's beautiful!'

'Stay back.' Pa drags a big, dead branch from the bush. He tips it in, he grabs my hand with his still, strong fingers. His breath is vrot.

A dassie's head pops over the mountain rock. Its bright little eyes watch with us.

The cobra slips its wet loops around the wood. It's as long as my body, it's as thick as Pa's neck, I'm not lying.

The Truth Lady shivers, 'Urgh.'

'Why are you saving him, Pa?' I ask.

'He lives far from the hut, he won't hurt us.'

The shining, wet monster hangs its yellow coils. It keeps its ugly kite wrapped in. It swings its head down, it uncurls in the air. It touches the grass and glides to the ground. Its huge head pulls. Its tail tangles out.

I whisper, 'Pa? You know the God part?'

'Huh?'

'You know we've got a God part and a mad part?

'Ja?'

The cobra keeps winding out.

'If people are busy being evil, where is their God part?'

Pa says, 'Mm … They forget it, that's all.'

'So is it always there?'

Pa nods slow, like he's not sure.

'*Why* do they forget it?'

The cobra's flat on the ground, poisonous and smooth. Pa can't answer.

I ask him again, '*Why* do they forget?'

The cobra smooths off the road, into the bush.

He's a beautiful, terrible monster, free on our farm.

Pa stretches his body across the canal. He fetches a bottle. Autumn Harvest Crackling!

He sits on the wall and screws the top off.

Now I know why Pa's not shaky. Now I know why he smells vrot.

He pours a big swallow into his mouth.

'Papa!'

Pa stares at the mountains cutting our sky. 'They feel like *useless*, Stella. That's why.'

He's a sad, sad man, sagging on the wall.

I sit on the cement. I hang my hand on his neck, like Grace hangs on me. 'Pa?'

'Ja.'

'How long does it take to remember?'

Pa can't talk. He's got hurt in his throat, I can feel it. It's like he tried to swallow a whole butternut. All Pa can do is shrug.

Pink streaks spread slippery across the sky. The sun drags silver off the mountain spikes. Down the hill, Jerry and Gustav drink together on the stair. Gustav's giggle runs up the hill to us.

'Pa, it's late,' I say.

But Pa just sips.

I leave him to drink, I go the long way.

The canal slides snaky next to my legs. I climb down the hill behind Jerry's house.

I creep along the side. I let my ears spy.

'I've got this silly song in my head,' Gustav says.

I crouch in the long grass, I spy through the stalks.

Jerry pours whisky, *blug blug blug*. 'Sing it for me.' He drops a ice block, *pulunk*. He gives it to Gustav. 'Come on. It's time I learned some German.'

Gustav's giggle goes on like a long chorus song. He climbs on the round telephone reel table. He splishes a tiny splash on Jerry's hair. Jerry frowns, 'Careful!' He whispers, 'Shit.'

Only I hear, because Gustav's singing his little boy song. I know it from Mevrou, she taught me when I was small. He dances a silly dance on the round wood table. '*Wie wahl ist mir am abend, Mir am abend, Wen zur roh die glocke läutet, Glocke läutet, Bim! Bam! Bim! Bam! Bim! Bam!*'

I tell the Truth Lady, 'I know what it means.'

'Mm?'

'*Oh, how good I feel in the evening, In the evening, When the bells ring for resting, Ring for resting, Bim! Bam! Bim! Bam! Bim! Bam!*'

Jerry grins and claps, he laughs at the crazy dance. Afterwards he helps Gustav down, like a rich princess from a cart.

In the night, Pa's arm is straight, but his legs are bendy. 'Stella, look at the moon.'

The moon looks like it fell and smashed on its side.

'People can't see it's a hundred percent. They think there's a whole piece missing.'

Ma talks like a cold, dead wife. 'Frank, go and sleep.'

Pa sways, he stares at the crooked moon. 'Even the moon gets a chance to show them.' He throws his loose arms, 'But not tonight.' Pa smiles his dimples at me in my tree. Me and Pa giggle about the dropped moon.

Pa points at me. 'You!'

We all wait.

'You and your music show. That's your chance!' he says.

Pa knows what I've been thinking! Even when he's stupid and drinking.

Ma sighs a hard sigh.

I climb down my tree, I push on his back. 'Come, Pa. Come sleep.'

Pa leans back against my hands. He staggers at the fire, he just misses it.

'Pa!'

Jerry floats out of the black shadows. 'Come, old pal,' he says. But he doesn't sound like a pal. He presses my pa's arms down to his sides. He forces him to the hut like he's a police. He shoves Pa on the bed. Pa falls down from the wine and the surprise.

Jerry does my pa's job at night. He drops our mattress on the floor. He gets my sister. He lies Gracie down with her milk bottle. Grace doesn't even cry. Her eyes go big, then they start dropping shut. She sucks quietly from the sleep and the surprise. Jerry covers her with her blanket. Ma leans against the door, she bends her head. She smiles a small, special smile that she kept. Jerry pats the place next to Grace. 'Bed time for you, too. Your mother needs a break.'

It's too early! I never sleep now.

But Ma doesn't say. She smiles her only smile. She leaves us with Jerry, like he's our father.

The air is thick and angry, it makes me crawl slow. The blanket is as heavy as cement. Jerry walks out of the door.

'You can't come to my concert.'

Jerry slides back. His eyes hide in the shadow.

'Only mothers and fathers are allowed.'

His head shoves to me, his eyes pop out. 'Liar!' he hisses.

Jerry shuts the door, even though I always, always go to sleep with it open.

I can't hear their words, they talk too soft. They switch the radio to KFM. It's a stupid, dumb station full of slow love songs. A stupid, slow song goes, '*Rock me gently* …' Pa is quiet because he's lying on his side. It's too early for me, but Gracie's breath is peaceful, it nearly strokes me to sleep.

I must stay awake! I'm the only one who knows!

I open the door, I don't care what he says.

I walk past to see if they're touching, but they're not. I force my pee out in the toilet. I walk like a tortoise back to the hut. The Greatest Love of All is singing now. It's Celine Dion. I stop in front of Ma.

'Don't worry, Stella,' Ma says. 'It won't happen again.'

But Ma is soft and shining.

I turn the knob to Radio 5. The DJ laughs in a empty room.

I leave the door open.

I try to stay awake, but they play Killing Me Softly. It's the fast mix, not the pretty, slow one, but Grace's breathing strokes me to sleep, like a small leaf falling, slowly this way, slowly that way, to the ground.

The Truth Lady asks, 'Well?'

'I don't want to say.'

She says, 'Come on, Stella. Don't chicken out now.'

Ma turned the radio back to KFM.

'Yes?'

The DJ was a British, his words were short and cut. He played Beethoven's moonlight song. I've heard it in Mevrou's kitchen.

'And?'

'I can't.'

'Come on!'

'They slid together.'

The Truth Lady dips, she whispers, '... like magnets.'

They hid behind the hut.

The moonlight song played its gold and silver instruments.

But the real moon hung like a thin, sorry strip.

The Truth Lady says, 'Come on.'

He pulled her down, she sat on the ground.

I stop.

The Truth Lady says, 'He opened her legs?'

He kneeled between them. He kissed my ma's neck, like when they had tea.

The Truth Lady ducks, 'He sucked on her breasts like a new born child.'

'Sies!'

'Sorry, Stella!' Her eyes stretch wide. 'Really, sorry kid.'

She says, 'And then?'

'I think they did something I've seen the dogs do.'

'You mean, on their hands and knees?'

I nod.

He jumped on her back. His hairy lip lifted.

A dog tjanks, 'Yip! yip! yip!' behind our hut.

I hear something hit, *fipp fipp fipp*.

But my chickens don't scream. Amy only mumbles.

It's just a stupid, chicken stealing dream.

My eyelids are black stones, they crush me to sleep.

The Truth Lady says, 'New day?'

I nod.

She drums for me, *BOOMM BOOMM*.

The nun doesn't trust us, she makes us stay late. She's got new roads going all over her face. She says, 'I want no mistakes. We've practised for weeks.' The nun points at us, but her bent finger points at the tree. 'God is always perfect for you. Try this *once* to be perfect for him.'

Something lands in my stomach like a eagle on a fish. I can feel its claws digging in. Even Mary's not perfect. She's got lucky beans on her dress and poo mess on her head.

'I want clean, neat hair, and perfect, polished shoes.' She stares at my broken shoes. She sighs hard like my ma. She grabs my hand, her hand is soft like cooked squash. She takes me to the hedge.

I think she's going to say rude things about my shoes, but she says, 'Stella, do you know why you're playing last?'

My hand hangs loose in her warm squash palm.

She says, 'Because you're the best.'

The heat starts cooking my cheeks like meat.

'Make sure you look smart tonight, alright?'

I stumble back to the others. The nun says to all of us, 'Come and get your choir gown from me when you leave. Keep them clean and neat.' She dusts off her nun habit. The nun's got a habit of dusting her habit, even though it's perfect and clean.

Pa also said it's my chance to be perfect, but he didn't say it like punishment. Pa says I'm as perfect as the moon, even when I'm not. Even when my shoes are peeling.

All day at school, I think, I'll play only for Pa.

I'll play much better than they've ever heard in Vyeboom.

I'll play like a angel in my white gown. My pa's angel, not the white porridge ones that the nun loves.

The Truth Lady says, Stella, *skip* school.'

Pa will feel rich like a mayor, not like a poor man who falls. I know my pa. He'll feel proud and rich, because I'm his daughter.

At break, Adrian …

The Truth Lady says, 'Stella!'

Pa dug inside his thick, sticky sweat. The sun boiled his head. It made his eyes blurry and white.

The Truth Lady says, '*Thank* you.'

Shuk! Shuk! Jerry slammed the grass with his stick. Five geese barked like dogs, they flew off the water.

The Truth Lady says, 'Five?' She sighs.

Hettie stamped down the hill with a sparkly, silver thing in her hands. Her dress was like a sail at the Vyeboom dam.

The Truth Lady says, 'Next door?'

I nod.

Jerry shouted from far, to Pa.

The Truth Lady yawns. 'What did he shout?'

'He said, Frankie! What's the bet …?'

The Truth Lady sits stiff. Now she listens.

The boerewors rolls were white and soft. Marais grabbed one in each hand, for only one man.

Jerry slid through their fence, he hid behind a tree.

'Hi!' he said. Hettie nearly fell at the poison tank.

The Truth Lady says, 'Poison?'

'Poison gas for the sand.'

Hettie stared at the blue lights in Jerry's eyes.

'Do you want to go for pie and chips?'

Hettie looked at her pa quick. She said, 'I *love* pie and chips.'

The Truth Lady sinks to her machine, 'Joy poured in Hettie's heart like …' She thinks. '… lovely, tasty gravy.'

I say, 'That's when he did it.'

'What?'

'He pointed to his pants where his winkie is. He rukked with his hips. He made those funny rude jerks the rappers make on TV.'

'Ooh. What did she do?'

'She sprayed him with the poison hose, but she missed.'

The Truth Lady laughs.

I watch until she stops.

Pa showed his palms, they were big and empty. 'Can I owe you?'

Jerry slapped Pa's flat hands. 'Frankie!' He even squeezed.

They laughed like they were still best, joking friends.

I shine my old shoes as bright as I can, but my pa's the best at polishing them. I tie my loose shoe strap tight with elastic.

Ma puts Velvetress leave on cream in my hair. She combs it with her own fingers. Ma puts her own hairclips in my fringe, the ones with the tortoise pattern. She gives me a surprise, she says, 'They need to see your pretty eyes.'

That makes me think, Pa's got brown eyes like mine. That makes me hope, maybe she still loves him.

But Pa is late.

Ma walks up the road with her hands on her hips. 'Frank!'

Grace copies Ma, shouting cross. She's in my old baby dress with waves of white frills. Mevrou bought it for me when I was born.

Ma's wearing her wedding clothes, they're her smartest. Her skirt is high on one side and dips down to her unkle.

The Truth Lady says, '*Ankle.*'

It's baby pink. Ma said she couldn't wear all white because of me in her stomach. Ma's white shirt is gathered between her titties. It's got three quarter sleeves that tip to the floor. She's got Velvetress wax in her hair, not the cream. It's combed back smart and glamorous like a model. Tonight you can see her beautiful eyes. But their furious wind messes them up. 'Frank!'

Ma's desperate shout makes me panic. We're late!

My flute is out of its box already. It's heavy and sweaty, but I am ready.

'Pa!' I also shout. The crickets shut up. The sand on the road is silent soft powder.

Ma pulls Gracie onto her hip. Gracie's shoes make dirty sand marks on her skirt. 'Come. Let's go,' Ma says.

'No!' I don't want to play without my pa. 'Paa-aa!'

All that answers is a engine.

Jerry's green car makes thick, rough dust. I stare through the glass to find Pa's face. But it's just Jerry, alone on his own. He stops next to us.

Ma asks, 'Where's Frank?'

'Pissed.'

Ma's mouth goes ugly like she bit a lemon.

Jerry shakes his head. 'Out for the count.'

'Useless!' Ma bombs the empty road with her word.

The Truth Lady says, 'Oh shit. In the village?'

'Uh uh.'

Zzimm, went Jerry's fridge.

A two litre box lay on its side. It had purple grapes painted on the white.

Pa's head hung like a horse that they kill for meat.

His heavy head dipped, his hands hung off his knees. I can hear his words leak, 'Ihavetogo. Nancy'n me.'

The Truth Lady says, 'Keep going, kid.'

He tried to stand, but he fell on his bum.

Pa stroked his face, but his skin had no feeling. 'My angel,' he said.

That's me.

Ma swings Gracie in like she's a bunch of feathers. She gets in the car next to Jerry. I stay on the road. 'Paa-a!'

'Get in.' Ma's voice is as hard as the ground when you fall out of a tree.

I get in the back, I turn and watch for Pa.

When we get to the grader at the gate, Ma says, 'Wait!'

She grabs Jerry's leg like he's her husband. Jerry drives backwards, *zeeeeee*, like hundreds of bees. Ma runs in the hut. Jerry waits like a husband in his smart blue shirt and his black business pants. Ma drops a white cardboard box in my lap. Jerry spins his wheels as we leave.

I open the box.

They're brand new and shining and black! They're the ones that I love, with the leaf holes and the buckle. Ma spits the words like they taste terrible, 'They're from your father.'

They are perfect new school shoes.

I put them on. My feet shine smooth and beautiful. The moon outside is beautiful. It's only my pa who is drunk.

I watch the smooth moon. It's full and fat and laughing at me.

But it's not as pretty as it thinks. It shines silver, not gold, because it's not properly dark.

And it shines for nothing, because Pa's not here.

Jerry stops his car outside the gate. I'm late! I jump out and run. When I get to the fire escape, I stop to tell Ma to go the front way. I wave in the light, but she doesn't see me. She's kissing Jerry under the lucky bean tree! Jerry and Ma are dressed smart, but they kiss like they're making sex in the bed. They kiss for so long, Gracie ducks under their kissing chins to see me. They kiss right at Mary's feet. Mary is stupid and stuck, what can she do? Vomit shoots up my pipe. I'm sick like Gustav, but I run up the stairs. I run fast down the corridor, faster than the sick can rise up. *Klupklupklupklupklup*, go my shiny new shoes. My legs pump like a scared duiker through the junior class. I run down the stairs to the stage. I pull open the heavy stage door. It swings, violent, it tries to crush me.

The choir sings, 'O *come all ye faithful, come let us adore him* …' The nun catches me in the stage wing. I can only see her white wrists in the dark, but I know the feel of her crooked claws. Tonight she's not nice, or soft like a squash. She hisses a whispery hiss, '*Hhhgggh*,' like a goose. She shoves me on the stage.

'*Come ye, o co-ome ye, to Beh-eth-lehem.*' The hall is packed full of parents. There's a video camera on three long legs watching us.

Ma and Jerry come in at the back. They're dressed very smart, but they're messy from kissing. Ma's hair is not so glamorous now. They stand guilty in the light, behind all the chairs. 'Stella!' the nun hisses like a horrible man goose. She opens her mouth wide, she points into it. She wants me to sing. I didn't know the nun had so many fillings. It looks like she chewed a whole lot of bullets.

I don't sing for her. I keep my mouth shut.

Gracie fights on Ma's hip, I can hear her whine. Jerry takes her from Ma, like Grace is his child. Grace gets good, she stares everywhere. The strange mothers and fathers are listening and neat. They smile with love at us on the stage. They are perfect parents.

'Stella!' The nun points at me, but her crooked finger aims at the back.

The choir sings, '*Sing choirs of angels, sing in exultation …*'

Ma looks worried. Jerry strokes her arm, he whispers in her ear. I can see them from here, do they think that I can't? Grace lies her head against Jerry's chest.

I don't sing a word.

The twins play first. Rudy gets scared, he keeps making mistakes. Bruce plays violent like he wants to snap his strings. Gracie fiddles with Jerry's buttons, she baby talks, '*Dup-dup-dup.*' Jerry puts his hand over her lips, but Gracie talks louder. Ma and Jerry get the giggles, like me and Nita used to. I feel like screaming. I stare at the stabbed Jesus, with his mouth also shut. His blood is as red as the orchids

I kicked. Jesus should be screaming. His mouth should be stretching wide from the pain.

David is next with his violin. He plays it nearly like a real Musician. His notes are good, but there's no feeling in his strings. Silent Night is meant to be gentle. Ma and Jerry have stopped giggling, but now Gracie wants to play. She puts her hand on Jerry's mouth, she thinks it's a game. Jerry takes it off and kisses it inside.

The nun hisses from the wing, 'Stella. Go!'

I walk to the front of the stage. Jerry's stroking my ma's backbone. Do they think I can't see? I want to scream like Jesus should, but I keep my mouth closed.

The audience is perfect. They put up their fist and go 'Uh-hmm,' instead of coughing. The video camera watches with its little red light. A small boy in front tries to crawl away. His pa catches him and wraps him on his lap. He points at me, he tells the boy, 'Ssh.'

I put the flute to my lips.

The people start to smile.

My eyes go to Ma and the man who's acting like my pa. They're not touching now.

I drop the flute down. I open my mouth, but I don't scream like Jesus should. I sing, '*Ama-zing Grace …*' My voice is hot from not screaming, it floats smooth to the roof. '*How sweet the sound …*' My flute hangs stupid and loose. My voice is hot like the sun's been on it. I sing the song true, it pours full of grace. It swells against the roof, it rings in our bones. But I sing it only to my mother. '*… Was blind, bu-ut noww, I seee.*' My song makes sore cracks in my ma's heart. Water runs from her eyes, I can see the shining stream. '*T'was Grace, tha-at taught, my heart to fear*

...' Grace grins, she waves her arms at her name. '*And Grace, my fear re-lieved* ...' She stretches like a snail away from Jerry. He pulls her back, he bounces her hard on his hip. Jerry sends silver splinters over the perfect people's heads. He stabs me from the back, just with his stare. But I sing so the splinters can't go in, '*The hour, I first, be-lieved.*' Jerry knows what I mean with those big, beautiful words. Jerry knows that I am screaming.

The audience clap like melted snow. They pour like a waterfall, but all that I see are Ma's wet cheeks. Amazing Grace echoes loud in the hall. It blurs the words of the nun's last prayer.

It echoes loud in the playground when we walk past Mary.

On the way home, it sings loud in the car. No one can even speak. Ma rubs her eyes. Grace falls to sleep. Jerry stabs through the window with his angry eyes. The moon rides home with us. Now it's gold from the dark, and it follows us fast. The moon is glad now, because my song was so strong.

I put the flute to bed in its box. Jerry lies Gracie down. He starts humming ugly, '*Hur hurr, hur-hur hurr* ...' He hums Amazing Grace in ugly hums in our hut. He's a mad, growling man. He drops our mattress on the ground. He throws our pillows down. He lies Grace on her pillow. He hums ugly at me, '*Hurr hurr* ...'

'I'm going to tell,' I say.

He shuts up.

I say, 'I don't care what happens.'

He stabs his eyes into mine. He spreads his huge hand over Gracie's face. Grace shakes her head, she gasps in her sleep. A scream jerks out of me, 'MAMIEEE!'

Jerry stands up quick. Ma rushes in. Jerry smiles, like I've just done something funny.

'Jerry's hurting Grace!'

But Gracie sleeps, sweet.

'And he hurt Nita's pa. I think he killed him.'

Jerry rolls his eyes up in his head. He gives my ma his big smile that can fix anything.

'Stella! Stop with your lies!'

'Ma, it's true.'

'Stop it! Stop it!' Ma hides her head, like I'm hitting her.

Jerry sings like he's putting a baby to sleep, 'Ea-sy. Ea-sy, Nance.' He pushes my ma gentle out of the door. He says soft to her, 'I'll talk to her. She's just jealous, for Frank.'

'I'm sorry,' she says.

Jerry sings sweet, 'Why don't you go and get Frankie so long?'

I swallow my sobs. They swell up huge, they block my breath.

'You little *bitch!* I told you to shut up.'

Jerry called me a bitch!

'Stella?' he says.

But I can't answer.

'I'll kill you *all* if you talk.'

My ears don't understand. His eyes are cold silver, I can't see what he means. His cross is small and cold, it hides in his hairs.

I can't find Jerry, whose eyes crinkle when he smiles. The one who says, That's my girl, like I'm his daughter.

'If you try that again, I'll kill everyone on this farm.'

I can't find Jerry, not even in his eyes. He must be lying.

'You'll go to jail forever,' I say.

He shakes his head. 'I'll say Frank did it. I'll say he went mad, like that man in Worcester.'

The man with the bandage sways towards me, the one who shot his girls with his hunting gun. I throw my arm over Grace. She baby talks, '*Ub ub ub*,' in her dreams.

'Do you believe me?' Jerry asks.

I look for his cross. 'No.'

'What?'

I can't look at his face full of hate. I look at his cross that won't shine. I want Jerry to love Jesus, like he said. I shake my head.

'You don't think so?' His question is like a hunting gun aimed at my face. My chest hunts for air.

That's when I feel her breathing.

The Truth Lady says, 'Who?'

The brown lady's in the hut! She's breathing for me. She's *here*, she's alive! Not strangled and dead!

I say to Jerry, 'Your mother's here.'

'Hey?' Jerry's hands crush into white fists. His face goes loose, like it might fall on the floor. It pulls tight again, his tight teeth glitter. Hate stinks in the hut, it smells like a dead mole. Jerry dives through the door. *Thik, thik, thik*, go his feet on the sand. They run faster, away, *thik, thik, thikthikthik* ...

'*Reeeee!*' A baby screams somewhere in the bush. *Thik thik thik thikthikthik*, his feet run back. Jerry stands in the door. The shadows stretch Mugabe's wings long on the walls. His screams are high sobs. He flaps his long wings, he walks his thick twig legs in the air. His flapping shadows fill the hut, but his screeches are weak. Some of his tail feathers land on the blanket.

I spring up and pull on Jerry's wrists. 'No!'

Jerry shoves me back. My head cracks, *BUKK!* on the cupboard. I'm a burning, broken head. I cry with my eyes open, I make myself see. 'Please leave him,' I beg.

But Jerry twists my rooster's head. It turns and turns until his beak is on wrong.

'Leave him! Leave him!' I shout. I grab, but all I get are his pretty tail feathers. Then there's a sound. It's not even loud.

It's a soft sound, *kik*.

Mugabe is pap. His head hangs bent. His beak points loose to the floor. I look for his mean look, but I can't see his eyes. His feathers hang like rags. My Mugabe hangs like a thin rooster suit.

I kneel down and cry like a baby. Gracie hears me and cries in her sleep. Jerry ruks my shoulders up. 'Shut up!' He bangs my face in my pillow. 'SHUT! UP!' Mugabe's suit hangs over my shoulder. His feathers stroke my neck.

Jerry throws it down in the doorway. 'Get into bed!' He rips the blanket up, he covers me to my chin. He tucks my blanket up. He lies over Grace and tucks her up, too. His white hands are too close to her nose. 'Do you believe me now?'

I nod too many times.

'Are you going to shut up?'

I nod and nod until he gets away from Grace. Jerry picks up my rooster. *Thik, thik* go his feet. *Shuk!* goes his car lid. His door slams, *klopp!* Jerry drives away with a gentle engine.

The Truth Lady's eyes look dizzy and drunk. 'God's truth!'

'What?'

'Seriously kid, there's enough here for a *book!*'

I lie in my choir gown and watch my sister breathe. Her nose holes swell in and out, just like my baby chicks. Her lips suck the air like it's a titty. Her soft hand is open next to her face, like Grace fell to sleep saying, 'Stop, stop, stop.'

I should have said, 'Yes, Jerry. I believe you.'

It's my fault Mugabe's dead. He was still young and strutting. He was the boss of everyone, with his mean eyes and his siren. My sobs can't come up. They make deep, sore bruises.

Later, Jerry comes back. I grab on my sister, I cover my head. He drags my pa past us. He drops him on the bed. Pa stinks of dirty wine and dirty feet. 'Orright, orright. Sokay,' Pa says.

Jerry talks to Ma outside, as sweet as Jesus. 'It's all sorted out, what did I say?'

My pa stinks.

My pillow's as sharp as a rock. I grip onto Grace.

Jerry is terrible. He's a monster who murders.

Jerry will kill us all if I talk.

The Truth Lady drums the tub, *BOOMM BOOMM.*

I wake up without a siren. My pillow is sore, like it hit me. When I lift my head, Mugabe's tail feathers still float on my feet.

Mugabe is dead.

Sadness digs a sore, dark hole inside me.

That's when I see the empty space. Gracie's missing!

I spring to my feet. Pain stabs my brain, my heart hits like a stick.

But Gracie's on the bed with spilt orange chips. Bright orange Bubbles crawl all over Pa. Gracie stuffs some in her mouth, her knees crush some. Pa lies like he's dead. I shake his heavy head. 'Pa?' I pull up his eye. It looks like a cooked egg. Pa grunts like a pig, '*Gggh*.' Gracie grabs Pa's eyelashes with her orange fingers. I say, 'Uh-uh, Grace. Leave.'

Ma's switched on the sprinklers. That's my pa's job. She crouches in the garden with her back curved to me.

I don't want to go to school, I must stay home and watch. I press my eyes to chase away Mugabe's loose, hanging beak. Everything's wrong. Grace's eating orange chips, but there's no rooster to steal them. I press my eyes hard to make the picture dark.

Ma's eyes are puffy seed sacks from crying in the night. She pulls spring onion shoots that came out in a crowd. Their hairy little roots try to hang on, but her fingers rip them, *crrip*.

'Ma, I'm feeling sick.'

'Where are you sick?' I see old disgust in her seed sack eyes. I know that look. It's how she looks at Pa.

I get dressed slowly. My brand new school shoes shine like nothing's wrong. I don't want to go to school. I don't want to leave Pa sleeping. I pull Pa's two eyes up together, 'Pa. Wake up!'

Pa snoffels like a baby, he pulls the blanket up. I get Grace's baby bottle off the floor. I drip it on his eyes, I make cold milk tears. Pa lifts his head, his eyes creak open. There's red and yellow in the whites. Pa looks terrified, like he saw the murder last night. 'Huh, huh, huh?' Pa sounds like Mugabe. My throat gets thick and stuck. My sad stomach spreads like hot porridge inside me. I say, 'Pa, it's late.' Grace shoves a snotty chip between Pa's teeth. She barks like a dog, 'Woof, woof.'

'Ma, Gracie's eating orange chips for breakfast.' Ma shrugs and rips the spring onion shoots. I'm scared to go to school. Not because of the concert, not because of the nun. I swallow and swallow. I rub my mouth. Now my throat hurts much worse than my head. It really *is* sore, but Ma won't believe me. She thinks I'm a ugly liar again.

'You…!' The nun's disgusted like Ma. It's like I'm not worth more words, but I hear her ending in my head, '… belong to the devil.'

When we're getting our books out and banging our desks, David says in front of the others, 'You can *sing*, hey?'

Some girls join in. 'Stella, you sang so well.'

'You sang it so *lovely*.'

The nun says, 'Quiet!' She strikes me with thunder in front of the others. 'What if one morning I just didn't feel like teaching?' She shouts like she wants a answer, 'What if I decided I just wasn't in the mood?'

She's going to send me home, like Cynthia, when she had scabs on her head. Her ma shaved her hair and painted her with purple paint.

The nun stabs her fingers in her eyelids. She tries to dig a tunnel behind her nose bone. She whines like a child, 'You just can't go through life thinking, me, me, me. I don't even need to even *be* here, you know. I could have stopped teaching ten years ago.' She opens her eyes, they've got new red threads. That's when I hear Nita in my head. I know what she would have said, 'Stella, you sang better than Beyoncé.' Nita always said silly things like that.

But Nita's far away in Swellendam, without any father.

The nun is right. I'm not a star. I belong to the devil, if there is one.

My throat hurts like Mugabe's, just before he died.

After school, the cars roar through my body. The wind warns me, Watch out. I get a stitch in my stomach. *Klip, klip, klip*, my new shoes hit the tar. *Dub, dub, dub* they stamp on the sand. Marais' wife drives past, she's as wide as the bakkie. Her lipstick is nearly as long as the bumper. A lump of silver crinkle paper glitters against the glass. The silver pile slides, she catches it as she drives. Her swerve of dust floats into my throat. It's dry like slangbos fire. I watch my bright, happy shoes running in the dust.

Ma's scrubbing our clothes in the tub. I can't see Grace. She's not on Ma's back. She's not on the sand. I check in the hut. I know it's dumb, but I look up my tree. 'Ma. Where's Grace?' There's disaster in my voice.

Ma's seed sack eyes have sunk. White washing bubbles climb up her arms. The bubbles pop soft, *tik, tik, tik*. Ma points her eyes at the hut.

I go and look again. I must be blind! Grace is there, on the bed. She's lying on her stomach, like when she was first born. She's much smaller than I thought. My Grace is the same size as the pillow. I touch her back, I feel her soft wind. 'My baby,' I whisper, even though I'm just her sister.

I can't find my pa.

I look at the dam. I look in the fields. The old pump's got its metal off. Its insides are showing.

A engine starts in my stomach. It pumps my legs, it shoots my shoes. Where *is* he?

I find him past the bend on the road to Mevrou's. He's fighting with the old afsluitkraan.

The Truth Lady asks, 'Old what?'

'It's a big, big tap.'

'Oh, stopcock.'

Pa's got oily black stuff all over his skin. Ropes stretch in his neck, he fights with the metal ring. Gustav flutters next to him. He's as white as Mevrou's flowers, he's sweating for nothing.

'Push, man!'

I nearly spring out of my skin.

Jerry stands above them. 'Push!' he shouts, like Pa is just lazy.

Violent water blasts Pa to the ground. It blasts Gustav to his knees. A brown waterfall shoots up to the sky. It drums hard like the hooves of a horse as it falls. Gustav crawls away, he hangs exhausted. The water turns clear and sparkling now. Pa bends back and laughs at the bursting water. Jerry grins with him. He's still clean and dry.

That's when I think, it must be a lie. Jerry wouldn't kill us.

There's a upside down waterfall gushing up to heaven. They're laughing like friends. Jerry wouldn't kill us, it's really not true.

I turn and run backwards to watch them having fun.

But Jerry's not laughing with Pa anymore. He's not even watching the water gush. He's watching me run, like *I'm* the dangerous one. His eyes flash the same terrible warning as before, 'Stella, I'll kill you all if you talk!'

The Truth Lady writes, *I'll Kill You All If …*
I ask, 'Why are you smiling?'

Her pen stops. Her smile drops. She says, 'I'm sorry Stella. This is just lovely Truth Stuff.'

Mevrou's kitchen smells like a happy day on the farm. It smells like onions and meat, the Magic Flute even plays. She's got a big pot on the stove full of funny bones with plastic ends.

'How was your concert?' she asks.

'Nice,' I lie.

'How did you play?'

I see Mugabe's hanging head.

I point at the bones. 'What's that?'

'Oxtail,' she says. 'How did it go?'

I see Mugabe's broken neck.

I stare in the pot. 'Do they fit together?' I choke.

Mevrou's big chopping knife waits in the air. 'What's wrong?'

Slangbos thorns prick my throat. Mevrou switches her opera off. 'Are you sick?'

I shake my head, I swallow the spikes. Mevrou takes some bones out. She makes a ox's tail on the board. 'There's the tail, see?'

She asks, 'Did something bad happen?'

I shake my head. I swallow and cough. I stare at the ox's tail. 'Shame,' I say.

I climb the dresser to my chicks, I stick porridge down their throats. All the way down, just like their ma. It makes my throat hurt even worse. On the CD, the three ladies try to make the prince talk. But the prince's got to glue his lips like Beyoncé and me. '*Stille, sag ich. Schweige still ...*' If he talks he'll never, never see his love again.

Downstairs, Gustav's boots walk in.

'What happened?' Mevrou asks him, also.

Gustav sounds like someone's sitting on him. 'Get me dry clothes, I need the toilet.' Gustav bumps and hurries, he slams the toilet door. Mevrou knocks, 'Gustav, don't you think you should go back to the doctor?'

'I told you, he doesn't know what's wrong.'

'What about Worcester hospital?'

'I haven't got time for hospital, *Mutti*, we're farming!'

'Well, if this carries on ...'

But Mevrou's not the boss. Everyone knows. Gustav does what he wants. The last time Mevrou was bossy, the piano went in the shed.

The Truth Lady says, 'Oh yes?'

'Because of Albert, the Piano Wizard.'

'Who?'

'He had his name on his car.'

He had a wet, side parting and a long, long fringe. He had special silver tools to fix piano strings. Gustav was happy and excited all the time. He asked Mevrou, '*Mutti* can you make us a eisbein for lunch?' Mevrou hated their duets.

The Truth Lady grins, 'Oh yes?'

They tangled up their hands, they crossed their legs over to reach the keys. Mevrou growled angry to me, 'Gott! Listen to them, squealing like mares!'

Mevrou hated it worse when they were quiet. She stamped in with tea, even when they didn't want.

One day Mevrou was using her Bosch, sucking up dust where the piano used to be.

'Where's the piano?' I asked.

She said, 'Gustav's angry with me. I phoned Albert's father. He's *very* Afrikaans.'

The Truth Lady asks, 'So then?'

Albert drived home to his Afrikaans pa, and Gustav hid in his room for two whole weeks. The piano went in the shed, under a thick, grey blanket. Pa said Gustav helped him move it on a trolley.

Mevrou put food on the floor outside Gustav's door. She worried and worried that he was going to turn into a person in a concentrate camp. But when Gustav came out, he wasn't starving and thin.

My chicks screech and screech.
Gustav shouts. 'Shut those birds up!'
'Sshh,' I say to them. I push the porridge down.
They're growing too fast. They need some meat.

I hear the toilet flush. Gustav's boots climb the stairs like a old, old man. *Klupp … klupp.* Suddenly Mevrou switches to Triumph, it's nearly the last song. '*Triumph! Triumph!*' It's bursting and glad. The magic flute got the prince through the fire and the floods. I hang my head through the hole. Mevrou curls her finger.

I drop soft to the dresser, 'Thanks.'

I say, 'I can't stay today, I've got to go and watch Grace.'

Mevrou looks worried. 'What's wrong with Grace?'

'I've just got to watch her.'

Mevrou looks at me funny, she wants to ask why. I go before she makes me lie.

Jerry brings real steak for Ma to fry. He stands and talks to her in our smoke. My pa is drunk before the moon even comes. I keep Grace safe with us against the hut. She bites my leg sore with her new teeth. 'Eina!' I say. Grace thinks it's funny, she dives with her mouth. 'Stop it!' I shout. Ma tries to take her, but I hang on. 'No, Ma, it's alright.'

Ma gives us Jerry's steak to eat. I gobble it quick. It's so delicious, it puts my stomach to sleep. Pa's scrubbed the black oil off his skin, but now he gets meat grease all over his face.

'Pa.' I point.

He tries to wipe it, but it's still slippery. Ma looks at him like he's something disgusting in a toilet. I wipe his face quick.

Gracie chews and she chews, nice and quiet. Suddenly she coughs, 'Kuk! Kuk!'

Pa's too drunk to see. 'Mamie!' I shout.

Ma runs to us.

Jerry swings Gracie up, he hangs her by her foot. *Thup!* *Thup!* he bangs her small back like he's trying to crack it.

The meat flies out. Gracie coughs and cries.

All of us laugh, because Grace is saved. Ma puts her on her titty, even though it's dry.

Jerry saved my sister! She could have *died*.

He's still the man who says Frankie, and says Bliksem, when they joke. He's our clever friend who saved Grace, not the one who hissed 'Bitch!'

I watch him from my tree, the man who saved my sister.

But he sits too close to Ma. He talks in her ear, with his big moustache touching. My pa doesn't see, he sleeps drunk against the hut. Gracie stretches Ma's titty with her lips. She lets go, *snup*. She climbs off Ma's titty and hangs on Jerry's leg. She smacks the flat bone of his knee like a drum.

A broken bottle hangs cruel near my face. That's when I see for the first time in my life.

The Truth Lady asks, 'What?'

They're not music notes.

They're just ugly green bottles that make my pa weak.

Ma lies back on her elbows. 'Where's Mugabe? I haven't seen him all day.'

Jerry stares up through the leaves. 'Have *you* seen Mugabe, Stella?'

My stupid bottles hang around my head. I see something terrible. It's nearly like a ghost. Jerry's wearing hate over his clothes. It's silver like his eyes, but it doesn't shine.

'Stella?' He strokes Gracie's neck. He rubs it with his thumbs.

A shout rips my throat, 'No!'

Ma frowns and clucks her tongue. She's sick of me.

Jerry lets go of Grace, he lies back like a husband. His lips touch Ma's ear, his soft words climb my tree. 'Maybe Mugabe went to find a new wife.'

I bang loud, *BOOMM BOOMM.*

It's Saturday again. Mevrou's playing her sad funeral march in the kitchen. She plays it every month on her grave days, but today I can hear the tears and the cries of the family.

'Are you going to the grave today?' I ask.

'I can't.' Mevrou looks up the stairs to Gustav's room. 'He can't even eat.'

It's like the piano is suffering on the CD. I feed my chicks lots of porridge, but they still shout and shout. 'Ssh,' I whisper, 'Gustav is sick.' The music notes sink deep in my skin, they march with the coffin. The slow, scared notes drum inside my ribs. It makes me too scared to even watch Music Mix. 'I've got to go home,' I say again.

Mevrou starts to ask, 'What's wrong?'

But I'm gone.

I run fast down the path. The birds sit close together, the trees hang sad. Even the river slides silent in its bed. The funeral march plays faster and faster in my head. I spring over the traps, like it's a emergency.

When I get near the hut, I hear my pa laugh. Gracie grabs Pa's bread every time he tries to bite. Ma's scrubbing herself at the tap. It looks like she's trying to wash her skin white. I don't stay and play. I've got to watch Jerry.

I run soft up the road. I creep through the trees. When I get close, I hide behind a trunk. It's so quiet I can hear the *zziimm* of his fridge. *Chushhh,* goes his toilet. It's a real one that flushes. Jerry hums with his new fridge. It's the song I switched off, The Greatest Love of All, by Celine

Dion. Jerry's new stairs are still only half plastered. A new window glass waits against the wall. I can see the white leg of the lady in red. Jerry walks past his window. He stops. He stares at the tree in front of me. I suck myself in to make myself thin.

Jerry marches to his car. He snaps the lid open, *clut*. He unrolls black plastic and lifts something up. It's teared and brown, like a old, ripped coat. He lets it swing in the sun.

Mugabe's colours are dull, like when I got him from Oom Piet. His wings hang dead. He's only got two tail feathers left. His red rubber crown shivers in the air. I can't see his eyes. Are they still mean? Are they shut? Please, please don't let them be scared. Please not! Jerry drops Mugabe on the table, *flup*. He goes inside whistling Celine Dion's song. My eyelashes burn from seeing my sweet, mean rooster.

Jerry comes out with a huge, rusty saw.

He drops it next to Mugabe. He sits his bum on the table. He flicks a Lucky Strike in his mouth. The match scratches, *ggitshh*, he curls his hand for the flame. Jerry blows his smoke straight towards my tree. I stand dead still like wood. I can see the truth now.

The Truth Lady asks, 'What?'

The tips of his moustache are not blonde, they're orange. And the streaks in his hair are just dirty rust.

Jerry stabs his cigarette on the table. He twists it and drops it back in his box. He picks up the rusty saw. He holds it high, like for a photo. He clamps his hand on Mugabe's feathers. He saws Mugabe's legs, *gga-ggi-gga-ggi*. The metal bites his thick twigs. I hear them go, *click click*. Mugabe's loose legs tangle on the table.

Jerry's going to eat Mugabe for spite.

His spite burns my eyes and my stomach inside. It makes me sick like Gustav, but I stand as still as wood. Jerry flips Mugabe over, he starts to saw his head. Even from here, I can see the leaking red. I can feel the old rusty teeth in my throat. I bite my itchy cough, to stop it. I squeeze my crying eyes shut.

When I open my eyes, they get a horrible shock.

The Truth Lady says, 'What?'

Mugabe's twig legs stand on the table. Mugabe's bleeding head is stuck on them.

Jerry is grinning at the tree in front of me.

I fall like a ball into the grass. Vomit stings my tongue.

Jerry's not cutting Mugabe to eat him. He's cutting him to hurt me.

He lifts the saw. He waits, like for a camera to click.

Mugabe's wings snaps, *crick*. I can't see, but I know from the spilling and the splitting. I know the truth from the terrible mess. Jerry is sawing through Mugabe's soft stomach.

I stand up and run, like when they ate each other's tongues. *Mu-ga-be-Mu-ga-be*, my legs pump as they run. Jerry is mad, he saws for violent spite. He wants to do worse. He meant what he said!

I run over the road, into my forest. I pump along the path. I spring over Sheek's trap chained to the ash tree. I push into the bushes that grow over Sheek's grave. Now there's no sun and no white disas in the middle. Now there's only a green sky of leaves. I shiver on Sheek's grave, I listen for the saw.

It's not like Ma who kills our chickens when they're old. She says she's gentle with them, even when they're dead. She plucks them, kind. She cuts off the meat. Pa always says their names when we eat. 'Thank you, Wilma. We know that you're not dead. But thank you for leaving us your meat.' Ma thinks Pa's mad to say that chickens have got souls. '*Eeeep*.' The thrush above me sings high like a flute, '*Oh lay oh leee.* ' 'Why are you hiding?' Another one asks, 'Why are you so scared?'

They didn't see Mugabe's head shoved on his legs. They didn't see Jerry's evil. I'm the only one who knows.

The Truth Lady gasps, '*Oh* my God!'

'Sorry?'

'Shit!' She jumps up, she sits, like it's hot under her bum. 'It just *hit* me! The old duck in Roodepoort!'

'Huh?'

'Heavenly Light Orphanage!' She says, 'I did this story before Christmas.' She growls, 'Bloody cops didn't let us print it.'

She twists, she digs her nail in my wrist. 'It was bright daylight, about ten o'clock. She was on her swinging seat, picking fleas off her cat.'

I nod, 'I know those seats, the farmers have got them on their stoep.'

'She was still in her night dress. I even got a photo. I remember what I wrote. She had the cat on its back. The cat saw him first, it jumped off her lap.' The Truth Lady hangs her heading in the air, 'The Cat Kept its Fleas!'

Her eyes glow like hot coals. 'He beat her skull against the swing seat. But she wouldn't go to sleep. So what did he do?'

I've got no answer.

The Truth Lady licks her lips. 'He held her down, he looked around. He snatched a bottle on the table. It was poison, for fleas. He snapped the lid off with his teeth.' The Truth Lady spits, 'He spat! He poured the whole bottle on the matron's curling tongue.'

She punches her page with her purple fist, 'Christ! Wouldn't that be insane?'

She cuts with her ink, *Heavenly Light! Check it out!*

Then she looks around, quick. 'Look, don't tell anyone, okay? If it's true, it's *mine. I* worked it out.'

She asks, soft, 'Promise, Stella?'

I nod.

'Just *forget* I said it. Carry on.'

'*Eep*,' the thrushes fly away to say, 'There's a girl on Sheek's grave.' The sun through the branches gets rusty and weak. Ma doesn't believe me. If I tell anyone else, Jerry will murder us.

The brandy man with the bandage nods his sore head.

I can't even tell God about my lie.

It's like Jerry said, God doesn't care. I'm not rich enough.

And I did a ugly sin.

I crawl to Sheek's rusty trap. I stamp my foot on its bottom jaw. I force my fingers between its teeth, I pull my hand into a cramp. They lift a tiny bit. They snap back, *prokk!* I stroke my fingers along the metal mouth. There's a little square there, like a rusted buckle. I get a stone and hit it, *buk buk buk*. The buckle hop hops, it makes silver tracks. I stop and listen to a *vip* in the bush. I hear a long slide, then a skoffel on the ground. It's a slithering snake, and a scared, kicking mouse.

There's a stick of ash tree on the path. I bite it tight between my teeth. I try the trap again. I don't care if my veins burst, I don't care about pain. My arms shake and burn right into my brain. I shove the stick in the gap, I let go, *grib!* The orange teeth bite deep. I stand on the stick, I pull the jaw up. My fingers sting like they're bleeding. But there's excited air inside me now. 'Pull!' I shout loud in my mind. I hear a soft sound, *kik*.

It's the same soft sound as Mugabe's neck.

I see stars in the grass, but the trap's alive again. I grip its red, rusted metal chain. The pain in my arms shoots to my ear bones. The grass on the path bursts, *kir-kir, tuk!* I crash against a tree, but I stay on my feet. I drag the trap off the path. I snap branches like Ma. I cover the hungry jaws. I know what it's called, it's called *camouflage*.

A mouse screams at the river. A whole flock of finches come to spy on me. They give each other looks, but they don't say a word. Next door at Marais', a tractor roars like a bully. From far away, the cars really do go *voom*. A bright green grasshopper flies *zzzaah* past my head. I creep past the trap. I crawl closer, I jump. The grasshopper pricks me, it kicks in my fingers. I grab the sharp, green spikes on its back legs. I smash its head with a stone. I put the squashed grasshopper in my pocket. My chicks need meat.

Pa sags to sleep early against our wall.

In bed, I see Mugabe's head stuck on his legs. I press my face in my pillow, I dive where it's dark. My mind says, *click click*, the sound of thick twigs snapping. I stick my fingers in my ears, I fall to sleep.

The Truth Lady says, 'And? While you slept?'

I shake my head.

'Come on, Stella.'

I say, 'My chickens got upset.'

'Yes?'

They squawked and they bumped like bombs were going to drop.

'Tell me.'

It was a soft sound that stabbed in Pa's brain, 'Huhh, huhh.'

Pa woke up.

He heard two trees creaking. He heard the fire die, *ssshhh*, like rain.

He looked up at my tree, he waited for a gust.

He gripped on our wall. He walked slow and listening. The moon listened, too.

I dream that someone's crying.

I make myself wake, I open my eyes.

Grace's feet are on my stomach. It's not *her* sobbing like a little boy whose mother is missing.

But it's not a boy, it's a grown man.

Maybe the wind brought it here from the squatters at the dump. My hens cluck like it's day time. Why aren't they sleeping yet?

I push Gracie's legs off.

'Ma?'

The bed is empty.

'Pa?'

The sobs stop. Pa's voice comes from the wrong side of the hut, 'Ja?'

'Pa, are you crying?'

'Go to sleep, my angel.'

I grip Gracie's hand tight, so she whines. The hens cluck in the dark. I listen for a while, but no man cries. Before my eyes fall to sleep, I see the man who swapped his car. His moustache is big and yellow. His pants have got stripes. He grabs my hand and says, 'Come. I'll buy you a Sprite.'

The Truth Lady asks, '*Who* was crying, Stella?'
The branches tangled up, they made zig zag shadows.
I stop.
The Truth Lady says, 'Come *on.*'
The moon painted silver stripes on his legs.
It gleamed his white bum into silver.
The Truth Lady gasps, 'Ja?'
Ma's thin brown arms hung tight around his neck.
Her smooth brown legs were wrapped around his back.
I don't want to tell the judge, but I must.
'What, Stella?'
'It was sex that made the branches creak.'
The Truth Lady dips, she nearly kisses her machine, 'It was sex that made her mother sigh.'

She bangs with her hand, *BOOMM BOOMM.*

There's a broken suitcase under my tree. It's Ma's from when she left Caledon. Pa's packed his clothes, a pink soap and our small pan. He's got a towel and a blanket in a black plastic bag.
He says, 'Stella, I'm going away for a while.'

The wind fills up my ears. Pa says other words, but the wind grabs them from his mouth and blows them backwards.

But there *is* no wind! My tree sags like it's cried out all its water, my ugly wine bottles hang still.

The worst thing in the world is happening.

Jerry comes to watch. His arms are folded, I can't see his killer hands. Ma's mouth is stiff like a bass fish. That's what happens when you try not to cry. Gracie knows, she hangs on Pa's legs. She bumps her cheek on his knee and starts to cry. Ma picks Gracie's hand off, but the other one grabs. Ma pulls hard to unstick her. I hear Grace cry, then the wind takes it.

There is no wind today.

Pa picks up his bags. He says something silent. He kisses me on my eyes. The wind blows my way again. 'Just there by the dump. Where the new shacks are.'

I don't nod. I don't even say no.

Pa tries to talk, but his throat also closes. He walks away from us. Gracie reaches for Pa, she knows, 'Papapa!'

When Pa gets to the grader, my legs start to pump.

'Stella!' Jerry shouts.

I jerk and turn. Jerry's got the same look he had when he cut Mugabe up. But his arms are folded. I can't see his hands.

I walk with my pa. Jerry's eyes bite my back. 'Papa, don't go.'

Pa puts both bags in one hand and hugs me to his chest. 'I told you, it's only until Ma loves me again.' He bends his knees so that he can see inside my eyes. 'And I'm not going to drink.'

He walks away, but I catch up. 'Don't go, Pa.'

Pa looks up to the sky, he says something else, but the wind steals his words.

Pa walks faster and faster, he leaves me behind. I shout, 'Papa-aa!'

This time, it echoes in the mountains. Pa walks backwards. 'I'll hear you,' he says. He points at Marais' telephone wire. He smiles a big, silly smile. 'You don't need a telephone.'

The last thing I see are Pa's deep dimple lines. I watch his back until he gets to the tar.

The Truth Lady sinks, she says sweet to her machine, 'Tears ran like a river, down the lines that she loved.'

Jerry's eyebrows are rusty. His eyes are razor blades. But I run through the gateposts, straight towards his hate. I run as close as I can to the killer man. I swerve away before I die.

I run into the hut. I dig my flute out of its box. I run up the road to Mevrou's. The flute flashes like a mirror, it sparks in the bush, it sparks on the sand. When I get to the dam, I swing my arm down and up to the sky. The flute twists and flashes, it spins and tries to fly. But it falls down, down, down. There's no wind to hold it. *Shlip* it goes, into the dark water.

It feels like it's *me* sinking. I've got no air left. My father is gone.

I fill up with water, my eyes and my ears. It feels like I'm drowning. I suck and I suck to try and stay alive. I suck air through my tears, it sucks into my lungs.

But I can't hear a thing, not even my breath.

I am not drowned. I am deaf.

There is fluffy white foam on Mevrou's kitchen floor. Mevrou mops it slowly. Her skin's got ugly veins and spots. She's tired and old. The kitchen stinks of Gustav's garlic soup. There's a tray on the table with dry, pink lamb and spilled Coke on the plate. I walk through the white foam. Mevrou says something, but I can't hear her words. I climb up the dresser. I feed grasshoppers to my chicks. They gobble the meat like it's steak from the shop.

I know what's through the window. It's a blue mountain with black smoke pouring up from the dump. It's my pa's new home. That's why I don't look.

When I climb down, Mevrou follows me. Her mouth opens and closes, she's ugly and old. She slips in the foam, she grabs on the door. She's too old and heavy to catch me.

I bang, *BOOMM BOOMM.*

I stare at the black board. The nun is teaching us more English things. I can't read today, I think I've forgotten.

The Truth Lady smiles. She guesses with her pen, *One man's meat is another man's poison.*

She sucks the top. *A apple never falls far from the tree.*

The nun sees I'm not writing. She pokes her crooked finger, but it aims outside. I wish I was Mary or her cement child.

Today I am jealous.

I wish my whole family was made of stone. I wish we could never move from our home.

The nun is loose, frowning skin. Her eyes are dirty smoke. She opens her mouth, she sinks her face close. Her fillings are chewed bullets, she smells like garlic soup. She's got a silver cross like him. She's got rosary beads on her hip like a gun. She shouts, still angry from the concert. I stare, but I don't care. I am deaf.

I walk past the bar, I don't move my head. I don't talk to Oom Piet, not even the chickens. I walk slow down the street without any sound. I can't hear my feet. Everyone else also moves slow. Their shopping bags are heavy. The cars glide slow, like they're all broken. I walk past the municipality with the red brick wall. I walk past the tannie in her glass money box, where people go to pay for their electricity.

The Truth Lady says, 'Hey! Isn't she the one who talked to the cops?'

I nod.

She's got giant fish lips, like the last one in the world they caught in Saldanha. Her lipstick is silver pink, like inside a oyster.

The Truth Lady asks, 'What did she say?'

He had his brown, shiny shoes with the flat tips. He had a brown crackly packet under his armpit.

He tipped his eyes on her chest, in the dip between her titties. He did it on purpose, to charm her, like Ma.

The Truth Lady asks, 'She said that?'

'No.'

'So what did the auntie tell the cops?'

He rattled his packet. 'So Gustav's the owner? On paper too?'

The municipality tannie got a rash on her neck. She forgot her English words, I think she talked Afrikaans. 'Definitief, ja.'

He said, 'And the manager?'

She said, 'There's no manager. Only Frank.'

Jerry's eyes turned to dead blue stones.

His packet crickle crackled as he walked out of the door.

Inside it, Mevrou showed me. It was only orange chips.

I walk slow past the Algemene Handelaar.

Dora's daughter's built from stone, with a stone till. She stares through red letters that say, Samoosas, Biltong, Vetkoek.

Something glitters at the end of the long glass box. I stop.

It's a silver cross!

I don't hear the door bell. I don't even hear the till *trring*.

I stare past a man's grey pants.

It's exactly like Jerry's! It's with all the lighters, and the knives that fold up. Made in China, they say. I've seen them before.

The Truth Lady says, 'Don't tell me he bought it there!'

I nod.

He stabbed the glass with his finger. Dora's daughter gave him the lighter with the white girl on it. The one with the long orange hair and huge balloon titties.

The Truth Lady grins, she dips her lips, 'He had a good, hard look.'

Jerry gave it back. He said, 'I'm trying to get to heaven here.'

'She told the cops?'

I nod.

He stabbed the glass again. He made a oily finger mark.

Dora's daughter says something, but I shake my head slow.

My eyes hunt and hunt. They stop next to Dora's head.

It's sitting with the Vicks and the sharp shaving blades. It's the last one. Christ is Among Us, I know what it says. Jesus stands in his dress. He holds up his stick with the umbrella tip. The same stupid sheep dig the hill with their feet.

I walk right past my ma's beautiful butternuts.

The Truth Lady guesses, 'They curved like Nancy's hips.'

I nod. 'They're the colour of our sun, just before it sinks.'

I ask her, 'Do you want a photo?'

'Of what?'

'Our butternuts.'

'No thanks.'

At home, Ma chases me with a plate. I walk past Jerry's feet. I climb up my tree. Ma's hair is wild, her arms are thin. She bends her head back. My potato rolls into the sand. Grace stares at it, like it's a fallen star. Ma talks to my potato, she says silent things.

The Truth Lady says, 'What did she say?'

'I think she said, Must I feed it to the chickens? I think she said, Mugabe's still missing. Everything's a mess.'

'And, did he stay?'

I don't want to say.

'They made sex, didn't they?'

I nod. 'Mevrou showed me.'

'Tell it, Stella.'

His moustache pricked her neck.

His hands were too soft, too white on her skin.

The Truth Lady says, 'Sies.'

Even his knees made her sweat.

She says, like she was there, 'A ugly cigarette smell stunk the air around the bed.'

Something huge and heavy steps over my head.

I wake.

Ma's sitting up in bed, she waves at empty air.

I stare and stare. But there are no snakes in the dark door.

There's no rooster. No Pa.

Only old moonlight, steamy and weak.

The Truth Lady asks suddenly, 'Hey, Stella, how's your bum?'

'Huh?'

'Isn't it sore?'

'I think it's turned into a bone.'

'Can't you get something for us?'

Ma's far away up the road, picking pine cones.

I run to the hut. I get the pillows from Ma and Pa's bed.

The Truth Lady says, 'Ahhh.' She sinks into it.

I sit on mine. 'Ahh. It's like a marshmellow.'

'*Marshmallow*.' She giggles, 'You're telling me.'

That makes me keep telling.

I bang, *BOOMM BOOMM*.

We're in assembly with the weavers. The new eggs have hatched. I can see the nests shake, but I can't hear the babies.

The Truth Lady says, 'You were still deaf?'

I nod my head.

Nita's mother's at the gate! I must be dreaming.

It's true! Nita's back!

Nita's thin, like her Ma. Her lips are stiff. Her plaits are so tight, they could split her head. The nun holds Nita's hand, she brings her to us. Nita looks at me, but her eyes are glass eyes. Everyone claps, but I can't hear their hands.

At break, Nita sits with me on the bench. She takes a white plastic thing out of her pocket.

I say to the Truth Lady, 'A MP3.'

Nita turns on a switch. The screen says, Pink.

She sits dead still through the song, shut up and weak. The other children dance, they make dust with their feet. They click their fingers, they watch for the nun. The boys dance past our knees. David shoves his face to us, he pulls his lips up. His teeth shock my heart into a bollemakiesie. They are big and broken and bleeding!

Then I see, they are plastic and fake. The others laugh with wide open mouths. Me and Nita sit like silent twins. David dances freaky, with his big, bleeding teeth. He still likes me, I can see.

But I don't care about him.

Nita's ma waits at the gate. She takes Nita's hand like she's a baby. She's got black tyre marks under her eyes. She smiles. She says something to me, but I don't hear her words. She gives me a funny wave, she walks away with her baby.

On the way home, I kill nine grasshoppers. That's too much meat for my chicks to eat.

Mevrou's kitchen smells of death, not delicious roasting like it used to. There are old chops dried up on the grill. There is old, hard chicken teared up on a plate. Mevrou stabs a huge leg of raw pork. She shoves garlic cloves in the holes. When she sees me, she snaps her music off. She waves her knife at me, but I climb past the blade. She points up the stairs, she cuts the kitchen in a circle.

I watch her from the dresser. I climb through the roof.

I feed my chicks smashed grasshoppers. I feed them so much, they've got to shut their beaks to make me stop. I climb down, I try to go, but Mevrou grabs my shirt. Her cheeks shake like her thighs when she does her star jumps. She stabs her thumbs into my hands. She squeezes me to speak, like the doll at the dump. Nothing comes out, so Mevrou lets me go.

When I'm out of the door, Mevrou's raw pork lands on the grass. A green apple comes flying after it. More apples fly, they bounce on the lawn. One rolls in the fountain and floats round and round. Mevrou stares through the window. I go in the kitchen, I stand on my tippy toes at the silver sink. The raw pork looks so lonely, so far from its ma. I laugh from my mouth, into my own ears.

I can hear!

I laugh and laugh, because it's really not funny. Mevrou laughs too, but tears boil in her eyes. She sits on the kitchen bench and sobs. I slide my arms around her stomach. My hands can't touch, but I hug her tight. Mevrou sobs like a big, hurt cow. I pull her arms open, I climb on her lap. Her tears drip on my head. Mevrou rocks me and rocks me against her pillow titties. She holds me like the sky. Her clouds press soft against my ears.

She asks, 'Stella, what's going on?'

The black smoke through the window pours up from the dump. I can't say the words, *My father's gone.*

Mevrou says a secret above my head, 'Stella, remember when I chased that Albert away?'

I sit still.

'Remember Gustav locked his room for two weeks?'

She says, 'When he came out, I was in my room, rubbing cream on my cheeks.' Mevrou stares at the stove glass. 'He said, *Mutti* …'

Mevrou chokes like there's swollen meat in her pipe. 'If you interfere again, I don't want to be your son.' Mevrou squeezes my ribs, I think she's going to crush me. 'Something strange happened, Stella. I started to rub out! I was like a *geist*! With no eyes, no nose, no mouth!' Mevrou claps her hand on her mouth, like to stick it back. She says, 'So I glued my lips shut. It wasn't hard, Stella. It was …'

I press my face into her titties. I stick my fingers in my ears.

When I take them out, I've got no sound. Mevrou talks more, but I don't hear her words.

I leave her on the bench, I fetch her lonely pork. I lie on my stomach and catch the floating apple. I stare up at the mother starling stuck in the tree. The Jackie Hanger's gobbled her to only bare bones.

We eat our supper, just me and Ma and Grace.

Jerry comes out of the dark in his smart concert clothes. His hair is brushed. He leans against my tree, he smiles like he's shy. But he grabs my ma's wrist, he kisses it hard with the inside of his lips.

Ma looks at me quick. His spit dries on her skin.

I want to tell my pa, but Pa is gone.

I leave Grace to bang the plates, I go and stand close. I wait at the fire, I stay in the way. I don't look at him, his eyes could peel my skin. Ma gets sick of me. She points at my sister, she pushes me to the hut. I can't hear her words, but I know what she says. 'Stella, make the bed.'

I make our bed quick before Jerry tries.

I lie with Grace while she drinks, but I watch through the door. Ma knows why I'm watching, I'm watching for Pa.

I miss him so much. I try to feel his hand on my face. I try to feel his kiss on my eyelids.

I fall to sleep by accident.

The Truth Lady says, 'And, while you slept?'
They played a song by dead Elvis Presley.'
'But weren't you still …?
I nod. 'Deaf.'
Ma whispered to him about her sisters, who she missed, and her ma who shouted Bible words at them. She said how the brown girls danced in a ring. She told how her mother shouted, Go. Get out!
I say to the Truth Lady, 'That was me in her stomach, you see.'

I wake up from the worry, not from dead Elvis Presley.

Jerry's tearing sticky tape with his long, sharp teeth. His moustache pricks like devil thorns. His face is orange from the flames.

Ma pushes the button that says Play.

The Truth Lady says, 'A tape?'

I nod. 'The one that I cut. I tried it the other day. Boney M played again, together and strong.'

'Hey?'

'Sometimes is goes, *veep*, but Boney M plays the same.'

I ask, 'Must I play it?'

'Uh uh. Go on.'

Through the door, Ma wriggles like she's still young. She dances with her arms up, shaky and snaky. Jerry dances to Ma, he ruks with his hips. His white hand strikes. He touches Ma's bum!

'Ma!' I shout, without any sound.

Ma creeps over our bed, she bruises my legs.

I catch her green, guilty eyes with mine. She shuts her eyelids tight.

I watch her for Pa.

I watch her eyelids until she falls to sleep.

I dream that I'm diving down to my flute. It rolls and makes a cloud of powder. I scratch in the powder.

I run out of air. I run out of time!

The water lily roots hang curly from the top. The dark lily pads grow over each other. I press my tongue flat against my teeth. My head swells up with old, exploding air.

I've got to breathe or I'm going to die!

I kick at the sand, I scratch with my hands. I swim up, up. I grab at a root, but it pulls out like hair. The dark lily pad pops to the top. I punch and I paddle. Water shoots up my nose, it floods down my throat.

The dam is as heavy as the world in me. My legs fill up, I can't move my arms. A frog pumps past bursting for breath. It explodes through the lily pad roof to the sun.

I sink to my flute, but I don't want it now.

I roll in the sand, I make brown clouds.

I'm dying.

Two thumbs press hard into my palms. Bubbles from her lips tickle my skin. The brown lady's hair is curly like mine, it twists like the water lily roots hanging down. She pulls as strong as a wind storm. She drags me so fast that the water blasts past. She rips the lilies away. I can see white clouds through the dam's silver skin. A black eagle aims its beak, it hunts with gold eyes. Its wings spread wide across the sun. It's got killing claws, but it's not hunting, it's calling, 'Come up, Stella, come up!'

I kick and kick.

I kick the leg of Ma and Pa's bed. I gasp like a summer wind, gusting.

I crawl on my knees, I find the candle. I feel the matches next to it. I light a match, *grittsh*. I look for the brown lady, but she's disappeared. I hear the flame go, *sshhhr* up the candle string.

I can hear again!

Gracie kicks like she's also swimming in water. Ma rolls on her back. Pa throws his arm over her.

The wrong picture shocks my eyes. It's not my pa!

I blow the flame out, but the picture stays bright. My heart beats for me, but I wish that it didn't. His hairy white arm was over Ma's titties. He had white muscle bumps up his back. His bushy moustache sat on her shoulder, like a ugly, yellow rat, come to steal while we sleep.

I listen for Ma's breath to make sure he didn't kill her. A whole world of water sits on my chest.

I carry it out of the hut, across the cement. It spills everywhere, but I carry it up the road to Mevrou's. The moon is thin and light. It looks like Pa's fingernails, the bits he clips on the sand.

Mevrou's house smells like sick animals. There's a moan from upstairs like a animal suffering. My chicks say nothing. I lift the heavy water up the stairs.

Eddie's white face watches me in his picture.

I stop at Gustav's door. Gustav's white arm brings the wrong picture back. The dam nearly pours.

Mevrou's hair sleeps in streaks across her pillow. The thin moon has turned it white. Her mouth is wide open, her neck is loose like rumpled bird feathers. Her breath comes out, *whrrr*, like when the boys put a peg on their bicycle tyres. The fingernail moon peeps at itself in the mirror. I kneel by the bed, the water makes me wobble. 'Mevrou.' I pat her on her cheek. 'Mevrou.' I take her chin and waggle it.

Mevrou lifts her head. 'Huh?' Her eyelids clip up. She strokes my hair, but she's still half sleeping. She stares at the moon in the mirror. She struggles to her side. She speaks slurry like she's drunk. 'Thtella, wath wrong?'

I sniff like Ma sniffs, but I can't smell any wine.

Mevrou reaches to her table. She sticks something in her mouth, *clat*. She pushes up with her thumb, *thut*. Now she sounds sober. 'Stella, what on earth are you doing here?'

'My pa is gone.' The dam swells huge. I've only got a tiny bit of dry air left. 'Jerry's stealing my mother.'

Mevrou flaps her arms like a big bird falling. I catch her hands, I help her up. Her big legs fall out of the bed. Her nightie flaps up past her panties.

My worry runs out like a river, 'Jerry's in the bed with my ma. He killed Mugabe. And he says he'll kill us all if I talk.'

Mevrou blinks. She feels my shoulders to see if I'm real. 'Gott! He killed who?'

'My rooster. He cut him in pieces to shut me up.'

Mevrou's not like Ma, she doesn't think I'm lying. 'Shut up about what?'

'About Nita's pa.' The dam gushes out. I get more air from talking. 'Nita's pa wanted to see Jerry's ID, then Jerry did something very, very bad to him.'

Mevrou presses my shoulders like she's a police. She asks me questions like a police. 'What did he do to Nita's pa?'

I can't say *killed*, it might make me deaf. 'I didn't see. '

'What did Nita's pa say to Jerry?'

'He was looking for a man who hurt a lady once.'

Now it's *Mevrou* who's drowning. 'What did Jerry do to him?' she asks again.

I can't say *killed*. I say instead, 'Jerry's from Joburg, not Hemel-en-Aarde like he said. And his mother's dead.'

Mevrou lets me go, I float up, up. But in her mirror, I'm still on my knees. Mevrou's hair hangs white streaks over her eyes. 'Aaaah,' she moans like she's got a bad cramp. She holds her mouth on, she rubs her lips. She starts to shake like she's doing a hard exercise. She catches her own hands, she squeezes them still. She pushes on her knees, she struggles to her feet. She walks her jerky legs to the light switch. The light surprises all the bendy blue worms in her skin.

Gustav groans next door. Mevrou stumbles to him. She tucks his blankets up. She's shivery and mumbly, she talks like I'm a ghost. 'I must find out the truth.' She strokes Gustav's fringe off his face.

I help Mevrou to make her own bed. It takes a long time, she wants it perfect. She sits on the bed and pulls her nightie up. Mevrou's got grey hairs curling under her arms. Her huge titties and her stomach cuddle each other. She puts on a huge bra to keep them apart. I help her with the hooks. She puts her feet in her stockings. Her toes are dry and powdery, they all look the wrong way. I roll her stockings to the top. She puts on a black onderrok.

I ask the Truth Lady, 'What's that called?'

'Petticoat.'

And the strong black dress she wears to see dead Eddie. I do the buttons up the front. Mevrou thinks I'm a ghost, she says, 'Stella's right about the truth.' She says other German words, 'Es ist immer das besten.' She tries to do the buttons that I've already done. She says, 'There's been too much damage.' I help her with her shoes. Mevrou's unkles are thick like big wood blocks. I buckle up her shoe straps.

Mevrou brushes her hair, it makes her pant. 'This time … I am not keeping quiet.' She looks straight at me in the mirror. Her hair is smooth and white. Her head is straight on her neck. 'Thank you, Stella.'

She pins her hair into a tearing, tight bun. She powders her face with a big fluffy puff. The powder floats in the room, it lands like white ash. Now *she* is like a ghost with her white, grave face. She ties her black scarf around her neck. She puts on her big black hat. It's a low, black roof in her small room. She sticks a sharp pin into it. She opens a round tub with cracked eggshells on the skin. She pulls out a silver watch. I duck under her hat, I help her clip it on. She mumbles in German, 'Meine Sünde steuer.'

The Truth Lady asks, 'What?'

'She didn't teach me.'

Mevrou says in English, 'One of my little gifts for shutting up.'

I stare at the watch.

Me and Mevrou are the same!

We did the same sin!

My gladness kicks me hard in my heart. I want to ask, 'Who gave it?' But I know it's dead Eddie.

She's dressing for Eddie in the middle of the night.

But a dead man can't tell the truth.

Maybe she's dressing for the police. Maybe she's going to tell them everything I said. But I can't ask Mevrou, in case she says, 'Yes.'

Kl-ock. *Kl-ock*, Mevrou's shoes go slow down the stairs. I wait on each stair, I touch her black dress.

Mevrou acts like it's daytime outside. She runs water in the bath, she pours soap powder in. White foam swells up, it tries to climb the side. She drops the dirty washing in. Her big white underpants float to the top. She leaves the foam to buzz, she takes a roast out of the freezer. She puts a opera on, it's The Magic Flute.

The Truth Lady says, 'It's *too* much, Stella. You must be joking!'

'I promise I'm not.'

Mevrou switches it to when the king's men chase the princess. Mevrou stands still and turns her ear to the speakers. She listens hard to the part where the princess's friend asks, 'What should we say? What should we say?' The princess sings, '*Die wahrheit, die wahrheit!*'

The Truth Lady says, 'Hey?'

'*The truth, the truth! Even if it's a crime!* Mevrou's told me the story lots of times.'

Mevrou makes us tea, we drink it with thick sugar. She stares through the door at the night outside. The sun tries to come quietly, but the birds shout about it. My greedy chicks wake, they start to go '*Scrawww.*' Mevrou sips her tea like a smart old queen.

'Is Gustav going to drive you?' I ask.

A seed of fury bursts in her eyes, 'Gustav's very, very sick!' She says, 'Stella, go upstairs and fetch my gloves in my drawer.'

Upstairs, her face powder floats like pollen in the light. Her black lacy gloves hide under her big, big bras. Mevrou looks confused when I bring them, like she forgot that she asked. She looks on the walls, like for something that she lost. She mumbles, 'There's no clock.' Her fingers are clumsy on her silver watch. She clips the watch off, she lies it on the table.

She says, 'If I'm not back in one hour, Stella, call the police.' She writes the number shaky on the In Season magazine. 021- 859771.

Now I ask, 'Where are you going?'

Mevrou's gone deaf like I was. She pulls her black gloves on. I start to do the buttons on her wrists. 'That's Gustav's job,' she says. A little smile wobbles off her lips. She says, 'Stella, I learned to shut up when I was very young.'

'It's okay,' I say.

'I didn't ever tell you what my father did.'

'Huh?'

'When he sent me to London.'

She sucks a big breath in my ear. 'He built special ovens in the concentrate camps. But they didn't bake bread like the ones in London.' She grunts like a punch, 'Right next to the showers. A funny place for ovens, don't you think?'

I nod.

She speaks her secret into my hair, 'The showers had special pipes for poison, you see.'

My fingers go cold and clumsy on her gloves.

She says, 'The people near the pipes died straight away.' Her bottom lip twists. Her words fall out, stiff, 'The others took much longer.'

'Mevrou!'

'They found their bodies crouched.'

'Oh no!'

'I saw the photos in the London News.' Her words punish us, 'They had foam on their mouths.' She starts to laugh, but it sucks like a sob. 'I thought, it's not true, it's a trick. The Jews just ate the soap, for the photo. But there was red down their necks. Their ears were bleeding.'

'Stop!' I bang my eyes shut. I rub them so hard that they squeak like a mouse.

Mevrou pulls my hands away. 'Tell them, Stella. If I can't.'

The Truth Lady gasps. She stabs her page with her pen, *Nazi Secrets Leaking! Ghosts Bleeding??*

Mevrou walks out of the door, 'Mevrou! Where are you going?'
She stops and stares. 'Don't come, Stella. It's dangerous.'
That's when I know, she's not going to see Eddie.
And not the police.
She's going to see Jerry.

She walks in her grave shoes out of the gate. The funeral march plays loud notes inside my mind. The first drums are slow, like a heavy, old lady.

I stare at the silver watch from dead Eddie. It's got no numbers, it's only got stripes! I know it's dumb, but I can't work it out. My birds start to squeak.
'Just wait!' I say.
I go to the lounge and pick up the phone. A warning strikes my fingers like electricity. I imagine cold handcuffs, sore on my wrists. I can't call the police. They'll lock me up.
I'll miss home so much, I'll die from crying. Please don't make me call the police, please.
I drop it back, *tak*.

Gustav's thrown off his red racing car cover. He's got a number watch on, it says 06:06. I must wait until seven. I read the writing on the trophy next to his head. Excellence in Music, it says.

I tell the Truth Lady, 'I've seen it in a old In Season magazine.'

Gustav grinned to the camera, he was still young with pimples. There was a giant watermelon on the same page. Mevrou said they grew it on drugs in Grabouw.

The Truth Lady says, 'Carry on, Stella.'

There's a paper on Gustav's table, with a silver pen. It's a old fountain pen like the nun's scratchy one. Gustav's written on the paper in leaning back letters, Piping 50 metres. Gaskets. Three way joints. There's a photo on the wall of him when he was small. He's on his pa's shoulders, he's got lots of missing teeth. He's got new, red sandals shining on his feet. Eddie's ears are big, his blue eyes are bossy. I think he's proud of the shiny red tractor behind him.

Gustav frowns in his sleep. He pulls his lips up so I can see his teeth. 'Thhhh,' he smiles, but it's only from pain. My birds squeak, they're starving for meat. I check Gustav's watch. 06:11. I visit Eddie's photo at the top of the stairs. His hair is forward like Gustav's. He's got Gustav's little chin. His eyes look grey, not blue today. And this time they're not bossy. This time they look sorry.

My birds won't shut up. I go down and mix their porridge. I check the silver watch, but I *still* can't read the stripes.

If the police come to get me, I'll run to the rocks where the huge cobra lives.

Must I phone the police?

Eddie's sorry eyes watch from the top. I run up the stairs. I ask, 'Must I phone the police?'

The Truth Lady says, 'You asked a *photo*?'

'I'll tell the judge I asked him because there was no one else.'

Eddie's ears are like trophies on the side of his head. His chin skin is smooth. His hair is combed forward, with thick oily cream. Eddie's top lip is crooked, even with no smile. His eyebrows lift up like they're trying to fly. But his eyes stay behind. They've got nowhere to hide.

That's when I see.

The Truth Lady asks, 'What?'

Eddie's scared, not sorry! He's keeping ugly secrets.

He knows there's trouble coming!

Gustav's curled up. I crouch down to see. 06:16. It's not seven yet, but time is dangerous.

Eddie's eyes say, Watch out. There's big trouble coming!

The Truth Lady asks, 'Stella, where was Mevrou?'

I run down to the phone. I press 0-2-1.

If I phone the police, they'll lock me away. I'll never see my ma.

I can't phone, I can't!

The Truth Lady says, 'Stella? Mevrou!'

Thum thum. Mevrou's grave shoes were like a slow drum. She nearly crushed a old tortoise …

The Truth Lady interrupts, 'Where did she go?'

Mevrou marched up the slashed, grass path.

She climbed, 'Ummff' up the stairs. She knocked so hard, her bones nearly broke.

My chicks scream like spoilt babies. 'Sshhh!' I spray my spit. Now I'm just as scared as dead Eddie on the stairs.

The Truth Lady says, 'Stella, stay at Jerry's.'

She cracked her knuckles, 'Jerry!'

Mevrou crushed her nose against the glass. She saw the naked lady on the car. She saw all the dirty clothes, and the plates with dry gravy.

The Truth Lady asks, 'Was he there?'

Jerry slid on his stomach across the floor. He slid all the way through the toilet door. He stood on his white toilet that flushes. His chest swayed through the gap, this way and that. He gripped with his thigh. He hung down to the pipe.

The window slammed, *batt!*

His head hit the grass, but he jumped up fast.

Mevrou's roast starts to sweat. It steams off its freeze as the sun warms it up. It makes me feel sick. It's like it's going to wake up and start walking.

The Truth Lady says, 'Stella, where the hell was Jerry?'

Mevrou marched her black clothes around the house.

She lifted the little window. Two huge naked titties stared with pink eyes.

The Truth Lady says, 'Hey?'

She bombed furious words at the girl's bare skin. 'Jerry! I know who you are!'

I stumble off the stoep.

I walk like I'm frozen through the gateposts.

Mevrou's screaming voice burns the air to white ash. It burns the leaves at the top of the trees. I make my fingers straight, I cut the scared air. I dig up red sand with my bare feet. Her shout pulls me like a rope, burning fast, by my heart. It pulls me down the road to Jerry's. I fly into the bush, I dive behind a tree.

I hear Mevrou exploding. 'I know about your mother!'

Mevrou tries to shout the house down. She roars like a horrible God, 'Are you *Rachel's* child?'

The Truth Lady whispers, 'Rachel?'

'My pa's ma. The one I got my music from.'

The Truth Lady writes, *Rachel = Frank's mother (Ran away when he was two)*

'You *are*, aren't you?' Mevrou shouts at the house.

Jerry shoots up in front of me.

He's got no shoes, his feet are bare and white. His knees are bent like he might spring. His flute fingers curl like a white wolf.

'Who do I *look* like?' Jerry asks.

Mevrou ploughs the dust with her black shoes. She marches past the car. Her grey eyes don't see me.

'Have a good look!' Jerry says.

I stare at his white hands and his white feet.

Mevrou's big stomach moves like she's hiding something alive. She says, 'I know about Eddie.'

Jerry sways like Mevrou shoved him. His fingers go soft like leeks. He blows a gust of shock, 'You *knew*?'

Mevrou nods a tiny nod.

'You BITCH!'

Jerry's scream rolls me up. It bangs Mevrou's bum hard on the car. After the echo goes, Jerry says, 'Did you know it was *rape*?'

Mevrou grabs her heart before it jumps right out. She hangs on the car like she's in a flood. Jerry walks to her with soft, hurting words. 'In his brand new Mercedes, on the back seat. He offered her a lift to the village. Ha! He tied her hands with his belt.'

The Truth Lady pants, she scrapes, *Brother to the Others! Made by Rape!*

'O, Gott, o, mein Gott,' Mevrou whispers. She grips on the car like she's being washed away. Her elbows shake, her knees collapse like waves are hitting them.

I know what rape means. In South Africa they rape babies. I've heard it on the radio. Pa always mumbles and looks like he's going to cry. Sometimes I ask why. Pa says he's so, so sorry for the whole country.

I know what rape means. It's how Eddie made Jerry.

The Truth Lady stabs her grape nail, 'Was he born at the hut?'

'Uh uh, at the river.'

'Say it, Stella. Go slow.'

Her hair stuck up wild, like she was caught in a war.

I can see on her leg, the blood on her thigh was thick and wet.

She wore a man's winter coat, but the sun was so hot it could melt metal.

'How do you know?'

'Mevrou.'

Mevrou heard a sweet, soft cry. She saw a fist of fingers, tiny and pink. But she sunk under the sink. She stared at the lines between the kitchen tiles. She crawled to the drawer. She fetched a fork.

The Truth Lady gasps, 'What for?'

She bent out one claw. She scraped like it was filthy dirt under her own nail.

Mevrou breathes like a wet fire, '*Whigg, whiggh, whiggh.*'

Jerry keeps talking the terrible truth. 'He stuck us on a train to Joburg.'

A soft yellow sun painted the brown lady's face. The baby was wrapped in a soft white cloth. The train roars through a tunnel. The train metal rocked her, rocked her in the dark.

There's a crying boy in Jerry's voice. 'She had to whore to feed us. She took pills to sleep it off. All I ever heard, was, Frank-ie, Frank-ie. She was always crying in her sleep, Frank-ie … Night and fucking day.'

But the Truth Lady just writes, *His Mother was a Whore!*

I tell her, furious 'I know how he feels! I know from Pa, when he drinks the whole day. You can't love and talk to someone who's snoring.'

'Okay, Stella. Relax.'

Mevrou's crying is snotty and hot, she doesn't even try to wipe it. She says, 'Sorry, sorry,' like a doll with a battery. Mevrou slides down against the tyre. She sits like a fat, sad doll with a crooked black hat.

My tears don't hurt. They come out free and fast because the brown lady's still alive. I've seen her lots of times. But Jerry's tears are ripping him. He makes a ugly noise, like Gracie when she choked. It's like Jerry's going to vomit his whole life on the grass. His back bends round, just like Gracie's did. His eyes pop wet, out of his head.

Jerry presses his eyeballs back in with his hands. He wipes and wipes like a car window wiper. Jerry's voice is not human, he speaks like a machine. 'I'm going to make him pay.'

Mevrou sounds confused, like her brain came out in her snot, 'Who?'

'Eddie.'

There's slime on Mevrou's glove. She points to the village, 'Eddie's dead.'

Jerry laughs like a evil machine.

She says, 'And the farm is Gustav's. It's the law.'

Jerry stalks Mevrou in his bare feet. 'Is it the law to rape? Is it the law to chuck a kid in a orphanage and pay the bitch to shut up?'

Mevrou says, 'It was a good home, for whites.'

Jerry jerks stiff, then blasts out, shocked, 'You knew?'

Mevrou digs her fingers in the grass, but Jerry crouches down. 'You knew he paid the matron?'

Jerry is too close. I crawl out of the bush, but they're both blind. Mevrou breathes right in his nose. 'She phoned the day she did it.'

The Truth Lady says, 'Wait, Stella. Who?'

Peep, *peep*, *peep*. The tickey box peeped like a truck reversing. Rachel drank her tears before she could talk.

Eddie swore, 'Fuck!' But I'll say eff to the judge. He kicked Mevrou's cupboard, there's still a dent.

Jerry rocks back like Eddie just kicked him.

Mevrou pulls on the tyre, she pushes on the grass. It's lucky about all her exercise.

Jerry rises so his chest is nearly touching Mevrou's titties. His eyes dig silver spikes, 'You're a evil bitch! Like *her*.'

Mevrou's looks desperate past his head. She sees me standing here. She acts like I'm not!

She makes herself straight, like a old queen. I think I make her strong.

She tries to walk past, but Jerry's in the way. She gives him a push, she talks in German, 'Geh weg!' Mevrou shakes her finger, 'You've done enough.'

I drop down in the grass as Mevrou marches past. Jerry runs and stops her with his metal chest. Mevrou doesn't care. She shoves him, 'Go now! Leave us alone!' She points at the mountains and shouts, 'Go! Get out!' Then she makes a quiet, secret deal. '*Go*. I know how to keep quiet.'

Jerry's laugh is as horrible as his hate. 'No way. *Someone's* going to pay.'

Something happens to Mevrou.

She turns into a huge, furious elephant. She's not the Mevrou I know. She screams 'GO-O-O!!' She throws her whole big body at him. Her black hat flies off, it floats gentle to me. Mevrou slaps him and slaps him, her arms wave and shake. She slaps Jerry in his face.

Jerry stands like a machine, switched off.

Mevrou stops slapping. She staggers back.

Jerry tackles her stomach. *Buduff!* She falls like a huge, heavy tree on her knees. Something cracks. I run to help her, but she storms me a look that screams, STOP! STOP!

Jerry laughs like Mevrou's crazy and strange.

Mevrou crawls with one shoe all the way to the table. She pulls herself up. Her fingers touch Mugabe's feathers, they slip in his black blood. Mevrou's missing shoe makes her stand bent. Jerry throws his arms wide like he's catching a big, dangerous animal. But it's *him* who's growling like a mad, yellow dog. I'm right behind Jerry, but Mevrou's eyes say, STOP!

Mevrou's eyes sink sad, like she sees a sad future. 'What do you want from us, Jerry?'

Jerry's white hands flash. They rip Mevrou's black scarf off her neck.

He wraps up his hands, they're see through and black. He springs on her like she's biting and dangerous.

My mouth opens wide, but no sound comes out.

Jerry's neck swells huge, his moustache lifts off his teeth. Mevrou's spotty hands tear at his fingers. I jump on Jerry, I eat my teeth in his neck.

I hang on Jerry's hands, but they're as strong as metal bars.

I tear his hair.

Jerry's like Jesus, he doesn't even scream. My own scream explodes, 'STOP IT!'

Nothing stops his strangling hands. Mevrou's grey eyes turn red, they try to burst from her head. 'STOP IT! STOP!' I scream. Mevrou goes to sleep on her feet.

Mevrou falls down in Mugabe's old blood. Her head hits *dukk!* as she collapses. Mevrou drops like black washing onto the grass. The washing sobs and groans, she's crying in her sleep. Jerry's shirt is bleeding where I bit him. He touches the red, he stares. I'm ready to run, but Jerry smiles at the blood. It's a lovely, kind smile.

'*Now* look what you've done.' Jerry crouches down, he holds Mevrou's head gently. 'You pushed me too far, Stella. I told you to shut up.'

I see my face in his eyes, and two blue skies. Jerry rolls Mevrou over. 'Let's help her,' he says. He sinks on his hands and his knees like a dog. He pulls on Mevrou's arm until her head lifts.

'Her head is bleeding!' I say.

Jerry pulls half of her body onto his back. She hangs like a big butchery sheep in a dress.

Her big legs drag. The ladders in her stockings climb to the top. Jerry crawls to the long grass, not to the car.

'That's the wrong way,' I say.

Jerry lets Mevrou slide, *thuk*, her poor head hits the ground. Her arms lie wide, like for her bicycle exercise.

'Aren't you going to take her in your car?' I ask.

Jerry says, 'She needs her hat. Just get her hat there, please Stella.'

'Take her to the doctor.'

Jerry strokes the hair off her face, like he's very, very sorry, 'First get her hat.' Her black hat is close. I walk backwards slowly. I bend down to fetch it. Her hat looks perfect and new.

He says, 'And her shoe please? Shame.'

I don't move.

'Get her shoe, then we'll fix her.'

I walk backwards, I watch. I can't find the shoe. I hunt in the grass.

'I can't find it,' I say.

Jerry waits for the shoe. I can't see his hands, only yellow grass stalks and Mevrou's big titties.

I say to the Truth Lady, 'I couldn't see.'

'What?'

My throat wants to talk, but my tongue gets stuck.

The Truth Lady swears, 'No! The bastard!'

She says, '*Tell* it, Stella!'

Deep in the grass, he pinched Mevrou's nose. His other hand crushed her hard on her mouth.

I stop.

The Truth Lady sinks, 'Her cheeks blew up big like balloons.'

She says, '*Tell* the judge, Stella.'

Her fingers cramped. Her feet jerked and kicked. She sucked like she was starving, but his flat, white fingers said, no, no, no!

I start to cry.

The Truth Lady twists to the hut, 'Sshh.'

She gives me a crushed tissue smudged with purple stuff. 'Sshh.'

I find Mevrou's shoe far under Jerry's car. I run back and push it on Mevrou's floppy foot. I do the buckle. Jerry stands up, he slides his belt from his pants. He straps it on Mevrou's unkles.

His feet dig the grass, his face swells purple red. 'Nnggh.' Jerry drags Mevrou the wrong way again!

'Where are you going?'

Mevrou's dress gets caught.

'Stop!' I grab Mevrou's arm, but Jerry won't stop. Her sore head bangs, *dup*, *dup*, *dup*. Red blood smears on the grass.

'You're hurting her!' I hop, I skip, I flap my hands and panic, 'Stop! Stop!'

Ditt! Mevrou's head hits a stone.

'You're *hurting* her!' I cry.

Mevrou's bun is broken, her hair tangles in the grass. Jerry pulls like he's ploughing. I throw myself on her body.

We're too heavy together, me and Mevrou. Jerry can't drag us, he has to let go. I pull her dress down. I try to fix her hair.

Jerry pants, 'She dropped dead, Stella. It was her heart.'

My own heart stops. 'She's not! She's not!'

I squeeze her cheeks. Now I can see what she took from her table. It's loose on her tongue. It's a thin silver wire, with three fake teeth. I take it out carefully, so she doesn't choke. I say into her mouth, 'Mevrou, wake up.' I pull her eyes open. They're red blood in white egg, like when a chick starts to grow. Her bleeding eyes make me terrified. Mevrou!' I press my ear on her titty, I listen for the drum. I put my ear on her mouth.

Maybe I'm just deaf. I shake my head and listen.

A grasshopper rubs its legs, *krrik, krrrik*. A gecko rushes through the bush, *shhrrip*.

Jerry says, 'You were out walking with her. She dropped dead.'

'No, no, no,' I say it like Grace.

Jerry lifts me off, he shoves me hard onto my bum. He grips my shoulders sore, worse than the nun. His fingers stab in me like they're stuck in a plum. I shake my head, 'No no no no,' like I've learned a new word.

'Fucking SHUT UP!' He kicks me to the grass.

I don't feel his foot. I don't care about his hate. I crawl on Mevrou, I blow in her mouth. I pat her fat cheeks, 'Mevrou, wake up.' I blow my air into her, but it spills back out. 'Mevrou, wake up!'

'Stella! Shut up! Listen!'

I hug Mevrou's dead head.

Jerry spits, 'Stella! This is your last, *last* chance!'

The Truth Lady writes it, *Stella's Last, Last Chance!*

I lie on Mevrou and cry. I don't care if he kicks me. I'll never lie. Never, never, never. I don't even care if he cuts off my head.

I'll tell the judge I wasn't scared. My Mevrou is dead.

Jerry pulls his belt off Mevrou's unkles, he slides it back in his pants. 'Come and tell Gustav that she dropped dead.' He rips my arm up like a wing, he makes me stand on my legs. Mevrou's fake teeth lie next to her head. Baby grasshoppers make green sparks on her black dress. Jerry drags me up the road, but I'm just loose pyjamas. I'm not even a girl.

Mevrou's got no heart beat. She's got no breath. That's what dead is.

I try to look back, but he ruks me straight.

Killer. Killer. Killer. Jerry's a Jackie Hanger. He breaks people's bodies. He'll never stop. Now I know, Jerry's a stinking, Lucky Strike killer.

I rip my wing out of his hand. I fly over the road, into the bush. My heart drums extra loud for Mevrou's dead one. *BOOMM. BOOMM.*

Jerry's roar is terrible, 'Aa-u-ggghh!'

I crash into my forest on scared, pumping legs. My forest catches me and speeds me. The green leaves and branches wave out of my way. They tangle behind me to hide me, they tell green lies. The birds scream, 'Run! Run!' I fly over a trap. *Swish, slick*, go the leaves. *Shet, shut*, go the bendy, thin branches across the path. I'm in a green storm, it slashes as I fly. The little thrushes screech Mevrou's words, 'Run child, run!' I spring across the stream. Then I run slow and listen. The forest goes, *sssshh.*

Only one nervous robin still worries for me. Jerry's feet run *thikthikthik* on the road. The bush speeds me to the edge, where Mevrou's lawn waits, nice and quiet.

The garden is still. The cherubs hold tight to their winkies. The grass pushes strong, it carries my feet. At the kitchen door, there's just silent air. 'Gustav?'

My chicks hear my voice, they scream for their meat. My feet are ghost feet, they're wind on the stairs.

I whisper, 'Gustav?'

Gustav makes sucky sounds like a old, sick man.

'Gustav, your *mutti*.'

Gustav takes ages to sit up. His hair is fluffy from his pillow.

Dip … dip, I hear slow feet in the kitchen. My heart forgets to beat. Even my chicks shush. There are footsteps on the stairs. I make my eyes think. Where can I hide?

I crumple to the floor. I slide under Gustav's bed. I hit a long, hard box. It's got a silver lock. I lift my knees past the suitcase. I stretch flat like a gecko against the cold wall. I watch over the top.

Jerry's feet walk in, listening.

'Where's Stella?' Jerry's voice is as dead as a grave.

'Jerry …' Gustav sighs out his relief. His metal springs sink, *keek*. 'Where's my *mutti*?'

The room feels bare, like Jerry teared off its skin. 'Where's Stella?'

Gustav falls back, *dug*, the bed bangs the wall. 'Stella?' Gustav's fluttery like a chick, calling the Jackie Hanger for help.

Jerry sits on the bed, *aa kik*. The metal sinks closer to my nose. The red cover slides up. Jerry's gentle now, tucking Gustav up. 'Never mind. Just sleep.' But I can feel his eyes chopping the scared room into pieces.

Jerry's bare toes grip the floor. The foot of Gustav's table looks like a wood paw. Gustav's boots face the wall, like they've done something wrong. His oupa's sword guards them in its long leather holder. Gustav's breath sinks deeper. Jerry's feet walk soft to the cupboard. The door opens, *urrr*. He turns, he stops.

His feet walk back. I shrink into the ice wall. Jerry whispers, 'Stella, if you're in here, you're *dead*.'

My breath swells up slowly, it beats in my ears. His knee bends, *kut*.

I force my face into the floor. There's a cool, tiny gust as Jerry lifts the cover. He drops the cloth, *fup*. His backbones straighten, *tik, tik, tik*. I'm drowning in dry air. I let a bit out, like I do with my flute. I do it nice and easy, just like he said. I smell the Lucky Strike breath that he left. I'm silent, I know. I don't make a sound.

Jerry's body crashes to the wood. He punches the suitcase, my air explodes, 'Huhh!' My head bangs the wall. I scramble so suddenly, it's like I left my tail. I scrape the meat off my unkle on the metal bed. Jerry screams at empty air, 'Stellaaa!'

My feet are flying ghost feet on the stairs. I hear Gustav ask, 'Jerry?'

Jerry's bare feet make bomb blasts on the stairs. It sounds like the papsaks, when me and Nita burst them. I dive behind the dresser. Jerry makes bombs on the kitchen floor, out of the door.

I'm a streak of white pyjamas, up through the roof.

My birds are mad from hunger. They thought I was dead. Two are up near the roof, on a high wood plank. I'm too scared to even think how they got so high. They float down to me on their baby wings. One lands on my head, it grips my broken braids. The tiles on the roof make thin, light stripes. I peep through the roof window.

He's there, at the shed!

He turns back to the house. I sink in the shadow. 'Papa please come.'

'Pa heard me,' I say to the Truth Lady.

'Really?'

The engine shook his teeth, *ggiddaggidda*. His tractor was dull, not shiny, from dirt.

'He had a job?'

I nod.

The tyres had thick, sticky stuff in the cracks.

The Truth Lady dips, 'Dog hair, and wet paper ...' She thinks. 'And slippery potato skins.' Her black eyes shine happy. I think she loves the dump.

He heard me in his head, 'Papa, please come.'

The chicks have finished cheering, now they beg me, 'Please, please!'

Dip, *dip* Jerry's feet go in the kitchen.

I peep through the cracks in the roof planks. The top of Jerry's head is like a yellow nest. He stops at the dresser.

My chicks try to charm me, they make sweet, begging *screeks*.

Far away, black smoke pours up the rock. It rides like a black train through the blue sky. 'Papa, please come.'

Pa stared at my tree, but it stood still.

He stared at the stripe between the slangbos and the dam. He shoved the dirty blade under some old, soggy boxes. He woke up the stink of sour milk.

The Truth Lady sinks, '… and green, rotting meat.'

I say it without sound. 'Papa. I'm going to die.'

The dresser moans. Jerry is too heavy. My heart twists into a hot, scared knot. I force the handle of the roof window up. I push the window wood, but it won't open. I shove and I shove. Sweat grows on me like a extra, hot skin. I watch the hole above the dresser. Jerry's white fingers clamp over the edge. I shove my shoulder against the window, but it pushes back at me.

Jerry says, 'Bitch!' He rises through the hole.

I hang on a plank, I shut my eyes. I kick the window wood with my two feet.

Jerry grabs for my hair, but I'm flying through the air. I'm falling with my arms spread wide to the sky. I land quiet, like a caracal. Mevrou's grass pushes up strong against my feet. It races me away. I look back while I'm running. Jerry kicks one of my poor, soft chicks. He springs in the air, he lands like a plank. He groans like maybe he bit his tongue. I pray loud 'Pa-paa!', I crash into the forest.

Jerry roars 'WAAARGH!' like a mad, murdering monster after me.

Pa kicked his brake, he swung in his seat.

He saw a child, but it wasn't me. Her doll was tied on her back with a towel. The doll's eyelids sagged. Its hair was white like Mevrou's hair, in the moonlight.

The Truth Lady says, 'That Xhosa kid?'

'Ja.'

She rolled leaky, old apples with her fingertips. She kept the ones with the small brown sores.

Pa slammed his foot. The hot metal roared. The rubbish broke on his blade like a filthy, stinking wave.

The killer catches up! He's panting at my back!
Suddenly there's a break in his beating feet.
I fly forward as he springs. '*Pa Paaaa!*'

His nails tear my leg, I smash down in front of him. My forest rips my face by mistake. He clamps on my leg, he's a metal bone crusher. I twist, I roll, I kick! kick! kick!

Cruch. Blood squirts on my foot.

I roll, I run. My forest opens like a green sea, but he runs behind me. My mind screams like a sky full of birds, Run, run, run! Run! I beg my own legs.

I can only think, Run! I've forgotten my own name.

I jump off the path, I smack through the long grass. The mother calls me to the peace in her ant eaten tree. I splash through the wet of the underground stream. I fly straight in. Dry sand showers down from the roof. I can't see a thing, but I smell snake surprise. Outside the trunk, Jerry pants with metal lungs. My eyes are blind from sunlight. All I can see are quick, twisty cramps. Then a dim light switches on.

They are baby snakes!

The huge mother snake waits flat against the back. The babies cramp away from my desperate breath. I'm sobbing like the mouse I heard at the river. Jerry's head slips in. His hair is blown back, there are spit bubbles on his lips. There's a burning, spinning look, a sizzling in his eyes. He crawls between the roots, he reaches for me. My body's as weak as a boiled chicken. Jerry's cruel claw slides to my throat. I sink away from his fingers.

'You'll go to jail forever,' I say.

Jerry growls like a dog with rabies, the ones that get white spit and eat the ones that they love. 'You fucked it all up!'

His fingers touch my throat. I jerk my head back. My body's boiled and weak, but I make my hand creep behind me. I make my pap fingers grip. I *make* my arm swing.

The baby snake slaps Jerry in the face. He screams like a girl, he collapses back. He smacks his own face with his hands. He thinks the baby snake is stuck, but it's not. It whips away from him.

Jerry stops.

His yellow hair flops. His ears stick out just like dead Eddie's. He's got scared eyes like Eddie in the photo on the stairs. It's his scared eyes that make me say, 'Cobras! They're cobras!' I throw another baby, *thup*. It lands on his shirt. I throw two more, *thup, thup*, they smack his winkie in his pants. 'Oh God!' Jerry ruks and he trips, he lands on his back. He jumps up, 'God! Fuck!', but I'll say eff to the judge. The babies glip and crinkle, they flick away. Jerry scrambles behind the fallen tree.

His hand creeps between two twisted roots. I throw another baby, but his hand sneaks again. I throw three more. The silence is terrible.

'Jerry? Why are you hurting us?'

Bom! Bom! Bom!

I scream from the shock. It's loud like a giant banging on a box! I throw the last two snakes into the sun.

The banging stops.

Now I know. That's what he wanted.

His blue shirt slides around bit by bit. He's got a glittering grey rock gripped in his fist. I crush myself in the stump, I press my bones against the back. Jerry's shirt blocks the light. I can see the snaky veins of wood on the walls. I can see the crusty sides, and the hanging hornets' nest. Jerry's fingers are metal hooks, stretching for my neck. I suck in snake air.

I breathe in hate instead.

Jerry's hate makes me strong. I dig the mother's middle off a big inside vein. She strains away from me, she's too wild to touch. I slide my hand along her cool, silky tail. I pull it from the wood. The mother snake panics. She shoots smooth and cool, fast towards the light. Jerry jerks his arm back, he swears a big one, 'FUCK!'

The mother snake licks for the light. She tries to sluip out, but I hang on tight. She drops off the vein, she lands, *fump* on my shoulders.

I'm covered by a dark, shining snake. I crawl out with my glowing, heavy coat.

The mother snake puts a scared spell on Jerry. He stands like cement. He can't move his feet, but he nearly breaks his back. As the sun hits my face, I let go of her tail. I crawl after the mother, through the dead roots. Jerry's a bent back statue, his heart looks stopped. His eyes are stuck forever on the huge black mother. She winds her body around a huge, reaching root. She dips her head down, she drops *DUF!* at his feet. Jerry's a useless statue.

I crawl between two thick, curly roots. I scrape past Jerry's knees.

There's only silence as I run. I don't think or scream or pray. I'm wind, that's why. I'm only rushing air. Jerry's hate made me strong. Now the silence makes me run. I don't hear a thing. But I'm not deaf, I'm running.

I hear no breaking branches, not even my own feet. I only hear Jerry's spit, sucking in, sucking out. There's a fire in my chest. His hate breath's on my head. I try to fly faster, but the air above me crushes. A mountain cracks my head!

I stay up! I run!

He grabs my shoulder. I spin, I smash into him. I shove and keep running. He grabs again, something snaps. My pyjamas flap. Cool air races on my chest. Jerry's going to get me. I dive off the path, I crash through some branches. There's a small fire burning in my hair where he hit. The bush hurts my skin by accident. I try to spring over the trap, but I'm too heavy. I fall down and listen.

Jerry's feet punch the path.

I crawl into Sheek's grave. I sit in my sweat. My eyes are dry and giant in my flaming head. They're as big as cymbals, they crash when I blink. I hang on my knees, they're slippery from my sweat. A trickle of something thick creeps down my cheek.

Crick, cruck, tuk. My forest warns me that he's here. Now there's only thin sticks and leaves between us. His metal breath saws. His rock is a shadow with cold silver sparks. Jerry's breath burns the leaves around the grave.

Jerry's going to kill me. I shut my eyes tight.

I try to find his proud eyes when I first played the flute. I say now before I die, 'We loved you when you came.'

Fury tears his throat, '*Hggg.*' I pee in my pants. Hot pee water runs. My tears make him blurry.

His hand lands on my head. He digs his fingers in.

He's going to lift my bleeding scalp off like a lid. I force my heels back, *shipp shipp*. It hurts much worse, but I lean into the leaves. I hang on his wrist, I feel his metal veins. His other hand lifts his terrible rock shadow.

I *ruk* on his arm with all my left over strength.

He staggers one small step. *Grukk!* Rusted teeth snap shut. Metal spikes chop into meat. 'AAAAGH!'

I tell the Truth Lady, 'It was pure hate and pure pain …'

She says, 'Exploding?'

He cries and he whines, he tries to feel what's eating him. The rusted jaw digs deep into his shin. Red blood leaks onto his toes.

I'm still alive! The gladness makes me crazy.

The old trap keeps eating, its mouth is full of blood. It hasn't eaten since Sheek. Jerry drags on the chain, but the chain pulls tight.

Jerry's locked to the tree forever. The trap will keep him and eat him. It will take years.

I crawl to the path, I run jerky and strange. My whole body shivers. My teeth try to bite my tongue for more blood. I think my relief is rusting my legs up. 'Pa,' I cry. It comes out soft and weak.

Buk! Buk! Buk! The sound shocks the forest like a gun. It shocks the bones in my head. Jerry's bashing metal!

The banging stops.

Chu-shukk, the chain hisses in the sand.

Jerry's free! Not even men eating teeth can stop him! *Chu-shukk*. It slams the powdery sand. I know where Jerry's going.

He's going to kill my ma and sister!

'JERRY!' I fill the forest with his name. 'JE-RRYYY!' I scream. I race to the road. The chain skids a long s-mark in the sand. 'Jerry! STOP! Please STOP!'

Jerry drags his trap.

'I *will* lie for you!'

Jerry stops, he bleeds on the sand.

'Jerry! I understand!'

His eyes slide to me, I can see the whites. He chews his moustache, maybe from the rusted pain.

'I'll lie about Mevrou. I'll *never* talk again.'

Jerry sags his head, like he's trying to decide.

He turns off the sand, he drags the trap towards the dam. He groans, 'Ahhhh.' The chain combs through the grass, just like Mevrou's hair.

'Do you believe me?' I ask.

His blood floats in the mud, it makes a still, orange cloud. It shuts all the birds and the insects up. Jerry splashes water, he tries to clean the bite. The dragonflies start to fly short flights. A brave swimmer frog dives down again. I wait behind Jerry, I watch the orange spread.

I think he believes me. I think he'll say yes.

Something clamps on my ankle, it sweeps my leg away. I fall on my face, *splussh!* Jerry buries me with blood. I stick my fingers in the mud, I try to push up. Water drowns my throat, it makes my lungs scream. I shove on my knees, but Jerry is too heavy.

I'm drowning, like in my dream, but the brown lady doesn't come. I can't feel her hands, only sucking, silky sand. I'll tell the judge the truth, even if he says I'm mad. She plays the warning song, but this time it's the real song from her CD. '*Stille, sag ich! Schweige still!*' It's German, but it means, 'Be still, Stella! Wait!'

I let my arms float. I'm a floating brown child, drowned in blood and mud. I glue my lips together, I bite the dam back. Black and green lights flash inside my eyes. Jerry's body lifts off me, but the song still sings, 'Sssh, Stella, wait.'

I say in my head, 'Stella, you are dead.'

I wait in the music. I float like the dead rat in the canal. My blood beats in my ears. I think they're bleeding. Then Mevrou shouts, '*Breathe!*'

Air rushes in like heaven, sweeter, even, than condensed milk. Mevrou shouts, 'GET UP! RUN!'

I've never, never heard Mevrou so furious. I crawl to the side with green lights in my eyes. I can't see Jerry. I stand up in the mud. I'm heavy from water. 'MOVE!' Mevrou shouts. She makes my heart pump the water out. I hang my heavy head. My legs follow me.

'Papa.' The word keeps me moving. 'Papa.' It keeps me alive.

'Jerry hated killing me.'
The Truth Lady says, 'What?'
'He hated the way my white pyjamas floated.'
'Oh?'
'I know from Mevrou.'
He tried to throw me out of his eyes, but he saw his own ma, swinging and dead. He saw her only breath left was the wind in her dress.

The Truth Lady just says, 'What happened next?'

Theeee, the bakkie wheels screamed on Marais farm. Marais' wife swelled up the whole bakkie front. Hettie's bum nearly bent the bakkie side.

The Truth Lady says, 'Stella?'

Ggwoik, *ggwooik*, Hettie crunched a green apple in two bites. She threw it over Oom Neville and all the sweating men.

Marais shouted to his wife, 'Give it power, girl!' But she wasn't a girl.

The Truth Lady's black eyebrows twist. 'Stella, where was Jerry?'

The tyres spinned a deep ditch.

Marais said 'Hettie, come stand by Pappie for a bit.'

The bakkie floated up. Hettie's dress was pink.

I open my arms to show the Truth Lady, 'It was as big as a tent at the Vyeboom dam. I think it was a bit see through, too.'

The Truth Lady says, 'Stella, what the hell's going on?'

Marais shouted, 'Dig!'

That's when Pa ran past.

The Truth Lady says, 'Ah.'

Oom Neville asked my pa, 'What's the hurry Frank?'

Pa stopped running, 'What's the hurry *here*?'

'They're going to give blood at the town hall.' Neville smiled a secret smile, 'They get free biscuits.'

Pa started to laugh, but fear poured from the sky. It haunted him worse, much worse, than his wine.

The Truth Lady leans to her machine, 'Worse, even, than Nancy's sighs in the trees.'

Pa's legs tangled up, he ran on the sand.

'Papa,' I whisper, but not with my lips. I slide down the bank. 'Papa.'

The word makes my pa real on the road! 'Pa?'

He hears my quiet cry. He skids on his feet, he kicks into the bush. Pa's got jumpy eyes and jumpy muscles in his face. He says, 'There's blood.'

'He's going to kill us.'

'Who?' Pa makes a safe roof, he holds me in the reeds. Pa smells disgusting like the dump. He feels in my hair like he's making braids.

'He wants to kill us, Pa.'

'Who?'

'Jerry wants to kill us.' I'm like a stuck CD.

'Where is he?'

'Ma …'

Pa lets me go, he runs. The world is too big, I'm dizzy without his arms. Pa runs for the hut, he believes everything I said. He spins, he runs backwards. 'Stella, call the police!'

Marais' tyres scream a scared, high scream. Pa points up the road to Mevrou's. 'Go to Mevrou! Now!'

I don't get a chance to say, Mevrou's dead.

I listen to Pa.

This time the forest holds still, because I'm dizzy. The warm air tries to dry me, but I'm soggy and slow. A dizzy pain beats, *thub, thub*, inside my brain.

When I get to Mevrou's, I go straight to the phone. This time I press the buttons all the way. 021- 859771. I tell the police lady, 'Quick! Come quick! Jerry's killing everyone on Nooitgedacht. He killed Mevrou …'

My throat shuts like a old lock.

'Who is this?' she sounds cross. I scrape a sore breath, I hear the *klank* of a jail. My name won't come out.

'Hello?'

But I see Jerry's thumbs on Grace's thin neck. 'I'm Stella.'

'Stella, this is not a joke. You can get into big trouble for lying to the police.'

I beg in a stuck together rush, 'I promise to God, I'm not lying. Please help us, please, please!'

'Get a grownup on the line.'

'Gustav!' I shout. 'Gustav!'

The Truth Lady speaks slow, like I'm a child, 'Stella. Where was Jerry?'

'I don't want to tell it.'

'You *have* to. For the judge.'

Ma fell on her knees. 'God! What happened?'

He gave her head a ugly shove, but Ma didn't see. She ran to fetch Grace from the green beans. She jigged Gracie hard on her hip, she started to run up the road to Mevrou's.

'NANCY!' Jerry's shout was horrible.

I tell the Truth Lady, 'It had sorry in it.'

'What?'

'The sorry people feel when they kill their own love.'

The Truth Lady shakes her head. 'You know, sometimes you don't sound like you're twelve.'

I run up the stairs. 'Jerry killed your *mutti*. The police don't believe me.'

'What?' Gustav struggles to his bum. He stands up tottery on his toes. He's as white as the wall, and he's thin, this Gustav. He's got a sad little stomach left, that's all. I pull on his hand, but it's floppy and soft. 'Come to the phone!'

He says, 'What?' like God gave him one note to say all his life.

'The police don't believe me! Jerry killed Mevrou!' I shout.

His brain suddenly works. 'Stella, is my *mutti* dead?'

'Yes!' I shout. 'Come to the phone!'

He collapses on the bed.

The Truth Lady says, 'Stella, the hut.'

'I can't.'

'You can.'

'Get in the hut!' Jerry said.

Ma turned back to help him. 'Go!' he choked. He picked up her axe against the wall.

I stop.

The Truth Lady says, '*Tell* it, Stella.'

He dribbled wet blood across the cement. He staggered inside, he locked our door.

'What was your ma *thinking*?'

'Ma thought the axe was to open the trap.'

Jerry barked like a mad dog. 'Get on the bed! You and Grace!'

She didn't see the ugly picture. She sat down with my sister.

The Truth Lady asks, 'How *could* she not *see*?'

It made Jerry sad, only me and Mevrou know.

He said, 'I don't want to, Nance.'

'What Jerry? What?'

Grace was quiet, like she knew more than our own ma.

Jerry stroked the blade. He prayed very hard to the God that he hated. Please let the pillow suck up the blood.

The Truth Lady says, 'No!'

'I promise he did! I know, from Mevrou.'

'Okay. What then?'

'Lie on your stomach!'

Ma saw it then, in his spinning mirror eyes.

She threw Gracie behind her on the bed.

Grace screamed, '*Waamamaa!*'

Ma shouts somewhere behind us, 'Stella, are you okay?'

The Truth Lady waves like it's a nice, happy day. She whispers, 'Don't stop.'

The police lady's gone! I push the number again.

'Gustav's too sick to come down the stairs. Please come. I don't care if I go to jail. Come and save my sister.'

'What's wrong with your sister?'

I put emergency in every, every word. I force it down the holes in the phone. 'Jerry's killing my family.'

She sighs. She's sick of my joke. 'Why?'

I'm desperate. The telephone wire stretches like elastic. It feels like it's going to snap. Then Mevrou rubs my back. I'll tell the judge, I don't care what he thinks. Mevrou is dead, but she rubs me like Ma used to. The words come suddenly, they crash against my teeth. 'He killed Inspector Booysen.' My breath stings my lips. The words march in circles around my brain. The police lady talks fast to someone else.

'Hey?' I say.

'We're sending someone right away.'

'Hurry! Please!'

Now all I want is the police.

The Truth Lady says, 'Stella. Finish at the hut!'

Pa *heard* Gracie scream. Pa ran as fast as a shooting star. *Dukgg! Dukgg!* He kicked our door like ten police!

The door punched Jerry onto Ma and my screaming sister.

He swung the axe up. The sun poured around my pa's thin body. It sparkled the blade, it made Pa think fast.

The Truth Lady writes with big, scary eyes, *Think fast or die ugly!*

Pa stared at Jerry's foot, smudged with blood. He stared at the jaws that chewed and chewed. Pa spoke sweet, like they were still friends. Maybe the angels helped him pretend. 'Jerry, what's happening here?'

Jerry played the same friendly game. 'Frank, why are you kicking the door to pieces?'

Gracie crawled to Pa, but Jerry pulled her to his lap. Gracie twisted and kicked like a tiny wrestler. 'Aaaeepapaa!' she screamed, like a crazy baby.

Pa held his hands out.

I stop.

The Truth Lady says, 'Come on, Stella!'

Jerry squeezed tighter. Grace shut her lips, her sore tears poured. The Truth Lady whispers, 'She was very, very brave, your little sister.'

I pray hard to God, I don't know which one. I pray, Save my ma! Save my sister! Speed the police wheels! Spin them like lightning!

The Truth Lady says, 'Stay with it, kid. Don't slip!'

Pa took his hands back. He rested them, relaxed.

He turned around to the lovely sun, 'Where's Stella?'

Ma saw Jerry's eyes zig and zag around our hut. 'No-o-o!!' she screamed.

Jerry threw Grace onto Ma. Her little cheek cracked, *krrek!* on Ma's knee.

The Truth Lady says, 'Poor baby.'

Jerry banged the cupboard with his back. The candle and the saucer smashed to the floor. My flute box hit the mirror, it split the glass in a circle of splinters.

Jerry lifted the axe above Ma's head.

The Truth Lady's eyes stretch wide. A dot of black make up swims in one eye.

I blink. 'He wanted the blade to split her brain. He wanted to pull it from her bones and chop Grace's soft body.'

Mevrou says, 'Sick!'

'But he didn't chop when he should have.'

His killing axe waited.

I crouch by the phone, I pull splinters off the wood. I prick my fingers deep, but they've got no feeling. I pray to the God who used to live in my heart. Hurry! Please come!

The Truth Lady says, 'The hut, the hut!'

Pa threw his whole body onto the trap. Jerry's knee nearly teared off his leg. 'Aaaaaaah!!' Jerry screamed. He fell down in the gap between the bed and the wall.

The axe sliced down.

Tears drip on my voice strings.

The Truth Lady gasps. 'What did it hit?'

I talk through stinging water, 'It missed Pa's backbone. It cut the soft part.'

The Truth Lady sinks, 'Just like a roast of Mevrou's.'

Pa cried deep like a bull, he bent away from the blade.

Ma nearly pulled Gracie's arm out of its skin. She threw her outside, into the safe, lovely sun.

I go in the kitchen, but the sun is too bright.

The Truth Lady says, 'Stella, get back to Frank!'

It makes my skin feel bare, like it's stolen my clothes. I climb under Mevrou's kitchen table. I hide in the shade. I pray.

The Truth Lady begs, 'Stella!'

Pa rolled on his bleeding back. The axe cut for his stomach, but Pa kicked hard. The blade jerked away.

The Truth Lady says, 'Is that when …?'

I nod. 'It chopped Pa's hand on the bed wood.'

Pa's little finger flew right off. I asked and I asked, 'How did it look?'

Ma wouldn't say, but Mevrou showed me.

The Truth Lady says, 'Yes?'

'It made a peeing curve, like the cherubs. Except it was red.'

I suck my fingers in the kitchen. They sting from the splinters.

I suck and I suck. I don't want to see blood.

The Truth Lady pokes my leg with her pen, 'Uh-uh! The hut!'

I jump, even though it's only plastic.

'Frank!' Ma screamed. She threw her body over Pa's.

I say to the Truth Lady, 'Will you write that for the judge?'

Jerry jerked the axe off the bed. He swung it up high.

The Truth Lady goes red, she's holding her breath.

But he dropped the axe instead.

The Truth Lady gasps, 'God!'

It made Pa's little finger bounce on the bed.

Kushukk, *kushukk*, the chain drags on the stoep!

Someone breathes creaky like a tree. Gracie cries with short, tripping whimpers.

Gracie's cry makes my dead legs climb the stairs. I lie down at the top.

Jerry falls in the kitchen. He jerks my ma with him, and my baby sister. My starlings shriek, 'Red! Red! Red!' They're all splashed with red. It can't be blood, there's too much.

I think it is!

Ma's clothes are bleeding, I think she's going to die! I can't even cry.

Jerry presses the air out of Ma's neck. Ma stumbles, choking and slow. She can hardly move her legs, but still she hangs onto my little sister. Jerry nearly falls every time he steps. It's like his dead father's hurting him on purpose.

Jerry drags Ma by the throat, he drags her up the stairs.

I creep past dead Eddie. I shrink to very small behind Mevrou's door.

Mevrou's bed is made up for her death. There's still a dent where she sat and got dressed. I can taste her face powder on my tongue. Jerry drags them to Gustav's room. I creep out and crouch under Eddie's head. I spy through the crack.

Jerry lets go of Ma's throat. Stuck air bursts out, she falls with Grace. Jerry jerks her straight. He bends her arm back so Ma gasps, 'Uhhh!' Gracie slides down her hip, nearly to the floor. Ma pulls her up slow. Gracie is weak, her voice has broken down. She cries like a broken doll with nearly flat batteries.

The Truth Lady says, 'Ag, shame.'

Jerry picks up the pen next to Gustav's head.

Gustav sees the terrible truth. He believes me now. He looks scared like Mevrou, before she slid in rooster blood. His eyes fall back into their holes. He croaks some words, but I don't think it's English. Jerry lifts the silver pen high in his fist. He punches it, *kitt!*

Ma screams, 'No-o-o-o!'

It snaps Gustav's skin, it stabs in his throat.

The Truth Lady says, 'He's *totally* psycho!'

Jerry rips the pen out. Blood pours out like a underground stream. He throws the paper on Gustav's legs. 'Write!' he shouts.

Ma is sobbing, her arm is bent wrong. Jerry bends it more, until she shuts up. Jerry's strong from the blood. He shouts to Gustav, 'Write!'

Then Jerry talks like he's making a speech in a hall. 'If die, I leave my farm Nooitgedacht …'

Gustav gasps blood instead of air. The red trickles on his titties. Jerry slaps Gustav's head, 'Write!'

Gustav writes. Blood drips on the paper.

'… to my brother, Jerome Titi.'

The Truth Lady says, 'Titty'?

'Titi. It was Rachel's name, when she was young.'

Ma's eyes are white and wild like a horse. Jerry's watching the words, he doesn't see Ma's white eyes on the sword. I stick my head around the door, as quick as a dassie. Ma's eyes turn bright from new terror. They say, 'Get away!'

I make myself as light as dust, even my feet. I creep. The sun shines right through me, all it shows is dust. It doesn't show my legs or my broken buttons or my bumps. It doesn't show the mud. I don't look at Ma in case I get heavy. I creep to the sword. *Shleek*. I slide it out of its leather.

It cuts the sunbeam as I lift it.

Jerry throws his arms open. He stands like a cross, from shock. My ma staggers free. Jerry thought I was floating with my mouth in brown mud. 'I'll cut you. I'll chop you!' I hold the heavy sword high above my head. I cry from my own violence. 'I'll kill you, I will!'

I say to the Truth Lady, 'I think I was a killer! Tell the judge, if you want.'

'Stella,' Jerry whispers. He covers his head like the roof is full of swords. He walks slow to me.

I'm not dust anymore. I'm a cutting, cruel sword. 'Get away! Get away!' I shake the sword high, I slice the sun into pieces.

'Stella, you're alive.'

Jerry smiles like he loves me, but I see his skin pull tight on his cheeks. I see silver glitter inside his blue eyes. I swing the sword, I sink it straight in his side! It sinks in like wet sand.

Jerry stares at the sword stuck in his side. He grabs the blade with his bare hands. He pulls it out.

But I don't let go. I won't.

Bright red blood drips from his fists. He swings the sword by the blade.

My knees crash, they drag on the wood. I hang on, I scramble up.

Jerry swings again.

I cry because my hands are slipping off. I cry because I'm furious.

Suddenly something soft wraps around my back. Strong brown arms tangle over mine. It's the octopus lady, but she's got my mother's smell of red pepper and rain. Her teeth grind in my ear. Her legs hold mine up. We join together, me and Ma. We're one huge woman with many arms and many hands. I'll tell the judge. Me and Ma were as strong as a Hindu God.

We force the sword out of Jerry's hands. The skin on his hands is sliced in white strips. Blood pours from the lines, it runs down his wrists. He holds out his hands, he begs. 'Nancy, I love you, man.'

The Truth Lady laughs like a thunder crack.

'What's funny?'

'He's *absolutely* mad!'

Ma whispers that, 'You're mad!'

Jerry says, 'We'll say it was Frankie.'

Ma lets go from the shock. She watches Jerry's blood dripping *tic*, *tic* on the wood. She stares at Gustav's red, bubbling neck. Jerry makes a bet, 'I won't touch the girls.'

Hot shock hits my heart. But my shock is a shiver compared to my ma. He shouldn't have said that.

'NO-O-O!' My ma ruks the sword out of my hands. She charges with the blade, its point is still pink from sinking in. Jerry can see my ma's crazy. Her eyes are metal green in the sunbeam. They can peel his whole skin, her scream can cut his meat, 'NO-O-O!'

He throws his trap leg down the stairs. It smashes the wood, it scrapes on the wall. Jerry falls after it like he can't feel it eating. At the bottom, he jumps up like a punch. But my ma is a killer, roaring after him. Jerry tries to run, but there's a axe in the way!

Pa's shirt is wrapped around his hand. It's a red, dirty rag. Pa's face is yellow. His eyes are black on each side of the axe. Pa stands like dangerous death with a blade.

Jerry swerves into the bathroom. Ma skids after him with her pink sword. Pa waits like a silent, yellow man at the door. Jerry screams, 'Nan-cy!!' but Ma stabs him in the ribs. 'Aaargh!' he blasts. Ma pulls the sword out, *slik*.

'Stop,' Jerry begs, but Ma charges again. He swings one leg in the bath, he lifts the trap with his hands. He presses his back into the white tiles. 'Nancy! NO!' But Ma stabs him in the titty.

'Nancy-y!' he cries, but Ma's mad from stabbing.

I shout, 'Mamie, STOP!'

Ma pulls the sword out.

'STOP!' I shout again.

She points the sword to the floor.

Jerry sinks to his bum. His blood turns Mevrou's white washing bubbles pink. It stains her huge white underpants floating on top.

Jerry cries like a little boy, 'Frankie. I'm sorry.'

Pa pulls Ma's arm. He whispers to me, 'Come, Stella.'

Pa's shirt is cut. I can see red meat!

I stop.

The Truth Lady says, '*Nearly* there, Stella, come on!'

The bum of his pants is just dark blood. Pa's a cut man standing. He takes the key out, he locks the door from our side. He slides down the wall onto his bloody bum. Pa lies the axe on his knees. He bleeds out more of his brown.

'I phoned the police,' I say to Ma and Pa.

But Pa's turning white. His eyes are like night in the hut with no moon. Ma slides down next to him. *Ka-chinng*, his axe sings against her sword. Ma pulls Pa's head onto her titties. She holds it tight like Mevrou did, when I was deaf. Ma says, 'Sorry, my baby,' like his head is baby Grace.

I run upstairs to look for my sister.

Gustav's rocking with his head on his legs. Red from his neck drips on his lily toes. I rub him on his back between his wings. Gracie's trying to put Gustav's boots on. She sits on the floor and sticks her legs in them. She tries to stand, but she falls on her nappy. 'Uh! Uh!' She frowns, cross. She huffs and she puffs, but she can't get up. Grace whines, she points at the boots. 'Tella,' she says.

I tell the Truth Lady, 'It's the first time that Gracie ever said my name!'

The Truth Lady says, 'Wow.' Then she says, 'Carry on.'

I go and fetch Mevrou's soft, white slippers. Grace wriggles out of the army boots. I put Mevrou's big slippers on her feet. 'There,' I say, 'Tella fixed it.'

Grace shuffles *shllof, shllof* across the floor. She walks on Gustav's letter, she picks it up. *Shllof shllof*, she gives it to Gustav like she's a little cleaner. She walks *shllof, shllof* to the top of the stairs. Gracie laughs loud, like there's a lovely surprise.

I hurry to see.

I stare straight into the black hole of a gun.

I grab Grace's shirt, but my muscles get stuck. I'm hypnotised by the gun.

'They're *children*!' Ma hisses. She points her sword to the bathroom door. 'He's in there.'

Then she begs, 'Get a ambulance! Frank's bleeding to death.'

But they aim their guns to Ma's head instead!

Ma sighs. She carried the blades past their black bullet eyes. *Chunng*, she lies the sword and the axe on the stair.

My pa can't even lift up his eyelids to watch.

The Truth Lady dips, 'It's like there was a evil spell in the house.'

'Huh?'

'Think about it, all the men were bleeding to … uh … sleep.'

Oom Roos twists the rusted key quick, quick. He slams the door back, *bakk!*

Now I run.

I jump over Gustav, fallen to sleep on the floor. I climb in his bed, I grip Gracie tight under the bleeding cover.

The Truth Lady asks, 'And downstairs?'

Oom Roos charged at the bath.

'Thank you, Jesus!' Jerry hissed. He acted like the police gun was only plastic. His eyes crashed with Ma's eyes through the open door. He said soft to Oom Roos, 'Frank's killing the whites.'

The Truth Lady scrapes on her page, *'Frank's Killing the Whites.'*

'He *wasn't!*'

'Relax, Stella. It's just a heading.' She says, 'And then?'

Oom Roos asked Jerry, 'Who the hell are you?'

'I'm Gustav's brother.'

Oom Roos frowned. He shouted over his shoulder, 'Who phoned the police?'

'Me,' I squeak, under the bleeding cover.

Ma answers him, 'My daughter. Stella.'

It smells like cow poo in Gustav's bed. Gracie plays with the slippers. Then she gets hot and kicks to get out. I hold her down, 'Shhh.'

There are footsteps on the stairs. There's quick breathing at the door. Gracie fights now like I'm trying to murder her. I peep over the top of the racing car cover.

The young policeman's got a very scared look. He's got light eyes like Ma. His hair is waxed flat with a zig zag parting. He crouches down, he touches Gustav's neck. He shouts, 'Another one here for the paramedics!' but his voice creaks like he wants to cry. Gracie kicks, she squawks like a chicken. She climbs out and laughs at the police's gun. He tries to smile, but his lips jerk on his gums. His moustache is thin and soft like the hair on a moth. This one's not going to take me to jail. That's when I remember.

The Truth Lady asks, 'What?'

The police don't even know!

I tuck in my top, I cover my bumps. I get out of bed and sit with Gustav. Gracie carries Mevrou's slippers like a doll. She tries to touch the police's gun. He clips it back in its holder, he rubs her head like a puppy. He smells like scared sweat. He wants to stay with us, but a ambulance siren nearly screams the farm down.

The scared police goes to look. I pick Gracie up, I creep careful down the stairs. Some men in white suits kneel down next to Pa. They've got a needle and a pipe. They've got a papsak on a pole that drips water, not wine. A man in a shining yellow jacket runs past me up the stairs. Gracie sits on Pa's foot. She waves her slippers, she chats to him with funny words.

Pa's veins suck water like a starving plant. Brown colour leaks back into his skin. His eyelids lift. There's a new, pale moon inside his eyes. Pa stares at Marais like he's dreaming in the day.

The Truth Lady asks, 'Marais?'

I nod. 'He came to see.'

Marais stretches his neck through the bathroom door. He watches the man touching Jerry's cuts. Marais pulls his neck back, he clucks like a Xhosa, 'Ey! That Jerry is a waste of white skin.'

Pa stares at Marais' giant white thighs. He stares at Marais' stomach hanging over his head. It swells through his buttons, as wide as a equator. Pa's eyes touch mine. If he had any air left in his breath, I know my pa. I know he would laugh.

Ma sees us suddenly, like me and Grace were only ghosts. She pushes me like a wheelbarrow to the white ladies on the grass. She orders Marais' wife and Hettie like they are just workers. 'Keep the children outside.'

Gracie loves Hettie's long hair. She pulls the blonde ends over her head. She peeps at us, then she pulls it hard.

'Eina!' Hettie says. She's got to pick Gracie's fingers off one by one. Hettie and Marais' wife think I'm mad when I shout, 'Look! Look! They can fly!' Only Grace understands, she waves her arms at my starlings. They fly short loops from the window to the tree, I think they learned it from me.

'Tella,' Gracie says. That's 'Stella' with no 's.'

Tella, maybe, because I told.

Marais' wife puts her arm around me to be nice, but it feels like a fat lady sitting on my back. It feels too much like Mevrou, with her soft arm and the cherubs. The sadness makes me shake. My lips go wobbly, my words shiver out. 'I stabbed him here.' I lift up my arm and show her my side, 'Just like Jesus.'

My starlings sit with their ma's bones in the fig tree.

I tell Marais' wife, 'He taught me Amazing Grace.'

Hettie's mouth hangs open as I talk. When she nods, her cheeks nod too. Her mother's arm is crushing me. She smells sweaty like a horse, not like garlic and rosemary like Mevrou. Mevrou's grave flowers still think it's a lovely day. The three cherubs keep peeing pretty water. I keep quiet and listen. I think I can hear something beautiful in their pee.

The Truth Lady says, 'Their pee?'

'It's Mevrou, without sound.'

It pours soft water on my heart. It makes me stop shivering. It's her new, hidden voice. I can sing it, but I can't say it. It's not for words.

I ask the Truth Lady, 'Will you try to write it, though?'

The Truth Lady nods.

It's like a little wind that's too shy to blow. I'll tell the judge, even if he laughs. Mevrou is still here in the prickle of the grass. She's in the silence of her own grave flowers. She's in the trees that speeded me, and stood dead still when I needed.

I'll tell the judge I want to cry because she died. But the truth is, I'm not sad enough.

The ambulance men lift Jerry's armpits. The scared police points his gun at Jerry's head. Sheek's trap still bites on Jerry's leg. Jerry tries to stop, but the policeman says, 'Walk!'

I want to cry for the Jerry who came to fix us, not this one with the handcuffs and the blood and the gun.

Suddenly, my ma screams from inside, 'Are you mad? *He* attacked *us!*' They carry Pa out on a plank bed. Oom Roos is pointing his gun at Pa's head. They're taking him to jail!

'Papa! Papa!' I scream. I throw off her sweaty, big arm. I beg Ma to stop them, 'Mamie!' I point at Jerry in the ambulance. '*He's* the killer! Ask Gustav!'

I run inside, I fall *flumm* against Marais' leg. I run past him up the stairs. Gustav's also on a plank with a papsak and a pipe. I try to shake him awake, but the ambulance man grabs me. I kick and I twist. He carries me out, he puts me on the grass. I spin away, I run to the ambulance. Pa's bled too much blood, he laughs slow and shallow. His voice is high like a lady, 'It's okay, my angel. Just tell the truth.'

Oom Roos guards him.

Ma begs, 'Mister Roos, you're making a mistake.'

'I'm sorry, I have to, until we've got the story.'

I shoot him with my eyes. I tell the truth to save my father. 'Jerry killed Nita's pa.'

Jerry laughs inside the ambulance, like I made a dumb joke. Oom Roos forgets to guard all the bleeding people. He bends his head like he *also* just heard Mevrou's song.

He looks helpless to Ma. 'We'll send a detective. *Someone's* lying on this farm.'

Marais offers us a lift in his bakkie. Ma's fighting to not cry, so I say, 'No thanks,' for us. Marais and his wife sink the front, Hettie sinks the back. Hettie's pink dress flies behind. It's the same light pink as Mevrou's washing foam.

Ma won't let me look inside the hut. She sits with me under my tree. She pats me softly, but it hurts my bones. Ma knows I'm praying hard for Pa. 'It's okay,' she says. 'The judge is a coloured.' But Ma's voice is as thin as water, I can't trust her words.

The Truth Lady twists, 'Uh-oh, your sister.'
Gracie's crying in the hut. We wait for her to shush, but she cries even louder.
'Ma?' I shout.
The Truth Lady points.
Ma's far in the garden, tying green beans with string.
I run and fetch Grace. She's still soft and sleepy. Her little arms creep around my bare neck.
The Truth Lady shows her teeth. She taps Grace's nose, 'Hello, sweetie.' She's got purple lipstick smudged on her chin.
Grace pinches my skin like she's seen a crocodile. She rubs her face against my bumps. She peeps with one eye.
The Truth Lady says, 'Is that the whole story?'
'No!'
'Okay, don't panic.'
She flicks her switch. 'I'm listening.'

Detective Saayman comes. He's a Xhosa with fat cheeks, I've seen him before.

The Truth Lady asks, 'Where?'

'After Nita's Pa, I saw him touch the grass. I saw him stare at Nita's pa's tyre marks.'

His eyes are small and clever. He stares at everything, even my ma. She shows him inside where I'm not allowed. His camera makes a white flash through the door. Ma tells him quiet, terrible secrets. I'm not supposed to hear, but my ears can hunt whispers. Her words sink in my meat. Ma tells how Jerry tried to chop her and Grace. Grace is bossy and strange, she sings a song with no tune. She cries then she shouts. She's a pain in the bum, but I pat her when she cries, I laugh when she laughs. I'm glad to have a sister.

When it's my turn to talk, the detective presses his book on the chopping block. He's got big black hands like Pa. He writes fast, but not neat, with a weak plastic pen. I tell him, 'Jerry choked Mevrou. He killed Mugabe. He punched Gustav with a pen.'

'Mugabe?'

'My rooster. He killed him for spite.'

He ignores Mugabe. 'How do you know that he killed Mevrou Viljoen?'

I tell him I woke Mevrou in the middle of the night. She got dressed in her grave clothes and when it was light, she went to shout at Jerry's house. I say that Jerry hid with all the snakes that he hated. I tell him everything that Jerry said about Eddie. I say Mevrou told him to go, but he tackled her down. I tell him Jerry choked her, so I bit him until he bled. I say, 'Mevrou fell to sleep in Mugabe's blood. It was black. Jerry dragged her by her unkles. She had no breath left.' I can't say the word, *dead*. 'He told me to lie again, but I ran away.'

His small, clever eyes aim inside my brain. '*Again?*'

His chest hair's got black knots, just like my pa. 'I lied once before.'

'For Jerry?'

I nod.

'What about?'

The police number shouts loud in my head. 021 - 59771.

'Stella? What did you lie about?' His gun is cold metal.

Ma rests her soft stomach against me. Gracie gets jealous, she tries to squeeze between us. Then she sees the detective's boots. She sits on her bum, she pulls on his laces.

The detective asks, 'Who did you lie to?'

My pa is in jail. I've got to get him out.

I can't look in his eyes, I stare at the knots on his chest, instead. 'Nita's pa.'

Ma says, 'Inspector Booysen.'

'What did you say to Inspector Booysen?' he asks.

'I said, Jerry's our family.'

The detective looks shocked.

'Even though he's white.' Now I watch his police eyes. 'I lied for Jerry and he gave me his flute.'

Detective Saayman doesn't pull out his gun. He doesn't say, 'You're under arrest!' He just writes with his pen. He writes it all down, but not very neat. Afterwards he doesn't touch his handcuffs. He just asks, 'Did a dog bite you when you were small?'

I stare at him. 'Yes.' How did he know about Sheek?

Ma strokes my scar, 'He didn't mean it,' she says. Gracie pulls his laces, she dribbles on his boots. The detective only chews his plastic pen.

'I'm *sorry* I lied.'

Ma says, 'It's okay, Stella.' She strokes my hair on top.

'Will they … put me in jail?'

The detective looks sad like Ma. 'Really, never. You're only a child.'

'Don't they put children in jail?'

'Never.'

I say, 'But I think Jerry killed him.'

The detective looks sad at our garden, like he's already guessed.

'What if he's …?' I just can't say, *dead*.

'She means …' Ma says.

The detective says, 'Dead? They won't blame you.'

'But I lied.'

'You're a child.'

'But Jerry said …'

'It's okay, Stella,' Ma says.

I lie my head against her stomach. The sky is white like the nun's eyes when she's being kind. When I sit up, Gracie's eating the detective's laces. I start to giggle.

I giggle and I hiccup, I can't stop.

The detective talks to Ma about Grace and the garden. I stop the laughing hiccups. I watch. But he doesn't make Ma laugh, he doesn't touch her where he mustn't. I try to make him write instead. I tell him I threw the flute in the dam. He nods. I tell him about Mugabe again, but the detective's not interested in a rooster.

When he stands up to go, I ask, 'Will they let my pa free?'

He doesn't answer. He just says to Ma, 'Gustav's still, uh, out, so he can't help us.'

He goes to take photos in Mevrou's house.

The Truth Lady grins with a smudged purple chin.

Ma takes Grace from me, 'Aren't you finished yet?'

'Uh uh.'

The Truth Lady laughs, 'She doesn't want to stop.'

Ma says, 'She's been practising. She says it's like a song.'

Ma walks away with Grace. Her back is straight and strong.

'It *is* like a song! I must say all the notes or I'll sing the song wrong.'

The Truth Lady sighs, 'I know kid, carry on.'

I bang, *BOOMM BOOMM*.

I stay home like Nita did. I practise my words, I say them in my head. Over and over, I must never forget. I must tell the perfect truth. They won't put me in jail, the detective said. But Pa's there instead.

I wait in my tree. I don't touch my bottles, they've got Jerry in them. I don't want any music, never, ever.

My eyes go mad from missing my pa. Over and over, I see him walk up the sand, drunk and crooked. I'm so glad he's home, I knock him over. I kiss him on the eyes, like he used to kiss me. I pray to the good God, the one that Pa loves. Please bring my pa back. His name is Frank.

But all my *real* eyes see, is a yellow van. The detective shuts his door *cluk*. He stands at his van like he wants to race away. Ma stops feeding sweet potato to Grace.

'I can't find finger marks.' The detective twists his palms to the sky like he lost something precious. Grace cries for food. Ma grips the spoon so tight, her fingertips go white.

'I tried my best,' he says.

'What about on Mevrou!'

The detective shakes his head.

'And the pen?'

'It was smudged with sweat and blood.'

'What about the note?'

'Jerry said Gustav wrote the note long ago.'

Grace starts to scream. Ma shoves sweet potato into her shouting mouth. 'There *must* be something ...'

The detective whines high, like a excuse, 'I wish the old lady wasn't dressed up like that. Her scarf and her gloves really messed things up.' He touches the plastic pen in his pocket. 'And I wish bladdy Gustav would open his eyes.'

The Truth Lady writes, *The Killer Snake Left No Trace!*

Ma's frown tangles and twists on her skin. She waits for good news, but nothing comes. The detective says, 'It's not like on TV where they've got machines that spin until they find some skin.' The detective checks our roof, but all he sees are green pumpkins in the sun, not a TV aerial like at Mevrou's.

Oom Neville comes to see us. Ma holds out Kool Aid, but he walks sideways, 'Wait, wait.' He washes his face and his hands at the tap. When he's nice and clean, he takes the glass from Ma. He sips small and careful, like its boiling hot. He says, 'The police are busy asking people what they think. I told them I never liked that white guy. I said to the police, look, Frank's a *drunk*.'

Ma ducks, like the word hit her.

'I can say it Nancy, because you know I was, also.'

Oom Neville finds me with his sober, sorry eyes. 'It's a sickness, my girl. It's not a sin.'

I nod like a grown up. I want to ask, 'Oom Neville. How did you *fix* it?'

But Oom Neville says, 'I said, he's a *drunk*. But Frank wouldn't hurt a ant.'

Ma nods. She whispers, 'Thanks.'

I'm scared that Oom Neville might love her and try to stay. But he says, 'I must get home to Susan. Do you want to eat by us?'

Ma shakes her head. 'No thanks. We've got supper.'

But Ma forgets to cook. Me and Gracie just eat lettuce and bread.

Detective Saayman comes again. 'Hi.'

I smile and let him touch my head. Then I creep up my tree, I hide in the leaves.

He talks fast, like he's guilty, 'Still no proof.'

The Truth Lady shakes her head, 'God's truth! The police are useless.'

The detective says to Ma, 'I don't just sit around on my bum. I mean, I'm working like a dog. I've spoken to everyone in Vyeboom.'

He tells Ma all the stories that he got.

The Truth Lady asks, 'Like what?'

About Dora's daughter and the silver cross in the shop. And the tannie at the municipality. And the doctor, with Gustav.

The Truth Lady's red tongue licks her lips, 'The DDT?'

I nod.

The detective says, 'The doctor thinks Jerry really loved his brother.' He sighs. 'Everyone says he was very friendly.' He rubs his huge cheeks like a bum. 'Right now, it's still up to the child.' He looks up at my tree. 'It all depends if the judge believes her.'

Ma asks, 'What do you mean?'

'I mean, if she makes things up, if the judge thinks she's imagining things, then ...' He shrugs.

I tell the Truth Lady, 'He was talking about me!'

'Calm down, kid.'

I dream my day dream about Pa on the sand, with his legs all bendy. But once I've kissed him on the eyes, there is nothing left. I know it's only a dumb, stupid dream. Then it feels like a tractor crushed me like Jenny, whose mother cried like a donkey at her funeral.

Ma says she was wrong. It's not the coloured judge in Worcester who decides who's right. It's a judge in a high court. She doesn't know what colour. But the high court's in the city.

'Is it on the mountain?' I ask.

That's the highest place in Cape Town.

'No, it's down by the shops.'

The detective keeps asking, 'Try to remember more. Maybe you heard something. Try to remember.' I try to remember.

'Keep trying,' he says, like maybe I'm lying. I try my best. I remember the waterfall sound of my joy. I say, 'It was like a big audience, clapping.' I tell him that silver flashes burst out of the box, and Ma's face was grateful when she saw my dream come true. I say, 'I blowed the flute for her, *pheee*, a dumb note without holes. Jerry's car engine went *vrrr-u-u-nnn*, fast past the apples. Pa came up from the garden, he thought the flute was from God. He said very serious, '*Someone's* looking after you.' Jerry's car engine was soft at the bend, *diga-diga-diga-diga*. Maybe it was *waiting.*' I tell the detective the truth, 'I *think* I remember. But it might be a dream.'

So they dig right at the Nooitgedacht gateposts. A new policeman comes with a dog. It looks like a wolf. It's got snarly sharp teeth and white fire in its eyes. It ruks on its leash, it tjanks, like for meat. I hide behind Ma, I hold onto Grace. 'Let's go home,' I beg. But Ma wants to stay.

The police wolf smells blood near the grader! That makes them dig fast. They pull the grader away, they dig under it. *Dung*, it goes, when the spade hits. They scrape the sand away. It's grey, like a bird's foot. It's still got all its fingers. Me and Ma run home like a thing with four legs.

Ma vomits in the toilet. I sit with Grace and shiver in the sunshine. Nita's pa's in the sand, with a grey, stiff hand. I'm still at home. But I'm a murderer.

Ma makes a tiny fire and boils us tea. I killed Nita's pa. It's my fault that he's stiff like the starling's mother. I don't say what I am, I just say, 'His hand was stiff like a claw.' That makes Ma go and vomit again.

Detective Saayman runs towards us. I climb up my tree, quick. I hide from his eyes.

'Where's Stella?' he asks. Ma points up at me. 'Well done Stella, well done.' But I know the words he should say. 'You killed him, Stella. You did it with your lies.'

He says to Ma, 'A shocking death.'

Ma points to me, 'Shhh.'

They walk to the garden, I watch from the top. I don't move a muscle or a bone. I breathe very soft, I sit very still so my bones don't creak.

Detective Saayman strokes his throat. 'His neck is just shreds. He must have bled out litres.'

The ground sucks me down, down down. My fingers sweat, my stomach rolls into a rock. It does a dead, heavy bollemakiesie.

The Truth Lady asks, gentle, 'Stella, what do you see?'

'I can't say, I can't!'

The Truth Lady says, 'You must kid! For the judge.'

Jerry ripped his head in. He slammed the window under his chin.

He stamped his foot hard on his carpet.

The Truth Lady asks, 'He dragged him?'

It was a terrible sound. Nita's pa cried like a slow, dying goat. I watched a wedding through the fence on Vermaaklikheid once. Their blade was too blunt, the goat cried and cried.

Ma says to the detective, 'Please …' She points at my tree. She bites her lip like she's eating her own meat. But the detective doesn't stop. His ugly police things drift up like burning stink. I hold tight to my branch, I don't even gasp.

Detective Saayman says, 'His foot was in pieces.'

'Oh God, oh my God,' Ma mumbles in her palms.

His unkle cracked, *krutt!*

The Truth Lady says, 'Ouch!'

It's like Jerry was trying to *kill* the God in him. He threw his body out. He teared off his shirt, he wrapped up his hands.

Now Nita's pa forced the glass. *Now* he was free.

My throat snaps closed. I cough and cough.

The Truth Lady says, 'It was too late?'

Detective Saayman shakes his head, 'There's bad, bad bruising, too. Rusted metal everywhere.'

The Truth Lady says, 'Metal?'

He let Nita's pa fall on the grader's claws.

I start to cry, 'He lay with his face on a terrible, sore bed!'

The Truth Lady says, 'Ssh, don't cry!'

I cry to the Truth Lady, 'I've got to tell the end, even if it chokes me.'

The Truth Lady's face is white, like the nappies on the line.

Jerry stamped his foot in his back. He sawed his head on the rough, rusted spikes. This way and that until he was dead.

The detective touches Ma on the arm. 'Sorry, man. But you're lucky.'

Ma's lips are clamped shut.

'They're sending the scrapes to Pretoria from under Booysen's nails. They'll get a expert to test for blood or skin.'

I whisper from my tree, 'He wrapped his hands.'

Detective Saaymen looks up, 'What?' He asks, 'How do you know?'

'Mevrou showed me.'

The detective laughs soft to Ma. 'Thank *God* they found the body!'

Ma smiles a tight smile to keep her vomit in.

Suddenly, the Truth Lady grins. 'Hiya,' she sings.

Pa walks to the hut with long, strong legs. His hand's got a bandage as big as my head. He lifts Grace with his good hand, he kisses the dip between her eyes. It's his favourite place to kiss my sister.

The Truth Lady asks me, 'Is that your pa?'

'Ja.'

My eyelids burn, I wish he would come and kiss them.

Pa tries to walk to us on the tub, but Ma grabs his pants. I hear her whisper, 'She's going to give us two thousand rand!'

The Truth Lady asks, 'Where's he been all day?'

'It's far away past Worcester. It's a place called AA.'

Pa's bandage looks just like the mad brandy man.

The Truth Lady says, 'They have that in the day?'

That's when I say, 'Melinda?'

It's the first time I've ever said the Truth Lady's name. She shocks very still, like she got stuck in a picture.

'What if they don't find any blood or any skin?'

'Hey?'

'Jerry could just catch a taxi from Worcester.'

The Truth Lady thinks. 'Look, kid. You've got to leave out all the voodoo.'

'Sorry?'

'The brown lady and Mevrou, all those dead oumas.'

'But ...'

'If you shut up about them, Jerry will sit.'

'Huh?'

'He'll stay in jail forever.'

'Forever?'

'I reckon.'

I stab my toes in the sand. 'What if he hangs himself?'

'Hey?'

'Jerry said that's what they do in jail. I think they tear up their sheets and make a rope.'

'You can't be serious.' She wipes her black make up, but it's creeped to her cheeks. 'I don't know, Stella.' She stares at the rock that's like a razor, cutting up the sun. 'It's all a bit much for me, I can't …'

Suddenly she swears, 'Ooh shit! *Shit!*' She flicks her red switch. She jumps up from the tub, 'Nancy! Frank! Bring the baby. Quick!'

Ma's arm makes dimples on Grace's bare bum. 'What?'

'The light! Come!'

Pa flaps a nappy, he hurries from the hut.

The Truth Lady puts her hand in her bag. Ma and Pa watch for the two thousand rand. She pulls out a big black camera instead. 'I need photos, quick!'

Ma ducks like she's shooting a gun. 'No! No! No photos!'

'I can't do this without photographs.'

Ma ruks hard on Pa's arm, 'My *ma* will see! And my sisters. No!'

'Sorry,' Pa says, shaking his head. 'Sorry.'

The Truth Lady doesn't listen. She keeps lifting the camera like a big gun. 'NO!' Ma screams. She drops Grace at her feet, she runs behind my tree.

The Truth Lady hangs her camera on her neck. Her grape lips suck thin, she flaps her hand, 'Come on now, don't be silly!'

She begs me like a friend, '*Tell* them, Stella.'

I walk slow past my ma. I climb my tree.

The Truth Lady's camera goes *klikka klikka.*

Ma waves her arms high in the sky, 'N-O-O-O!!' she roars like a lion, with green freezing eyes. The Truth Lady scrambles back, her camera clicks *klikka klikka.*

Gracie starts to cry.

Pa clamps his big hand on the camera, 'Rather go.'

The lady from the Truth is a bad driver. She swerves in the thick sand, she nearly smashes the gateposts.

Pa doesn't laugh, he just stands with sagging hands.

My pa's very sad to see the money go.

The End

Glossary

Guide to foreign languages and slang as they appear in the text. Unless indicated otherwise, the translations below are either Afrikaans, German or Xhosa to English.

Afrikaans

Algemene Handelaar: General dealer
Bakkie: Light truck
Biltong: Dried meat snack
Bliksem: Damn
Boerewors: Traditional sausage
Dassie: Small rock-rabbit
Donner: Curse word, derived from 'thunder'
Doos: Profanity, literal meaning 'box'
Eina: Ouch
Fynbos: Indigenous vegetation
Glips: Slips
Hemel-en-Aarde: Heaven-and-Earth
Ja: Yes
Kloof: Gorge
Koeksuster: Syrupy doughnut
Lekker: Lovely
Mevrou: Missus
Miggies: Insects
Moeder: Mother
Mielie: Corn
Oom: Uncle, often used as a respectful term for a man
Ouma: Granny
Pap: soft
Papsak: Wine sack
Ruks: Rips

Sies: Sis
Skoffels: Scuffles
Slangbos: Snakebush
Sluips: Slides
Snoffels: Snuffles
Stoep: Porch
Tannie: Aunt, often used as a respectful term for a woman
Tjanks: Howls/Cries
Vetkoek: Fried batter
Voetsek: Curse word meaning 'get away'
Vrot: Rotten
Vyeboom: Fig tree

German

Mein Gott: My God
Gott sei Dank: Thank God
Zu Hülfe: A snake
Gut getan: Well done
Mutti: Mother
Mein liebling: My darling
Eisbein: Meat dish
Geist: Ghost
Es ist immer das besten: It's always the best
Meine Sünde steuer: My sin tax

Xhosa

Enkosi: Thank you

Acknowledgements

Thanks to my brother, Mark.
Without you, I would not have been able to start.

Thanks to David for his quizzical, infinite patience.

Thank you to my children, Tao, Grace and even Kai for
accepting Stella as imaginary family.

I am deeply grateful to Karen Jennings and Maire Fisher
for editing this strange book. Thank you to Karen for your
calming ways, your sense of shape, and your defense of Stella's
innocence. Thank you Maire for your lightbulb mind, your hours
of listening to a child speak, and your weird flair for inhabiting
character.

Thanks to Colleen Crawford Cousins for that liberating axe, and
to Gillian Gimberg for your brilliant, improving eye.

Thank you Colleen (and the Rain Queen) for 'getting' my writing.

The following artists were not credited in the text:

Don't Cha: Pussycat Dolls
Fluorescent Adolescent: Arctic Monkeys
Green Grass of Home: Tom Jones
Killing Me Softly: Roberta Flack
Lady in Red: Eric Clapton
Les Misérables: Composer – Claude-Michel Schonberg
Somewhere Over the Rainbow: Judy Garland
You Light Up My Life: Debbie Boone

whiplash

'Tracey Farren's striking debut novel … gives a visceral, street smart and wonderfully authentic voice to the difficulties faced by women who are victims of poverty, abuse and stigmatisation.' – *Sunday Times*

'This novel…creates a sensation wherever it goes. Tracey Farren has hit a raw nerve … – *Sunday Independent*

'… marks the debut of a startling new voice on the South African literary scene.' – *The Star*

Recipient of a White Ribbon Award from Women Demand Dignity Advocacy Group. Short listed for the Sunday Times Fiction Award.

'… intimate and frank, simple and colloquial, as well as cold and brutal, hallucinatory and complex …' – *Business Day*

'Raw, gritty and with a rhythm that takes you from the staccato edges of prose to the poetry of an exotic rainbow …' – *Cape Times*

'… a powerful story, which leaves you feeling first sympathetic, then heartbroken, hopeful and finally fulfilled …' – *Cape Argus*

Other fiction titles by Modjaji Books

This Place I Call Home
by Meg Vandermerwe

The Thin Line
by Arja Salafranca

The Bed Book of Short Stories
edited by Joanne Hichens

Whiplash
by Tracey Farren

Go Tell the Sun
by Wame Molefhe

Bom Boy
by Yewande Omotoso

www.modjajibooks.co.za